When Kingmakers Speak

When Kingmakers Speak

by Nathan Veerasamy

iUniverse, Inc.
New York   Bloomington

When Kingmakers Speak

iUniverse books may be ordered through booksellers or by contacting:

iUniverse
1663 Liberty Drive
Bloomington, IN 47403
www.iuniverse.com
1-800-Authors (1-800-288-4677)

Because of the dynamic nature of the Internet, any Web addresses or links contained in this book may have changed since publication and may no longer be valid. The views expressed in this work are solely those of the author and do not necessarily reflect the views of the publisher, and the publisher hereby disclaims any responsibility for them.

ISBN: 978-1-4401-3892-8 (pbk)
ISBN: 978-1-4401-3891-1 (ebk)

Printed in the United States of America

iUniverse rev. date: 5/22/2009

For my father, Mr S. Veerasamy

*Special Thanks to my friends Milad and Prem
and my sister Shen*

Introduction

The whip rose in a huge arc above his head and snapped down ferociously on his own back. Relentlessly he struck. Though his body quivered with pain, he uttered not a whimper. Again he struck. Mercilessly. Dark, red, angry welts erupted from his skin. It was brutal and masochistic.

She watched mesmerised. Every stroke of the whip that hit his back stung her. Down it came again and as he raised the whip she could see streaks of red. He had drawn blood.

Was this what the Jesuits went through, she asked herself? Could such mindless torture expunge sin? So much self inflicted pain cannot be the Lord's way, she momentarily thought. Just as quickly as the thought formed, she put it out of her mind. It would be wrong of her to question or doubt.

Then a hooded figure appeared at the end of the corridor. It seemed to have detached itself from the shadows. Only a soft rustle betrayed its movement as it glided slowly towards them. It stopped suddenly and turned towards her.

For a moment she felt afraid. Had she done something wrong?

The stance of the figure seemed reproachful even though it remained silent. The hooded face turned away from her and then moved closer to the man.

She drew in a sharp intake of breath as an arm from the hooded figure reached out. A frail, wrinkled hand caught the man's tightened fist.

"Enough," said the hooded figure. An old, calm voice but firm and authoritative. "You have lashed yourself far more than usual. Why? Ten lashes no more. That is what you set yourself. Why have you exceeded your punishment?"

"To absolve the sins, I am about to commit."

"You absolve them through prayer not..."

"No," the man interrupted, "prayer is not enough. Not for these sins. Cleansing myself of my future sins requires more."

"Then why commit them."

"Because it is part of the Lord's work. I must fulfil my duties as the Lord's servant. Vengeance is mine says the Lord and I," he said pointing to his chest, "am the instrument of that vengeance."

She heard the hooded figure sigh in exasperation. They had heard this argument so many times before. Refuting it would be futile. The hooded figure gestured to her to move forward.

Carefully she placed the bowl she had been holding on the table, just beside the man. She could not resist looking at his face, solemn and sad as usual. Poor tormented soul she thought. She wanted to put her arms around him, comfort and reassure him but this was forbidden. Painfully she wrenched herself away and took her place behind the hooded figure.

They waited in silence as the man dabbed some cotton wool in the bowl and started cleaning his wounds. She helped him clean the wounds on his back which he could not reach. When she finished they both said a prayer which the man repeated. There was so much sincerity and spiritual emotion in his words that she felt moved.

"We shall pray again later. Together?" he asked.

"Yes, yes, we will," replied the hooded figure. "We shall ask the Lord for guidance and forgiveness for you dear brother".

For as long as she could remember, the man had carried out this same ritual. He would wait a fortnight for his wounds to heal and then flagellate himself again. Surely he has done enough to absolve himself she thought. Whatever grievous sin he had committed must have been pardoned by now. Sadly she knew that this self torture was still not enough for the man.

"Dinner will be ready in half an hour," said the dark figure next to her, breaking her reverie.

"Thank you," replied the man bowing low.

And that was the last she saw of the man for a long time. She could not bring herself to see so much pain and suffering. The next time she would see him, he would be dying on that very table.

1. Dusk at Changi Air Base

The tide was coming in as two guards walked the moonlit path towards the generator house. Hidden among the shadows, a man watched them closely. It was uncomfortably warm and humid. The clinging silence of the still air was only broken by the murmur of waves on the nearby beach. The man's neck ached, the muscles on his back were strained and taut, the tingling sensation in his toes had given way to a dull numbness but he stoically ignored the pain and remained still.

It was quite a long time ago when he had spent nights crouched in the same position for hours, waiting in ambush during the war. He remembered how the ground always felt warm and heaved in disapproval with every explosion. The wind howled a deathly dirge as the artillery and mortar shells screeched and flashed. Scorched flesh reeking of sulphur, glassy-eyed soldiers weary and blood stained, wandering aimlessly like dervishes. The screams of women, the screams of children and the screaming mortar shells. Why did they scream? Would it have made the pain more bearable or postpone the inevitable? Why did they scream?

The war had ended a long time ago but he must not forget. Tonight the legacy of the war was about to be resolved. The souls who had suffered at the hands of treachery would finally rest eternally.

"Damn mosquitoes," said one of the guards, slapping the back of his neck.

"Yes, just like that new Captain's wife," replied the other, "a merciless bloodsucker. Beneath those stunningly sexy curves breathes a vindictive soul. I know you're not religious but the devil has left his mark on that woman. She's always at the centre of any RAF social gathering, always influencing proceedings and stealing the limelight. She created quite a stir when she strode in with her Marilyn Monroe red dress. All for effect, I'm sure."

"That's probably more than a rumour. I've heard she was a debutante in Chelsea before coming here. I'm surprised that a woman of her stature and background wouldn't prefer the social circle of the colonials trussed up in the Raffles Hotel. There could be an ulterior motive but what could she want from RAF Changi?"

They had now reached the generator house. It was a small white building nestled between two gentle slopes. Across one slope, a single path snaked its way through the murky lights of a few lampposts. The path led to the main buildings almost half a mile away. Only a few shadowy trees and some bushes dotted the large expanse between the generator house and the other buildings. The other side of the generator house was a stretch of grass and thorns extending right up to the perimeter fence. Running parallel to the fence was the beach. The beach, though frequented by many, was quiet here and the generator house was similarly desolate. It was an ideal spot for sinister work.

The heavy clicking of the guards' boots stopped momentarily as they paused to sign the prowlers' perimeter logbook. Just behind them, the man began to count silently. Eighteen, nineteen, twenty. It was always the same. The guards always took twenty seconds to turn the corner around the generator house and up the path. That was all the time that they allowed him. Only twenty seconds for him to run from the tree and around the building to the entrance. It was more than sufficient but if they broke their routine and decided to double back, he knew he would be caught.

There were no trees close to that side of the building and a lamppost illuminated the entrance; but it could be done. Five seconds to run to the entrance and fifteen to unlock the door and enter. He might have to pick the lock but he could do that in ten seconds. He sat quietly behind the tree and waited, rehearsing every move he had to make and studying the terrain over which he had to make his run. The next time the guards went past he would make his move.

They would be back in fifteen minutes after filling in their entry in the last book on the perimeter fence. He had timed them on the last two occasions. Without realising it, the guards were patrolling at almost the same time intervals. Security in this camp had slackened since he left but that was years ago during the war. No one would suspect an infiltrator now the war was over.

He could hear voices. The guards were coming back but they were taking a slightly different route, walking along the path instead of over the grass. He watched them pass under the lampposts that lined the footpath. There were swarms of flying ants around each lamp totally confused into a mating frenzy by the buzzing, flickering light of the lamps. Then he noticed the flying ants moving away as the guards approached. That would be a useful early warning system, he thought, when the guards were on his blind side. They reached the generator house. Eighteen, nineteen, twenty.

Now!

Swiftly, silently, keeping low all the time he ran around the corner of the building. He dropped his short sword under a bush and continued towards the entrance. If he was caught and lost his knife, the sword would give him a second option. It was probably unnecessary but he had to take every precaution.

He had been silent so far but as he turned the key in the lock, the slight sound seemed to clatter raucously. Then to his surprise, the door would not open. He pushed against the door but it was still locked. In a few moments the guards would appear on the far side of the building. Desperately he turned the key as hard as he could but the lock held. There was hardly any time left. The flying ants were beginning to move away from the lamppost at the edge of the building. He would have to abandon this attempt and try again. Quickly he turned the key the other way to remove it and then he heard a click as the door suddenly opened. He silently cursed his stupidity in turning the key the wrong way. As he jumped in and closed the door behind him, he could just catch a glimpse of the back of one of the guards.

He was quite sure they had not seen him. If they heard him they would investigate or worse, inform the commander in the guardroom. He waited by the door with a knife in one hand, listening for footsteps. After a few minutes he moved towards a window and peered outside. He could not see the guards but there was no one on the path leading to the entrance. It was safe.

Removing his torch from his belt, he set to work. His watch showed he had ten minutes to locate the cables and plant his time delay device. The light from his torch lanced through the darkness as he searched. He carefully placed his knife against the sides of all the machinery. Then he felt a gentle tug on his knife. He had located the magnets of the emergency generator. The cables he wanted should be running out of the generator to the adjacent transformer but he could not see them. Carefully he ran his fingers behind the generator and smiled as he found them. Hurriedly he unpacked the tools he needed for his task.

He checked his watch when he finished the job. Two minutes left.

There was no one outside as he slowly opened the door and peeked. Everything had gone according to plan. He walked briskly towards the bush.

"Halt," a voice shouted out.

He turned around and saw the two guards behind him. One had his rifle aimed at him while the other was circling towards his back. Through the corner of his eyes he could see the short sword neatly tucked under the bush but the guards were not within striking distance. There was no alternative. He had to try to convince them that he was not an intruder.

"Put your rifle down, soldier," he commanded in as imperious a voice as he could muster.

"I said put your rifle down, and if you speak to a superior rank in that tone, I'll charge you with insubordination."

They lowered their rifles hesitantly and he could read confusion in their faces.

His impression of a domineering British colonel had obviously caused uncertainty. He turned abruptly as if to walk away, slipping the knife behind his left forearm in one smooth movement.

"Wait … please," one of the guards shouted, "what were you doing in the generator room?"

He turned slowly pretending to huff in impatience. They were walking towards him. Very slowly he raised his arms in feigned disgust and protested.

"I told you not to address me in that..."

The sentence was left incomplete. There was a rush through the air and one of the guards groaned and bent over, a knife sticking out of his thigh. As he had expected, neither guard reacted. He could see they were stunned in suspended animation, their minds refusing to accept danger. Their faces were white and pleading and their tongues dangled ridiculously at the tip of their open mouths. They were obviously national servicemen, still fresh from England. The usual fresh recruits who had hoped their term would be a tropical holiday rather than a true soldier's training.

He picked up the sword under the bush and slashed at the arm of the second guard as he fumbled and tried to aim his rifle. The other guard was slobbering, begging with both hands clutching his thigh and staring at the long knife that had pierced his leg. A disgrace to the thousands of British soldiers who had fought so valiantly against the Japanese. He would save their officers the humiliation of having such soldiers in their ranks. With uncanny speed he aimed a sharp blow to a pressure point on the guard's head. The guard slumped into a heap and was silent. Turning quickly he saw the remaining guard staring open mouthed at him in horror.

"No, please, no," the guard choked and turned to run.

He slapped him with the hilt of his sword and as the guard fell, he kicked him in the midriff, winding him.

"Get up and don't make a sound." The guard was coughing and whimpering.

"Now pick your friend up."

They moved towards the shadow under the trees and he pushed them roughly to the ground.

"Don't move and I won't kill you. I'm going to leave soon but I want some honest answers to my questions. If you tell me the truth I'll let you live but if you don't, I'll cut your lying tongue out. Do you understand?"

The guard nodded.

"When is the next change of prowlers?"

"Next change? Um ... in a few minutes. We were on our way back to the guardroom..." Thud! He hit the guard on the back of his head and kicked him.

"Don't lie. I know you've just changed patrol. Now tell me the truth."

"In two hours," the guard coughed painfully.

"How many guards are patrolling this side of the air base?"

"Just two. Two for each shift. Who are you and why are you doing this?"

"Shut up," he spat out. "Just answer my questions."

So far he had only been testing the guard for his willingness to divulge information. He had to win the guard's confidence or terrify him and make him feel that truth was the only way he would carry on living. There was only one crucial fact he wanted. He must choose his questions with care.

"Why are there so many officers in ceremonial dress?"

"A party. There's a party in the officers' mess."

"Is there a telephone in the officers' mess?"

The guard shook his head.

"Where is the nearest telephone to the officers' mess?"

"The signals room on the top floor of the next building."

He turned suddenly. Was that a flicker of movement behind him? Someone hiding? Watching? The air base looked still. He crouched low and hurriedly bound both guards. If there was someone close by he would have to be dealt with quickly. It was too easy to dismiss it as just his imagination. He had to be sure. He circled the generator house once, scanning in all directions. Nothing.

When he returned to the guards he noticed one of the lamps blink momentarily. Was that what he had sensed? It was plausible but he could not convince himself that he was absolutely sure. He had instinctively felt he was being watched. If indeed there were someone hiding in the darkness, then that person would have to be just as adept at concealment as he was. The scarcity of trees offered little cover and it was not sufficiently dark to move freely without being noticed. He had lain in wait for a long time and only seen the guards prowling up and down. No one else. If there was an unseen watcher in the darkness, he would have been stalked. From the back! That was the only area he could not have placed sufficient attention to as he watched the guards.

Then another thought encroached into his mind alarmingly. Who would creep up stealthily and watch him? No one could know that he was here. For the first time that night he felt a little uneasy.

He had to dismiss these thoughts. Valuable minutes were slipping past. He resumed questioning the guard who was still conscious. There was an encouraging tone of supplication in the guard's voice. It was time to ask the all-important question but he had to manoeuvre the guard away from the true purpose of his interrogation if he was to gain full advantage of this situation. It was far better to acquire a few concrete facts than to be muddled by a bag of half-truths.

"Who is the CO of this camp?"

"Colonel Dexter."

"Lies!" He raised his sword. "Tell me the truth or I'll chop your head off."

"I am telling you the truth," the guard cried.

He pulled out the guard's left arm and with one quick stroke cut off his little finger. The guard screamed and twitched like a mutilated worm, his face contorting into incredulous terror. He stuffed a handkerchief into the guard's mouth to muffle the scream, scanning the nearby area for any movement. No one seemed to have heard the scream. The watcher, if there was one, obviously preferred a passive role. He pushed the guard back on the ground roughly. There was no resistance as the guard slumped backwards. It was the same during the war. Men who thought themselves strong and courageous would collapse completely when confronted by death.

"The truth. I want the truth. Who is the CO of this camp?"

"Air Marshall Collins. I'm not lying. The CO is Air Marshall Collins." He could see tears streaming down the guard's cheeks. The guard was beginning to shake convulsively. No hesitation. He had to ask his questions quickly and allow no time for the guard to think.

"The next time you lie to me, I'll chop your arm off. Who's manning the signals' room?"

"Sergeant Peters."

"Where is the emergency standby vehicle?"

"Next to the NCO's mess."

The hilt of the sword was raised once more and brought down heavily on the guard's head. The guard slumped to the ground.

He paused, looked around and listened.

An eerie silence had caught hold of the night and held it disagreeably. Even the crickets stopped their incessant chirping. He made sure the guards would remain silent and then plotted his next move.

He had the information he wanted. The nearest telephone for the guests at the party was the signal room, which was manned by Sergeant Peters.

Cleaning his sword on the guards' clothes, he made his way to the officers' mess. Behind him, the door of the generator house seemed to move imperceptibly.

Melanie Hartson got up from her chair as the dance began in the officers' mess. She had heard enough frivolous gossip from the officers' wives. They were all the same to her. Weak women with no real ambition for themselves or their husbands, wallowing in the contentment of colonial life. It was time for her to fulfil her real purpose in attending this party.

As she crossed the room, she could sense heads turning. She knew she looked stunning in her low cut crimson dress, drawn tight across her waist to amplify the sensuous curves of her buttocks and breasts. At the centre of the dance floor she turned abruptly and glided to the bar. With that one simple gesture she had become the centre of attention of the whole party.

It resembled a bar in a London pub. She could see most of the unmarried national servicemen huddled around it. They were seeking comfort in a mediocre imitation of a token icon which reminded them of home. The men were surreptitiously eyeing the single women but now they stared at her hungrily. She swung her hips majestically, looking at them directly, teasingly issuing a challenge and then turned away again. She enjoyed playing the temptress when she felt like it but something else had caught her attention.

The duty officer, Captain Jenkins had just walked up to the far side of the bar. Some inner instinct told her that this was a situation that could be exploited to her own ends. There was something about the Captain that disturbed her ever since he arrived at Changi Air Base. She had never been able to influence him like the others. His rugged handsome features seemed to mirror an inner hardness and resilience. She knew many of the women among the small British community were totally taken in by his charismatic charm. The lower ranks respected his demanding but benevolent leadership. Worst of all, his public school background easily established himself within the CO's inner circle and he now stood directly in the way of her husband's success.

The party was being held in honour of Squadron Leader Cribbs who after thirty-four years of service as the MPO was resigning because of ill health. There were two candidates for the post of Manpower Officer, her husband Captain Giles Hartson and Captain Hayward Jenkins. It was common knowledge that Jenkins was a clear favourite but Melanie was determined that the post would be given to her husband.

She remembered her first meeting with the elegantly dressed, officer cadet Giles Hartson. Giles had strolled in, naive, virginal and half-drunk, into her brothel in Soho. He was completely mesmerised by her right from the start and was soon sending her chocolates and flowers. It did not come as a surprise to her when he proposed marriage. Many men had proposed to her before and some were in earnest. She knew that if she waited long enough the right man would come along, a man who would take her away from her gutter existence in sleazy Soho. She knew Giles's family was wealthy but had wrongly guessed from his accent that he was upper middle class or possibly an aristocrat. It was only after their engagement that she found out that the Hartsons were a family of merchants who had profited from various ventures in the Far East. When Giles graduated from Sandhurst, his father used all his influence to send his son to a military base in that region to look after the family's business there.

The Hartsons were slightly suspicious of Melanie when Giles announced his engagement. Giles kept Melanie's background secret but Nigel, Melanie's son from her first marriage was an impediment and the Hartsons initially refused to have a daughter-in-law who already had a son. Finally Giles sent Nigel to a boarding school and his absence persuaded the Hartsons to agree to a marriage.

Shortly after marriage, Giles received his posting orders to Singapore. Melanie was devastated by the news. She was only just enjoying moving around in London's fashionable circles and beginning to make herself known. Now her hopes of establishing herself among the elite in London were dashed. She hated her husband's family from that day onwards.

True to her ambitious nature she was determined to make an impact in Singapore when they arrived.

Captain Jenkins looked up as she approached and smiled politely.

"Good evening, Mrs Hartson," Jenkins greeted her.

"Good evening, Captain. If you're looking for something, maybe I can help you." Her smouldering lips curled into a smile, parting slightly. Most men would have blushed or showed some signs of being ill at ease but Jenkins simply smiled. Mockingly she asked herself? Somehow he had always been able to side-step her.

"Thank you. Most gracious of you but I have to pass a message to the CO," Jenkins replied.

"Would you like to try some punch? It's my own special recipe." She held out a glass.

"No, thank you, Mrs Hartson, I'm on duty tonight and if you'll excuse me I have to return to the guardroom."

Melanie watched him leaving. Always confident, always correct and charming but she would trip him up someday.

"Good man Jenkins."

The commanding officer, Air Marshall Collins and Squadron Leader Cribbs had joined her at the bar.

"Oh yes, an excellent officer and so charming to the women," she answered.

She noticed the two men exchange glances.

"I noticed him standing by the bar. Did he..."

"No, no. Captain Jenkins would never drink on duty," she replied. "I offered him some punch but he refused. He's very much an officer that goes by the book. Well respected by both men and women."

The CO continued. "I was going to ask whether he had a message for me. I did tell him to inform me as soon as the signals operator sent him a message from RAF Seletar."

"Oh I don't know. He might have. RAF routine simply bores me. I hardly listen to a word my husband says when he comes back from working late. I'm more interested in the present and what it has to offer. Would you like to dance, Air Marshall?"

Before he could answer she had seized him by the arm and pulled him towards the dance floor. She held him close as they danced. He moved stiffly and shuffled uncomfortably but soon she could feel him relax. Halfway through the dance she could see the Air Marshall's gaze straying towards her cleavage.

"Let's go outside. I need some air," she whispered before the dance was over. She whisked him through the side door before he could protest.

She stood very close to the Air Marshall on the veranda outside the officers' mess.

"It's a lovely night. I just love looking at the moon,

don't you?" She could feel his eyes burning into her breasts. She turned slightly so that her nipples brushed gently against his arm. She began talking about her early days in Singapore as if unaware of their closeness and could hear his breathing becoming harsh and ragged.

Then his hand moved quickly and cupped her breast.

She did not push him away immediately but paused just long enough to tempt him further before jumping to one side.

"Air Marshall! What are you doing? What will your wife say?"

"I'm s...sorry Mrs Hartson. I don't know what came over me. I apologise."

"This is highly irregular. It's not something expected of a man in your high position, Air Marshall. If word gets out, there could be a scandal." So far so good she thought. In a moment he'll be putty in my hands.

"I hope you're not contemplating mentioning this to anyone Mrs Hartson. It could... It wouldn't do either of us any good."

"No, of course I won't mention your attempted rape to anyone if you insist; but quite a few guests saw us walking out of the door together and a woman has got her reputation and dignity to uphold."

His face was red with embarrassment and he was fidgeting uneasily. She had never seen him like this before. He was always confident and aloof whenever she had visited the base.

"It wasn't attempted rape, Mrs Hartson, just a moment of weakness. Please forgive me and let's try to forget this unpleasant moment of indiscretion."

"I could hardly call fondling my tits a moment of indiscretion, Air Marshall"

"Fondling what, Melanie?" Captain Hartson walked through the door with another officer. The CO looked open mouthed at them and turned to Melanie with a look of abject capitulation.

"Oh hello, Giles. Not fondling, darling. Pondering. Pondering bits of information. The Air Marshall was talking about how much Squadron Leader Cribbs would be missed and how he has to select the new Manpower Officer carefully."

She turned to look at the Air Marshall meaningfully and added, "I believe he knows you are applying for the post."

The Air Marshall spluttered and then found his voice.

"Yes, yes. A difficult decision. If you'll please excuse me I've got to talk to Cribbs again."

He wiped his brow and hurriedly walked back into the officers' mess. The officer who accompanied Captain Hartson looked at Melanie strangely and then followed his CO back into the dance room.

"What happened Mel? It sounded like a…"

"I'm just making sure the Air Marshall chooses his next MPO correctly Giles dearest."

"What do you mean? You're up to something Mel. Tell me what it is?"

"Never you mind your silly head. Just leave everything to me. I'll take care of everything."

Captain Jenkins was checking the guards' patrol book when he noticed a civilian rushing out of the officers' mess on the opposite side of the parade ground. He could see it was an elderly gentleman walking towards the signals' office and wondered why a civilian would be wandering in that direction. He was unaccompanied and therefore must be familiar with the layout of the base. Probably an ex-officer he thought. As he watched the man, something at the edge of his vision caught his attention. Something had fallen or moved he thought. He replaced the guards' patrol book and walked towards the parade ground keeping his eye on the elderly man.

Then he saw a shadow running quickly, stopping behind the trees. As the elderly man moved, the shadow seemed to hesitate and then move. The shadow kept along a path parallel to the elderly man. Two men, one following the other. Why? Who were they? The follower's actions certainly suggested an insidious motive. A sinister premonition crept into the Captain's mind and he began to run. They were at least fifty yards away and the elderly gentleman was leaving the signals room as Jenkins crossed the parade ground. He could see the shadow vaguely hidden behind a bush waiting silently. As he ran he mentally calculated the distances they both had to cover and he was confident he would reach the man first.

Then suddenly all the lights went out. He slowed down and stumbled forward a step at a time. The whole base was blacked out. He knew that the emergency generator would start operating in a few seconds. He stood waiting for a minute but it was still pitch black. His eyes took some time to get accustomed to the darkness as he made his way forward. There was the sound of movement just ahead of him.

He felt certain that the blackout and the two men

were somehow connected. Darkness was always the perfect cover to creep up on an adversary. Something dreadful was about to happen. Robbery? Assault? No, probably worse, he thought.

Keeping very still he withdrew his revolver. Click! He pointed his revolver in the direction of the sound ahead. It became quiet almost as soon as he did so. The grass behind him rustled or was it the wind? Then he heard the sound of movement and a thud to his left. His firing arm moved towards the sound, rotating through a half circle so that he covered both positions. This was a dangerous game but he had to keep alert.

Cautiously he moved towards the path between the officers' mess and the signal block. The man was probably not armed otherwise he would have been shot by now, he thought, unless he wanted to operate silently and not alert the guards.

He could see a light in the far distance. Someone in the guardroom had the presence of mind to light a paraffin lamp.

"Guards," he shouted.

Then he saw him.

A mere shadow gliding in between the buildings, less than twenty yards in front of him at first but moving fast in the direction of the guardroom. He ran with a certainty of purpose and a familiarity with the air base. The familiarity chilled Jenkins. This was not a stranger to RAF Changi. Was he an ex-RAF serviceman or a local Singaporean? What terrible deed had he committed in the darkness? What guilt made him flee? Jenkins wanted to know. He fired a warning shot high above the man's head.

"Stop. Stop or I'll…" Jenkins shouted but the man had already ducked behind a building.

Jenkins gave chase. If he lost sight of the man for too long he might lose him altogether under the cover of darkness. As he turned around the corner of the building he saw the deadly gleam of a long blade descending on his neck. He twisted out of the way but the blade caught a glancing blow on his right arm. He crashed heavily onto the ground dropping his revolver as the searing pain shot through him. He tried to roll as he saw the blade being raised once more. He knew he could not get out of range fast enough but instead of another slash the man kicked his ribs. Numbed by the pain he laid on the ground for a few seconds as he heard retreating footsteps. He had to alert the guards as he searched for his revolver. It was gone. Slowly he straightened up and staggered forward.

Then he heard another shot.

Still in pain, he staggered forward and reached the front of the building. He could see torch light. There were soldiers running everywhere but no one was coming towards him. Surely they must have heard the two shots fired. The man could still be stopped but he had to be quick. It was difficult to run with an injured arm so Jenkins shouted out.

"Over here. Quickly over here."

There was a considerable pause before he noticed one of the lights moving towards him. Then he realised why they had not searched his area. He was in the middle of three buildings. The buildings must have deflected the sound of the gunshots and confused the guards.

"Captain Jenkins? Are you all right?" The guard 2 I/C Sergeant Williams was shining his torch at Jenkins' face.

"Put that torch down, Sergeant. We have to organise a search."

He briefly told the Sergeant what had happened as they hurried to the guardroom. Jenkins could see that the CO and the other officers from the party had already arrived and were issuing orders. There was no time to talk to them. He could still get the mysterious intruder if he acted quickly.

"The front entrance seems secure, Sergeant. Get the standby land rover and check the side entrance."

He paused by the back of the officers' mess as Williams walked away quickly. The fastest way out of the air base was via the main or side entrance. The intruder could have cut a hole through the fence but eventually would have to make his way back to the main road. It would have been far quicker to reach the road from the entrances. He obviously could not have passed all the airmen and soldiers at the main entrance unnoticed so that alternative could be eliminated. The side entrance was more than half a mile away. Sergeant Williams would definitely have reached it in time to stop anyone from leaving.

Escape was virtually impossible unless there was something he had overlooked. The entrances or the fence? Beyond the fences was jungle and... the sea. Jenkins felt his pulse pounding. The sea! The intruder could cut through the fence and escape in a boat. He had to inform someone.

"Jenkins," a muffled voice called out. He could see someone standing in the alley next to the officers' mess. He hurried towards the voice. His mind was so preoccupied that he failed to notice someone move behind him. Then he was hit on the head and his mouth covered. He tried to turn around but his legs buckled and as he passed out he could smell a whiff of something vaguely familiar.

2. An Inspector calls

Captain Jenkins held the back of his head in pain as he woke up. His clothes had been removed and he had been left in bed with only his underwear. Looking around him, he realised he was in the medical centre and called out to the medical orderly standing near the entrance.

"Why am I here, medic? Where are my clothes?"

"They have been taken away, sir."

The 'sir' was added in, almost as an afterthought and Captain Jenkins felt annoyed. The medic was a Singaporean and it was unusual for Singaporean soldiers to show any sign of disrespect to an English officer. He tried to recall what had happened and noticed that the lights were on.

"I can't walk around like this. Get me my clothes, medic."

"Your clothes have been taken away, sir, but the Quartermasters' Sergeant gave me these for you." The orderly handed him some clothes.

"Why were my clothes removed medic?"

"The CO will inform you. He told me to tell you to see him as soon as you regained consciousness."

"How long have I been unconscious?"

The medic looked at his watch and answered with a smile, "About two hours."

Jenkins walked hurriedly up the steep road leading from the medical hospital to the administrative block. It was past midnight but the air base was buzzing with activity. He wondered what had happened while he was unconscious and why the medic had showed him scant respect. When he arrived at the CO's office he could see police cars parked near the entrance to the air base. The CO received him coldly when he greeted him.

"Sit down, Jenkins. I thought I'd better talk to you first before those Chinese policemen get their hands on you," began the CO. He paused and lit his pipe.

"Awkward business this. I'll have to talk to the High Commission's officials first and make sure that the RAF's interests are not jeopardised. What I want to know from you is why?"

"Why what, sir?" Jenkins could see the CO was struggling with something difficult.

"The RAF will be behind you 100%, Jenkins, but I can't help you unless you're totally honest with me."

Jenkins waited while the CO glared at him. If he's attempting some sort of interrogation he's doing a bad job of it, thought Jenkins. He looked straight back at the CO indifferently.

Finally the CO straightened up. His manner changed slightly as he spoke.

"Tell me what happened, Jenkins."

Jenkins narrated the events leading up to the moment

when he passed out. The CO twirled his moustache and did not look very pleased.

"I want you to tell me again what happened in every detail."

"Sir. I already have. In fact I want to know what happened myself."

The CO swivelled around in his chair. "We'll have to end this discussion now, Jenkins. The police want to talk to you in the conference room. You'll find out from them what happened tonight."

As the CO led the way, Jenkins noticed a policeman standing just outside the door. The policeman had obviously eavesdropped on their conversation. As they were about to enter, the CO laid a hand on his shoulder.

"I hope what you told me was the full story. For all our sakes."

"This is Inspector Prem from the CID," said the CO, introducing him to a tall, big Indian. The Inspector smiled warmly as they shook hands. Jenkins could see that behind the kindly expression was an intelligent man whose quick darting eyes searched and missed nothing.

"Just a few routine questions to help us with our investigations Captain. Sergeant Lee here is my colleague and will be recording your answers to help you present your formal statement later on. The medical officer has told me that you sustained some injuries. So if you're not quite ready, we could postpone this to a later time. However, it would expedite matters if you could help us as quickly as possible."

"I'm prepared to answer all your questions now, Inspector," replied Jenkins. The Inspector's testing my willingness to co-operate, he thought, but why should that be questionable?

"Good. A serious crime has been committed, Captain, and you could possibly be an important witness." A pause, then the Inspector continued.

"The victim was a civilian and that's why the CID is heading the investigation."

Another pause as the Inspector looked at the CO who grunted and showed his annoyance. Jenkins knew that the CO did not like having civilians disrupting his air base.

"Did you see the victim tonight, Captain?"

An obvious trap, thought Jenkins.

"Which victim?"

"Are you saying there might be more than one?"

"I thought I was a victim but you seem to imply that another exists. I'm not sure what happened tonight and in fact I don't even know what crime has been committed other than the obvious sabotage or vandalism of the lights."

"Oh. I'm sorry, Captain. I thought your CO might have told you what we found." The Inspector tapped his pen against the table and continued.

"We found a body, Captain. Dead in a pool of blood. Obviously murdered during the blackout. We are trying to establish alibis at the moment. You are the duty officer tonight?"

"Was," the CO interrupted, "Flight Lieutenant Flynn has relieved him for the rest of the night."

The Inspector looked at the CO with annoyance. "Yes, fine. While you were on duty, Captain, were you carrying a revolver?"

"Yes."

"At all times?"

"Yes."

"Loaded?"

"Yes."

The Inspector was asking questions at a measured pace. A typical police interrogation thought Jenkins. He matched the inspector's brevity and speed. It was necessary in order to convey openness and genuine honesty.

"Did you fire your weapon at any time?"

"Yes."

"You fired your weapon?" the CO interrupted again, looking at Jenkins in disbelief.

"Yes, I did, sir, but I did not kill anyone."

There was a horrible pause as the Inspector raised his hands to stop any further conversation.

Tap, tap, tap. The inspector's pen hit the table three times before he spoke.

His next words jolted everyone in the room but Jenkins.

"What makes you think the victim was shot, Captain?"

Jenkins could see the Sergeant next to the Inspector smile triumphantly but he answered in an even tone.

"Because I heard another shot."

"You heard another shot! What the devil are you playing at man?" the CO shouted looking angrily at Jenkins.

Once more the Inspector raised his hand as a gesture to restore order. His voice was as calm as ever but firm as he put the CO in his place.

"I must beg your indulgence, Air Marshall Collins. I

cannot carry out a proper investigation if you interrupt continuously. I do not wish to remind you that it is against the law to hinder the police in an investigation. Please show some restraint otherwise I'll be compelled to carry out the rest of this uh ... at the police station."

The Air Marshall face was bright red as he stared menacingly at the Inspector. Jenkins watched the horrible tension between the two men. Both were trying to appear calm but the twisted wrinkles of the CO's face betrayed his feelings. For a moment Jenkins thought he was going to hit the Inspector but quite suddenly he slumped back in his seat and waved dismissively at the Inspector to continue.

"Thank you, Air Marshall." The Inspector turned to Jenkins.

"You say you heard a shot, Captain. Please explain the circumstances. When and where?"

Captain Jenkins related the events of that night. The Inspector remained impassive throughout his narration but his darting eyes seemed to be carefully weighing everything that was said.

"Did you recognise the man who was tracking the civilian, Captain?"

"No. I couldn't recognise the civilian because he was too far away but he walked into the signals block unchallenged so I assumed he was a known guest. Was he the victim?"

"Yes. He was an ex-officer of the RAF and an old friend of Squadron Leader Cribbs. A Major Hughes. He came all the way from Britain for Squadron Leader Cribbs farewell party. It is indeed unfortunate that he should be the victim of such a callous crime."

The Inspector paused and whispered something to Sergeant Lee sitting next to him who immediately left the room.

"According to your story, Captain, you fired a warning shot and then lost your revolver." He paused and looked at Jenkins.

"I fired a warning shot and then the revolver was knocked from my hand by the murderer."

"Well we don't know whether the mysterious follower was the murderer yet. That's what we are trying to establish. After the revolver was..."

The Inspector paused and checked his notes, "... knocked from your hand, you heard another shot and assumed that it was the shot that killed the victim."

Captain Jenkins phrased his answer carefully. He could somehow sense that he was slowly being led into a trap. "I don't know whether the victim was shot. The victim was shot wasn't he?"

"Yes, he was. Relax, Captain. It's only natural to attribute some sinister motive to the mysterious man's suspicious actions. You were right in assuming that the shot you heard was the mystery man firing at the victim but if he had a gun why did he not shoot you?"

A difficult question. He had to think fast but he could not find a satisfactory answer. The inspector's pen tapped the table again. Tap, tap, tap.

"I don't know, Inspector." Then Jenkins felt a sudden flash of inspiration.

"Maybe he did not have a gun. Yes that must be it. He saw me holding a gun, decided to disarm me and then used my gun to kill the Major."

"Certainly a plausible explanation, Captain, but

aren't we dealing with pre-meditated murder here. The murderer stalked his victim, intent on murder. He must therefore possess a weapon of sorts. That conflicts with your theory."

Jenkins said nothing. The line of questioning was aimed at a suspect and not a witness. He felt outraged but to defend himself would be an acquiescence of guilt. The safest strategy would be to only answer the direct question and avoid making any comments when a question was not being asked.

"Don't you think that if the stalker intended murder he would have carried a weapon of his own?" asked the Inspector.

"He probably did but might have changed his mind when he saw my revolver. I wouldn't know what went on in the murderer's mind, Inspector."

"Well I'm not an expert myself, Captain, although I have dealt with numerous murders and murderers. Why do you think he would prefer a noisy weapon like a gun? Why would he want to attract so much attention after stalking his victim so carefully?"

Jenkins felt the web of suspicion closing in on him but he had to place his trust in the truth. He must stick to the facts.

"I don't know, Inspector. I can only relate the facts. It's up to you to fill in the gaps."

The CO leaned forward and was on the verge of saying something. A quick castigating look from the Inspector silenced him and the CO leaned back, twisting his walrus moustache in frustration.

"We'll leave that for the moment Captain but there is something else you mentioned which is slightly perplexing. You said you looked for your revolver but couldn't find it after it was knocked out of your hand. So how could the murderer have found it?"

A pause as Sergeant Lee entered the room with a large brown paper bag. Then the Inspector's steely eyes lifted and looked at the Captain.

"How could he have found your revolver in the dark?"

"Once more, I can only guess, Inspector. It might have fallen close to his feet or maybe it wasn't knocked very far away. I don't really know. Maybe I was wrong. How do you know it was my revolver that was used in the murder? Maybe he did have a gun of his own and for some unknown reason chose not to shoot me."

"We do know it was your revolver that was used." Dramatically he emptied the contents of the brown bag Sergeant Lee was holding on the table. It clattered on the table and Jenkins recognised with trepidation the high power Browning, his personal service revolver. He looked first at the Sergeant and then the Inspector. Their eyes stared back menacingly. Confess, the eyes urged him!

"Where did you find this, Inspector?" asked Jenkins.

The answer came quickly. "Where you dropped it, Captain. You remember where that was?"

Jenkins' mind was whirling with images. Accusing eyes were still glaring at him. Confess!

"I did not drop it, Inspector. It was knocked from my hand."

The Inspector interrupted. "Knocked from your hand as you fired the shot?"

Once again the accusing look. Confess!

"No, I told you before. The murderer knocked it from my hand."

"And then you shot him?"

"No. How dare you accuse me of murder?"

"I am not accusing you, Captain. Just trying to establish the facts."

"I've told you the facts Inspector but I find your line of reasoning objectionable and insulting. I'm here to co-operate with the police in finding the murderer but if you persist with these veiled accusations then I have nothing to say to you."

The Inspector stared hard and long at Jenkins as he spoke.

"I'm simply trying to verify your story, Captain, not accuse you. You must try to understand the difficulty I'm having. The other evidence we've collected so far does not give much credence to your story. Everyone else's versions of tonight's events support each other but yours is ... uh ... well rather different."

Jenkins suddenly remembered something.

"Sergeant Williams!" he interrupted. "Sergeant Williams, the guard 2 I/C, will be able to verify my story or at least part of it."

"Sergeant Williams, Captain?"

The Inspector and Sergeant Lee exchanged glances.

"Yes. I told you earlier on that Sergeant Williams found me and helped me to the guardroom. He might still be at the side entrance where I sent him."

The Inspector swivelled the revolver on the table as Jenkins waited for him to reply. Once, twice the revolver turned and then the inspector stopped it. The barrel of the gun was dramatically pointing at Jenkins.

"Sergeant Williams was missing for quite sometime when the lights were restored. He was later found dead in his land rover. Close to the side entrance. No one knew he would be there. No one except you, Captain."

The Inspectors words hit Jenkins with a cold splash. He was no longer a suspect of one murder but two. No one spoke for sometime but Jenkins sensed the condemning gazes of everyone in the room on him. Finally he spoke.

"Was Williams shot?" he asked, anticipating the answer.

"Yes, with the same revolver. How well did you know the former Major Hughes?"

"I met him for the first time last night when we were introduced. I can't say I really know him."

"You might not know him intimately but he could possibly have been in the same RAF base as you, in England."

Trying to find out the motive, now that he had established the opportunity to murder, thought Jenkins.

"I very much doubt whether he was in the same base in England or whether our paths crossed. You can easily verify this through the Foreign Office"

"Oh I will, Captain. I will." The Inspector was interrupted by a policeman who walked in and handed him a piece of paper.

"Please excuse us for a moment, gentlemen. Something important has turned up." Sergeant Lee followed the Inspector as he left the room. Jenkins could see them through an open window, standing in the corridor and talking in whispers. The Inspector looked disturbed while the Sergeant glanced at the Captain several times.

"Why, in God's name, did you do it, Jenkins?" Air Marshall Collins asked suddenly.

"I didn't, sir. You must believe me," replied Jenkins.

"We've just found the two missing guards," said the Inspector returning.

Both Jenkins and Air Marshall Collins turned to him expectantly.

"Two guards were reported missing when we arrived, Captain. They have just been found dead and hidden under a bush near the emergency generator."

"Were they shot by some other revolver, Inspector?" enquired Jenkins.

"No, we don't know yet. One of them had knife wounds. The pathologist is having a look at the bodies and I have to check them myself. Sergeant Lee here will record your statement, Captain."

"You mean he's cleared of any suspicion of murder," interrupted the CO.

"Not quite, Air Marshall, but the two dead guards complicate matters," replied the Inspector as he left.

Jenkins was pensive as he walked back to the guardroom. Through the two rows of barracks he could see the air base runway lying serenely in moonlight. The sound of the sea in the distance reminded him of his home in Wales. He recalled the numerous occasions he had spent as a young boy watching the tides coming in late in the evening with his Uncle Raymond. It was his uncle who had introduced him and encouraged his progress in the civil service and then the military. What would he say now if he found out his favourite nephew was a murder suspect?

An inner curiosity made him turn towards the signals block. There could be a vital clue which the police could have overlooked. He started from the parade ground and retraced his steps, searching the ground carefully. It took him nearly ten minutes before he found the first spot of blood in the dim light. The scene of the murder itself was marked by a huge stain next to a bougainvillaea bush. As Jenkins looked at it, a voice made him jump.

"A criminal always returns to the scene of the crime," said the Inspector emerging from behind the building with two other policemen. "I thought you might return."

Jenkins realised that he had been watched since leaving the CO's office and now he was caught in the Inspector's subtle manipulations.

"Is that why you let me off? To set this trap?" he asked.

"This is not a trap, Captain, but merely confirmation."

"That I'm a suspect?"

"No, Captain. This is confirmation that you are not the murderer. Either that or you're devilishly clever and have acted out your innocence to perfection. The murderer would have reached this spot without any difficulty but we saw you searching the ground and following the trail of blood stains towards this spot, clearly indicating you did not know where the crime was committed."

"Why did you return here, Captain?"

"To piece together what happened. No one has even told me what happened while I was unconscious."

"Well, when we arrived the electricians were busy finishing the repairs to the electricity mains box. The murderer it seems had blown that up with a timed incendiary device and cut the wires in the emergency generator room. He is obviously someone who knew the camp well and my first suspicions fell on the personnel present in the air base tonight. A difficulty arose when we found out that no one knew the victim well except for Squadron Leader Cribbs who had a perfect alibi.

According to some guests, Major Hughes was given a message signed by you informing him that there was an overseas telephone call for him in the signals block. The power cut occurred soon after he left the signals operator. The murderer timed the whole operation almost to perfection. First he killed two guards who probably got in his way. Although one of them had a horrible knife wound, the pathologist confirmed they died from bullet wounds. Hughes was killed right there with a knife."

The Inspector pointed to Jenkins' feet.

"Then the killer must have made good his escape in the land rover by disposing of Sergeant Williams with a single bullet through his head. Shortly after, a guard found you unconscious behind the officers' mess. Your shirt it seems was drenched with whisky."

"Whisky? I don't touch the stuff."

"I found that out. It was clear to me then that you were being framed and therefore not the murderer."

"If you did not suspect me from the start then what is the reason for the aggressive interrogation in the CO's office?"

"My apologies, Captain. I had to create certain impressions with your CO. I didn't want it to be common knowledge that someone was setting you up and that we knew. I have now informed the CO that you are no longer a suspect as a gesture of goodwill. I know that your name has been put up for promotion and I certainly don't want your career to be compromised."

Jenkins was placated but suspected that the Inspector's calm manner and slow drawl concealed a devious motive.

"You have been busy, Inspector. What else did you find out about me?" asked Jenkins.

"More than you imagine, Captain. I know you have powerful friends in the Foreign Office in Singapore."

Jenkins suddenly became wary. This last revelation was leading the Inspector too close to the confidentiality of his special orders. No one should know, not even suspect. He had to be careful and smiled nonchalantly as he spoke.

"Not friends of mine, Inspector, but my father does have a habit of pulling a few strings on my behalf."

"I don't enjoy prying, Captain, but this is not an ordinary murder investigation. It is far too complex and we are completely in the dark about the motive. There is so little that we do know."

"So what have you found out?"

"Almost nothing to help us proceed. Motive, Captain, the all-important motive. Once that is revealed, everything will fall in place."

"If I can help in any way, I'll be only too pleased, Inspector."

"I'm glad you said that, Captain, because we do need your help."

"Yes, of course, Inspector. What do you want me to do?"

"You can be our eyes and ears, Captain. You can inform us if anyone behaves suspiciously. I can see two things happening, Captain, and you must be alert when they do. Firstly you will find that someone in the RAF is involved in these murders and he will benefit in some way. Secondly, and I regret having to say this Captain, but you will be watched closely by whoever is involved."

Jenkins considered the Inspector's words carefully. Was the Inspector simply being melodramatic or had he found out something about RAF Changi that he himself had overlooked? As he watched the Inspector and the two policemen walk away he began to realise that he had been manipulated all along. The Inspector had intentionally made him look suspicious in front of the CO hoping that Jenkins would then want to clear his name and become involved in the investigation. Jenkins smiled to himself. If only the Inspector knew that he wanted to be involved in the case anyway.

3. Voices #1

Is it raining?

It will rain when the time is right.

Are you referring to the weather or the enemy?

*The enemy? Such a strong word. Little Impediments.
Nothing more. Not even a minor setback.*

You sound concerned.

Something has happened.

Changi?

Yes.

Another ripple to break the pattern?

A complication by the name of Captain Hayward Jenkins.

*One person? Surely one person cannot complicate matters
beyond resolution?*

No but there is a simple solution.

State it

I recommend simplification by elimination.

*Too direct. Have you considered the repercussions and
consequences? What about his background?*

*The RAF transferred him to Changi just a month
ago. He is their liaison officer with the British High
Commission. He has a non-military background and was*

recruited directly into the air force through the British civil service. A clean record and an able officer.

Liaison Officer. A very convenient title. Duties vague enough to involve himself with too much.

Surely you don't suspect.

I do. When Major Hughes was eliminated, Jenkins was an eyewitness. Major Hughes was the gambit but the presence of Jenkins could have turned the gambit into a poisoned sacrifice.

Why?

If he is what I think he is.

The probability must be a million to one.

Coincidences have been known to wreck lesser schemes. We must place him on the chess board.

As a pawn or a major piece?

What rank did you confer the CID representative?

Inspector Prem is a pawn who does not even realise it. Shall I give the same weight to Jenkins?

No, we must find out more about him instead. He might be more important than he seems.

I am anticipating some reactions to Changi. So far we have been right but events are beginning to accelerate.

Can our resources cope?

Easily but we may need more manpower for surveillance. I propose we re- allocate the men's duties after this week.

Agreed. None of them will be able to visualise the whole puzzle if we expose them to unrelated bits. Have you sorted out the messengers?

The messengers for the last assignment have been sent on a fishing trip.

Drowned?

Yes.

4. Forensics

The forensic department at CID headquarters was a relatively new addition. Inspector Prem and Sergeant Lee had started early that morning scrutinising the pathologist's report amidst the smell of new furniture and whitewashed walls.

Inspector Prem turned to the first page of the forensic report and read it again.

"... deep lacerations that could only have been created by a long and sharp implement, for example a sword."

He was struck by the similarity of the last section of the report to a murder a few years or two ago. Searching in the records department he soon found the file of the murder. The file cover was stamped 'Investigation terminated'. When he read the forensic report, he found the same words, ' deep lacerations, probably caused by a sword.'

The report was signed A. De Souza, the same pathologist as the present case.

"De Souza? Isn't he based at Alexandra hospital?" asked Prem.

De Souza put down his cup of coffee and looked at the Inspector over the top of his glasses when they arrived at the hospital.

"Dr De Souza? Hello, I'm Inspector Prem. Thank you for your prompt report. Would it be a convenient time to discuss it now?"

Prem knew that the pathologist liked to play the king in his tiny castle. Any visitor to his domain was quickly put in his rightful place. The rightful place according to De Souza was the position of subservience. His mannerism certainly indicated that he considered the inspector's presence an intrusion.

"Sit down, Inspector." De Souza's tone was almost brusque. His hand moved over his shiny scalp. It was a habit retained from the days when he had a full head of hair.

"Now a busy man like me goes through dozens of reports in a week. Dozens literally. Dozens. Which report were you referring to?"

Prem handed him the two reports.

Pointing at them the inspector added, "The two cases are separated by more than a year but notice the similarity of the wounds."

De Souza looked at the two reports carefully. Prem detected a glint of precognition in the pathologist's which disappeared when he looked up and spoke.

"And your reasons for showing me this?"

Always unhelpful, thought Inspector Prem, but he calmly replied, "I was hoping you might recall something about the earlier murder. The report states that the victim was a member of UMNO, United Malay Nationalist Organisation. The motive for the murder was unknown.

Is it possible that you might remember other, unwritten, details of the case?"

"Ah yes. Memory, Inspector. Memory. My memory has yet to fail me. You know I have six children and I remember every single one of their birthdays. Every single one. Not many fathers can manage that."

Inspector Prem simply nodded and waited patiently.

"I do remember something about that case, Inspector. The victim was more than a member of UMNO. He was a political aspirant, a high flyer and most importantly a suspected member of the MCP."

"MCP? Malayan Communist Party? Why did the report not state this?"

"Political reasons, Inspector. UMNO would never acknowledge publicly that their ranks had been infiltrated by a communist."

"Someone would have known. The government considers the communists a serious threat," said Prem.

"It was all hushed up. The government agreed to a cover up."

"You're very brave to say something like that about the government."

"I have nothing to lose, Inspector, and a man like me can stand up to anything. Even the government."

De Souza had a well-paid job and respected status in society. It was strange that he spoke like a man with a chip on his shoulder, thought Inspector Prem.

"So a suspected communist was murdered with a sword?" Prem pretended to be thinking aloud. He did not want to sound be too eager.

"In my expert opinion, Inspector, most definitely. A

long knife could inflict the same injuries but a long knife is the same thing as a sword."

Prem was deep in thought. Two murders, identical but separated by several years.

He looked at the report again, searching for the location of the murder. His pulse was racing when he found it. The victim was found in Changi! There had to be a connection but what was it? Did De Souza know?

"Do you recall any other similar cases during the past few years?"

"No, I would certainly remember if there were. Memory, Inspector, and mine is flawless. The two cases are very similar and very unique."

"Same murderer?"

"Almost certainly."

A few hours later, Inspector Prem was back at perimeter fence in Changi airbase together with Sergeant Lee. It was a hot sunny day and the beach was crowded as usual with families from the RAF enjoying a pleasant day at the beach.

A few children were bemused at the sight of the two CID men walking fully clothed up and down the beach. Some of them started shouting and made abusive cat calls.

"Why are we walking along the fence, inspector?" asked Sergeant Lee feeling slightly self conscious.

The inspector ignored Sergeant Lee's discomfort.

"Let's go through the sequence of events," suggested the inspector.

"The cause of death from the forensic report was

'severe inter-cranial trauma' from a single bullet wound," the inspector quoted.

He continued, "The same cause of deaths for the two guards and Sergeant Williams. They were killed by a bullet but Major Hughes was killed by a single knife wound. If a killer kills with a knife he will always use a knife."

"Maybe he lost his gun and switched over to a sword?" Sergeant Lee offered. "He shot the two guards and then killed Major Hughes with a knife and then shot Sergeant Williams with ..." His voice trailed off

"You see the problem now?"

Sergeant Lee nodded. "Yes, switching weapons twice in a short time span. A killer would never do that."

They were close to the end of the perimeter fence. Just around the corner was a road, Nicholl Drive, where their police car was parked.

"It is indeed strange but there must be an explanation," said Sergeant Lee.

Inspector Prem stopped suddenly, turned and smiled triumphantly back at Sergeant Lee

"There is an explanation and it is right here"

The inspector pointed at the fence.

Examining the fence, Sergeant Lee found that it had been neatly cut halfway down the post right down to the ground. The cut section had been bent back into place and held by a large rock.

"This could have been cut days ago," said Sergeant Lee.

"No rust on the cuts," Inspector Prem replied. "This is a recent cut."

"So the killer escaped through this?"

"No, not one killer."

"What?"

"No, I think there were two killers!"

"You deduced that from a cut in the fence?"

"One killer used a gun while the other used a sword. Obviously the sword killer is the same as De Souza's UMNO murderer. There simply isn't enough time for the second shooting and a long run to this fence. Only one killer must have escaped here."

"The sword killer of course. What about the gunman?"

"I don't know. I'm not sure if he even attempted to escape."

"Meaning he is still in the base?"

"Possibly or maybe he was invited into the base and assisted the knife killer."

"The triads use ordinary knives or meat cleavers but who would use a sword to commit murder?"

The Inspector pondered the question.

He remembered where he had seen swords.

The party at the air base. Some of the officers of the RAF wore ceremonial swords! Once more his thoughts were redirected towards Jenkins. An officer and a Captain, but he carried a gun not a sword. Maybe one of the other officers was involved. If so, why?

5. Colonials

Jenkins was determined not to fritter away the two days medical leave that he had been granted. The previous night's events were still being constantly replayed in his mind.

He felt certain that only one murder, that of Major Hughes, was premeditated. The other three were incidental when air base personnel got in the way of the killer. Jenkins recalled with chilling vividness how he had chased the killer in that fearful darkness. Why did the killer spare his life but killed the other three?

The killer was without a doubt a professional but did he act out of his own volition or was he hired? The answer Jenkins felt must lie with Major Hughes and the motive for murder.

Hughes had only been in Singapore for a few days, a pleasant reserved man with no known enemies. That was the view of Changi Air Base. Who would want to kill him? Maybe his past could reveal something, thought Jenkins. He picked up the telephone and dialled. The voice at the other end was deep and cultivated.

"Thomson? Jenkins here."

John Thomson was Jenkins' contact in Singapore and provided a direct link with his boss in London. When Jenkins had first met him on his arrival he was surprised at how young Thomson looked for a man of forty. His faced was smoothed and unlined with a receding hairline and a curved forehead that matched his hooked nose. They had spoken for less than five minutes at the airport but Thomson's instructions were lucid and unhurried. Jenkins felt he had a competent and reliable man as back up.

"Oh, hello, Jenkins and how is Changi treating you?"

"Not too well, I'm afraid."

Thomson's voice was less frivolous when he replied.

"Has something happened Jenkins?"

"Well... yes, but first do you have any information on a Major James Hughes?"

Thomson's reply surprised Jenkins.

"I don't think I know a Major Hughes. Why do you want information on him, Jenkins?"

The tone in Thomson's voice was unmistakable. Jenkins was sure that Thomson was hiding something.

"I'm sure you'll find him quite easily in your files, Thomson."

"I dare say I might. There are thousands of files here and I certainly cannot recall every name but why the interest?" Thomson's words were tinged with a slight irritation.

Jenkins paused and considered Thomson's words carefully. Thomson's reaction to what he had to say would be interesting and informative.

"Major Hughes was murdered last night."

"Murdered? What? How did it happen? Hold on a minute, Jenkins."

Jenkins could hear angry voices in the background.

"Jenkins? I've found the document about Major Hughes's death. Some idiot left it lying under a pile of junk. The police were here sometime ago and reported it but no one informed me. Tell me what happened briefly, Jenkins."

As Jenkins related the past events he made sure that he sounded like a stricken man unburdening himself and even sighed at the end of his narration. It would be easier to acquire Thomson's assistance through sympathy.

"That's quite an unfortunate set of circumstances, Jenkins, but we can't really discuss matters on the phone. I finish in a couple of hours. Could you meet me in the Tanglin Club then?"

"Let's make that three hours then. It will give you plenty of time to find the Major's files."

In the mean time there was another important person he had to meet, thought Jenkins.

An hour later, he was walking between the twin palm trees that straddled the entrance of Raffles Hotel, nodding politely to the turbaned doorman.

Just as he was about to consult the concierge, a familiar figure caught the corner of his eye.

It was Inspector Prem

Quickly he turned away towards the bar. He did not want to be seen, least of all by the crafty inspector. Keeping his head down, he could see the inspector and two other CID men walk up the main staircase. They were probably here for the same reason, he thought.

He watched them through the white marbled banisters, up two flights and then disappearing past the clump of elegantly shaped occidental topiary in oriental pots. An incongruous fusion of East and West, he thought, very much against the beliefs of Kipling.

He would wait by the bar until they had left.

The sign on top of the bar read, STRICTLY NO UNIFORMED PERSONNEL. Jenkins was not wearing his RAF uniform but shook his head at the snobbery and class distinction in colonial Singapore. The non military colonials saw themselves as the cultured elite. They did not wish to be sullied by the assumed excesses of the military and kept them at arm's length. The local Singaporeans were even more ostracised and were only allowed to serve at the bar but not drink or be a patron. These were only tacit rules. An iconoclast would occasionally violate these rules but he was soon cold-shouldered and ignored, usually by his own community.

Jenkins ordered a Singapore sling, keeping an eye on the staircase. The golden coloured ceiling fans were spinning rapidly but it was still warm indoors. There were a few tourists lounging on cushioned rattan chairs, under the palm trees in the quadrangle, next to the bar. One of them stepped up to him.

"The empire where the Sun never sets," the man grunted in the distinct Australian accent.

"Problem is these pommies don't know a sun rise even if they see one,"

He had moved to the side of the bar, blocking his view. Jenkins smiled politely and moved towards a table where he would be in sight of the staircase.

Someone was coming down the main stairs.

It was one of the CID men but where was the inspector? Carefully he repositioned his chair behind one of the large potted tropical plants that dotted the hotel. The man seemed to be looking his way but it was obvious he could not see Jenkins clearly.

Then Jenkins felt a hand on his shoulder.

"Captain Jenkins. What brings you here?"

Jenkins spun back and grabbed the hand.

It was Melanie Hartson who almost shrieked in surprise.

"Mrs Hartson! I do beg your pardon but you startled me," replied Jenkins.

Out of the corner of his eye he could see Inspector Prem descending the staircase. Hurriedly he exchanged a few pleasantries with Melanie Hartson and then excused himself. It was time for an important meeting.

Mrs Hughes agreed to meet him in her room. She was a handsome woman in her mid-forties and although she wore black, her clothes were elegantly cut. Her hair was a dyed platinum blond and she spoke with a throaty masculine voice. She seemed to be a woman of strength and did not appear to be the grieving widow he had expected.

"I came here to make sure you were all right and I thought you might like some help in organising transportation and freight for your flight home."

"Oh no, all that's been taken care of by Air Marshall Collins. Most kind of you to offer. Would you like some tea, Captain?"

Jenkins graciously accepted. Even though the

temperature was a humid 30 degrees, a hot cup of tea was still irresistible to an Englishman.

"I told him not to come to this God forsaken place. I hated it when we were here just before the war. I left after only a year but James stayed on and was captured by the Japanese. I don't know how he managed. The heat, the bugs and the awful natives."

"I didn't know your husband was a POW during the war."

"Yes, he was in Changi with Major Cribbs. Thankfully it was for only a few months towards the end of the war."

Changi! The same area as the murder. Was it significant?

"Were all British prisoners held in Changi?"

"Yes, I think so, but I'm not absolutely sure."

Mrs Hughes seemed reasonably chatty so Jenkins decided to press on with his inquiry.

"I suppose Major Cribbs and your husband must have known each other for a long time for him to have taken the trouble to travel all this way."

"Well, the war brought them together. Friendships are not made during a crisis, they are forged. James and Major Cribbs remained good friends even after the war. He often talked about how Major Cribbs and the chaplain tried to maintain morale in the tiny hut they called the chapel. It's still there in Changi. Have you visited it?"

"Yes, a very poignant and sad place. What was your husband's state of mind shortly after arriving in Singapore?"

"He was quite pleased at the prospect of meeting old friends, I think, but strangely despondent when he came back from a church he visited. Memories of the hard times in Changi must have come back to him."

Mrs Hughes became silent. Her face showed strained lines of pain. Jenkins could see that she had kept her grief in check all the time. It would be wrong for him to press Mrs Hughes for more information but he did not want to leave yet.

"Could I have another cup please, Mrs Hughes?" he asked.

"Yes, of course, Captain. The milk's not very good, unfortunately. It's that awful condensed milk they used during the war."

"I don't mind really. That's what they use at RAF Changi. It certainly isn't as good as the milk we had in Wales." He paused as he sipped his tea. "Have you been to Wales, Mrs Hughes?"

"Oh yes, several times. We live in Bristol. Wales is the ideal place for our summer holidays. I didn't realise you were from Wales. Your accent is hardly regional." She stopped and seemed uncertain whether she had caused offence.

"Quite all right, Mrs Hughes. I do have a trace of the Welsh accent which I'm proud to retain but I'm still puzzled about what you told me."

"Puzzled?"

"Yes. About the church visit. Was it to the POW chapel in Changi?"

"No. He had gone out on his own to visit some of the 'old places' as he put it. I didn't go with him. The heat you see. It just doesn't agree with me."

Mrs Hughes was back to her voluble self and Jenkins nodded encouragingly.

"When he came back he mentioned something about a convent and a mystery or a puzzle. I can't remember which. James always loved conundrums. He would spend hours trying to solve puzzles. He was a thinker, you see. That's why he rose so quickly up the ranks in the RAF. I didn't pay much attention to him at first but he spent the whole of the next day going around the island. I think he was looking for something but I don't think he found it."

"Did he mention this to anyone?"

"No, I don't think he did. It's not in his nature. He prefers to solve a problem completely and wait to the last before presenting the solution. The thrill of seeing shocked faces after an unexpected revelation never ceased to please him. Do you think he stumbled on to something he shouldn't have and it resulted in his ...?"

Jenkins interrupted as Mrs Hughes paused. "I don't know Mrs Hughes but what he found out could be important."

"That's what the Inspector said."

"Inspector Prem? Was he here earlier?"

"I don't remember his name, Captain. I've never trusted these locals. He wanted to take away some of James' possessions. That's why I didn't tell him about the diary."

"Major Hughes kept a diary?"

"Yes. He bought this one especially for the trip and he spent a night writing in it."

Jenkins felt he was close to discovering something important.

"What did the Inspector take away?"

"Nothing. He said he was trying to help me by finding

my husband's killer, but I don't trust these foreigners no matter how polite they may appear to be. Do you think I made the right decision?"

"I've talked to Inspector Prem and I'm sure he can be trusted but what about the diary."

"Oh, lots of gibberish. Would you like to see it?"

Before Jenkins could answer she had gone into the bedroom. Jenkins tried to gather the swirling bits of information he had obtained into a clear picture. He felt sure that there was something crucial in Mrs Hughes account. Perhaps the diary might shed some light.

He flicked through the pages quickly when Mrs Hughes handed it to him. There was only a single page where comments were written. When he read it he found it hard to conceal his disappointment. There was hardly a hint of anything extraordinary. Maybe it's too much to expect incriminating names, he thought.

"I told you it's gibberish," Mrs Hughes commented.

"I can't find anything here which suggests he found out something important."

"Neither can I, Captain and yet I distinctly recall James saying that he had written everything in the diary. Everything. He spent almost a whole night writing in his diary. He said it was important."

"Would you mind if I keep this diary for the time being, Mrs Hughes? There might be something in here we've both overlooked."

"Not at all, Captain. If it helps in any way I'm only too glad."

Jenkins was deep in thought as he walked back to the lounge bar of Raffles Hotel.

Two men were huddled together around the furthest table, deep in conversation. Everything looked perfectly normal until he moved closer. Then a face turned towards him. A face which he recognised.

"Hello, Giles," Jenkins announced.

Captain Giles Hartson's face became deathly pale for a few seconds before he recovered.

"J…JJ… Jenkins! Uh… Hello."

Jenkins noticed the man next to Hartson was Malay.

"*Apa khabar*," Jenkins greeted the man in Malay.

"*Khabar baik*." The reply was polite and formal but the man was clearly ill at ease and left immediately.

"I didn't know you had any Malay friends, Giles. As a matter of fact I don't ever recall you saying anything good about Singaporeans."

"He is not a friend as such, Hayward. More a friend of a friend and one does have to be polite to the locals. After all, we have left them in charge of this country. What brings you to Raffles anyway?"

"Mrs Hughes. I offered to help her with transportation but Air Marshall Collins it seems, has beaten me to it."

"Jolly generous of you to offer. It's sad and tragic what happened to Major Hughes."

He looked up to see Melanie walking through the door.

"Giles, dearest, we really have to leave soon. Please excuse us, Captain Jenkins we have an appointment at the Britannia Club."

Melanie whisked away her husband before he could reply. Captain Hartson looked back nervously just as he left. Was there some dark secret they wished to hide?

Jenkins remembered the sign near the entrance. Maybe the Hartsons were merely embarrassed of being seen with a local in the Raffles hotel. Maybe there was something more?

These questions raged through Jenkins' mind as he sat in the taxi to the Tanglin Club.

The Tanglin Club was a colonial favourite especially with military personnel and their families. It was located close to the central business district and was just over an hour's drive from all the main bases that dotted the periphery of the island. Although membership was open to everyone, the segregation was painfully obvious. Officers and the wealthy colonials congregated around the bar overlooking the bowling green and the tea rooms. The NCOs and lower ranks drank beer in the 'pub' near the entrance foyer, next to the smoke-filled billiards room. The handful of local members intermingled uneasily between the two groups, unable to find a comfortable niche.

Jenkins had observed all this with mild displeasure when he had first visited the club. He thought it strange that the colonials who had decided to live here could not simply enjoy what the region had to offer. They seemingly had to create little milieus to remind them of 'dear old England'. He walked up the broad winding staircase to the tea rooms wondering why Thomson had chosen this club for their rendezvous.

He found Thomson seated by the veranda, smoking his pipe and reading a copy of the *Times*.

"Hope you've got used to the humidity and mosquitoes, Jenkins," said Thomson slapping his forearm. "I've been here years and my skin still comes out in a rash." He held up his forearm revealing a motley of splotches and red bumps.

"I'm more fortunate in that respect, Thomson," He lowered his voice and got straight to the point." Have you got the information I asked for? Is it safe to talk here or do we have to go elsewhere."

"Safe enough, old boy, but let's not make it too obvious that we are discussing something important."

He leaned over the railings and gestured at the bowling green beneath them. Jenkins followed his lead and pretended to look with interest at the men in white flannels bowling. To anyone in the room they would appear to be two ordinary gentlemen discussing the game of bowls.

"The information you wanted is classified and I had to get clearance from London before I could release it."

"I understand perfectly."

Thomson cleared his throat and proceeded with a lengthy exposition.

"Briefly, Jenkins, Major Hughes was a member of M15. To fully understand his mission here we must go back to the nineteen forties. During the war the British army supplied arms to the resistance movement in Malaya to help them fight the Japanese. We knew that the movement had a communist faction but we had little choice. They were the only effective guerrillas in Malaya. We did not expect that they would rise in power so quickly to a position of dominance.

Soon after the war ended, the communists became a threat to national security. Our military intelligence thought that their activities were confined to the jungle but their various acts of subversion suggested a much bigger network.

The British governor here in Singapore requested help and MI5 set up a counter intelligence department for this region. It took us quite some time to discover the extent of communist infiltration. When we finally made some inroads into the communist movement, the revelations were quite staggering. The communists had agents working in important positions in the civil service."

He looked squarely at Jenkins.

"In the British civil service. Can you believe it?"

Jenkins already knew most of this story so he simply waited patiently as Thomson continued.

"It is rumoured that the communists actually influenced the independence talks in '58. That's why the British government decided to maintain a military presence here.

Then rather unexpectedly, we had a defection from someone in MCP."

"Malayan Communist Party? Are you sure?" asked Jenkins.

"Yes, absolutely. Why do you ask?" Thomson paused. When Jenkins merely shrugged, Thomson continued.

"It was an important break. A big break. The defector was willing to provide us with quite a few names of the Singapore communist network. Instead of moving in swiftly, the Head of Directorate 'E', the Far East Operations, decided to gather further evidence and then smash the communists in one mighty blow. It was a tragic mistake because the defector was murdered before we could even verify all of his important contacts."

Thomson paused to fill his pipe with more tobacco.

"How did they find out about the defector? Was there a leak?" Jenkins inquired.

"Was that what they told you?" Thomson looked hard at Jenkins who nodded and smiled.

Jenkins' pause was long enough to compel Thomson to continue.

"There was a leak. A rather embarrassing leak for us all. Most communists in this region, known or suspected, had so far been local Malayans and Singaporeans. No one suspected that the leak would be British and someone with access to confidential papers. Suddenly the whole M15 operation here was threatened and that's where Major Hughes comes in. He was sent here to investigate and uncover this security leak."

"But I thought he was here on a social visit?"

"That was his cover. He was supposed to have decided to settle here for a few years under the guise of a retired gentleman."

"Surely your department would be able to pin point the person responsible for the leak now. There can't be many people who knew that Major Hughes was coming."

Thomson winced. Jenkins could see that Thomson felt he was indirectly being accused. Thomson's tone became expectedly incensed.

"I'm of the opinion that his murder is probably not related to his investigative duties."

"How can you be sure? First a defector was killed because of a leak. Now Major Hughes who was sent here to investigate that leak is killed. It certainly looks like a connection to me."

"Possibly but I still don't think so. Major Hughes reported to me on the day he was killed and requested a postponement of a scheduled debriefing meeting. He said something about an old POW friend and a private matter. Of course I had to agree to the postponement. I personally feel that this private matter, whatever it is, has more to do with the murder than Major Hughes investigative duties."

Thomson had confirmed what Jenkins had only just found out from Mrs Hughes. Major Hughes had found out something important.

"Did he explain what the private matter was about?"

"No."

"Surely he must have at least hinted at it."

"Not in the least."

Thomson was clearly becoming less willing to talk. Jenkins could see Thomson watching him closely all the time. Then Jenkins realised that Thomson actually suspected Jenkins to be part of MI6. An operative from MI6's main duty was to check MI5 agents.

"I'm not working with MI6 Thomson."

Thomson did not reply but stared back hard at Jenkins.

"Your phone call to London would have confirmed that."

Still Thomson remained quiet but he seemed to relax slightly.

"I find it rather strange that Major Hughes should be secretive about his movements considering the nature of his duties."

Not expecting a reply, Jenkins was surprised when Thomson leaned forward and answered him.

"The major was a very private person, Jenkins. Highly introverted. The type that would never allow personal matters to mix with work."

"Maybe that was why he was chosen for the job, Thomson. His diary contradicts what you've just told me."

"I don't see how ..." Thomson's voice trailed away as he realised his mistake.

Jenkins smiled. He had dangled a red herring as bait and Thomson had swallowed it whole.

"What then is your opinion of his diary, Thomson?"

Pausing for effect he added, "... now that we both know your department has read it."

Thomson's composure appeared to be restored but Jenkins knew he was struggling beneath it.

"Well we did not really scrutinise it properly. A quick flip through. I thought it would be better to be discreet and leave it with his missus for the time being. One has to be sensitive about these things. A diary is rather personal. It would be highly uncivilised to impound it from the grieving Mrs Hughes. What did you find out from the diary, Jenkins?"

"That depends on what exactly he told you about this so called private matter you mentioned earlier."

For a moment he thought that Thomson would see through his small bluff but after a long pause, Thomson sighed and shook his head in apparent defeat.

"I'll be totally candid with you as a friend. This is strictly unofficial you understand. Absolutely no one should know."

"Of course, Thomson. I have no intention of making

a mountain out of a molehill. London is constantly making mistakes and looking for scapegoats elsewhere."

"Yes, quite. I'm glad you understand. On the day before Hughes was murdered he visited me at home. It's best if I take you there."

Thomson led Jenkins out of the club across the street and along several rural paths. Finally he stopped by the pillared gates of a large old house.

It was a typical old colonial house in Singapore. The whole building floated off the ground, raised by several pillars. This would prevent flooding from heavy rain. The paint was peeling off its white walls. Little geckoes were darting through the cobwebs that clung under the boards of a spacious veranda. Grim fluted vertical iron bars covered the louvered wooden windows. The woodwork appeared to be rotting. The garden was choked by tall *lalang* grass and weeds from years of neglect. A washing line with clothes on it was the only indication that the house was still inhabited.

"An old, cantankerous but proud man used to live here just before the war," said Thomson.

"He spent many hours lovingly tending and designing this huge garden. The garden now bears little resemblance to its lush splendour of the past. During the preparations before Singapore was invaded, soldiers from the nearby Tanglin barracks were ordered to set up defence lines by digging trenches.

A platoon of soldiers led by a Captain was detailed to extend these trenches through this garden. When they arrived with their tools the old man came storming out in anger. No one was going to touch his garden. The Captain pointed out that war had broken out and that he was empowered to dig the garden but the old man vehemently drove them out insisting that the soldiers would be fined if they tried to dig up his garden. Can you believe that Jenkins? The Japanese were virtually up the road and this man was threatening the army with a fine. A fine during a war!

The old man twisted a few arms and phoned his contacts and got his own way. The Captain and his platoon were forced to leave. He was livid and has since recited this story as one of the reasons why Singapore fell on that fateful February of '42."

Thomson sighed. "Do you know the name of the Captain, Jenkins?"

Jenkins shook his head.

"James Hughes. He was a Captain then. He was so disgusted with the incident that he requested to be posted out of the Z-force of Malaya and Singapore. The authorities compromised and sent him to Borneo where he lasted only two years before the Japanese captured him and brought him back here."

Thomson pushed aside the bush covering one of the pillars of the gate to reveal a plaque. "You're probably wondering why I told you this story. Look at the plaque."

Jenkins leaned forward and read the name on the black cast iron plaque.

Mr G. Thomson.

"The old man was my father, Jenkins, and Major Hughes knew that. That's why he disliked me and was unwilling to tell me what he had found out. I could tell by Major Hughes' manner that he had found out something important. Whatever it was he discovered, he's carried it with him into his grave."

6. The diary,
Flynn and Geylang

Jenkins sipped his tea thoughtfully in his living room. As an officer of the RAF, he was entitled to the best accommodation available but since he was single he was given a small bungalow off Nicholl Drive just outside Changi Air Base. It was in a quiet cul-de-sac and suited his needs of privacy and quiet, perfectly. The sea was only a short walk away and Jenkins spent most weekends lounging on the beach or swimming. It was not an unpleasant life for the British and although many of them were serving time in national service, the exotic, idyllic environment very much alleviated the tedious routine of military life.

The Malay maid Jenkins employed, was still busy cleaning the kitchen. The Malays were often employed by the British in their homes. They were quietly respectful but not obsequious. This made them popular as domestics.

Jenkins picked up Major Hughes's diary and moved to the veranda at the back of the house. It would be far more pleasant to read by the shade of the tall coconut trees flanking the house.

"*Sudah habis, tuan?*" asked the maid.

"Thank you, Milah. That will be all for today," Jenkins replied in Malay. It was an easy language. Unlike most of the English in Singapore, Jenkins had learnt the language rather quickly and his basic vocabulary enabled him to converse to a limited extent.

He stretched himself on the old settee on the veranda and scanned through the pages of the diary but found nothing of importance. Perhaps there might be a hidden message concealed somewhere else. He carefully searched in between the covers of the diary hoping to find a scribbled message or a hidden sheet of paper but there was nothing hidden. Major Hughes had written only a single page.

Basking in the sun, the city has changed so much since we left after the war ended and peace began. Elegant buildings and a few landmarks still stand but none of the peaceful colonial atmosphere that we all loved exists anymore. Everyone here seems to have forgotten the war but the scars remain. There are still quite a number of colonials who chose to stay behind, unable to part with a lifetime's habit of tiffin and tea in spite of this island's looming independence. Hours frittered away in the blazing sunshine. Opulence and extravagance still dominate their pretentious activities. Very few would gladly embrace the changes that are sweeping through this island and accept that they are no longer masters of this nation. Even the churches and convents face an up hill task in coping with progress and crime. No longer can they provide the spiritual comfort for people who work from 9 to 6.

The diary was a disappointment but he distinctly

remembered Mrs Hughes telling him that her husband had said that he had written all his important findings in the diary.

The phone rang. It was probably Thomson.

"Hello Thomson?"

"It's me, old boy," replied a nasal voice. It was Flight Lieutenant Flynn.

"Oh, Peter, I thought you were someone else."

"I thought you might need some cheering up after what happened yesterday. I've found this really charming place where we can have a nice drink and pick up a few fillies."

"I'm sorry, Peter, I've had my share of drinking for today. I think I'll just relax at home."

"Don't be such a bore, Hayward. You'll only get depressed if you stay at home. If you don't fancy a night out drinking, there's something else I've got in mind. I'll pick you up in half an hour. Okay?"

Flynn, regretfully, was going to be persistent.

"Come around if you want to, Peter."

An hour later, they were speeding along Changi Road towards the city. Jenkins could see that Flynn was in one of his fiendishly conniving moods. A lovely but quaint surprise Flynn had said. He had flatly refused to answer any further enquiries until Jenkins agreed to accompany him. Jenkins had finally given in to his curiosity and consented. Flynn's preoccupation with the macabre was well known throughout the RAF and Jenkins felt he did need some sort of distraction from his present worries.

"I'm not familiar with these streets we're driving through. Where are we going Peter?" Jenkins enquired.

"Well, you don't want to be familiar with these streets, old boy. This is the worst part of Geylang. Believe me you don't want to be here on your own," smiled Flynn.

When the car finally stopped, Flynn jumped out and rushed into a house leaving Jenkins waiting outside. Two dark shapes were circling above the trees. Bats! They were huge and he stared at them in fascination.

"We eat them, you know."

He turned. Standing by the door was a young woman who was looking at him in amusement. She looked Chinese but Jenkins picked out some prominent differences. She was tall, with a high-bridged nose and her long black hair cascaded in neat little curls over ample breasts. Her eyes, though, were distinctly Chinese and glittered as she spoke. As Jenkins studied her he was momentarily stunned by her quaint attractiveness.

"You don't have to look so appalled. Those flying foxes are fruit eaters and very clean. I've been told they taste very much like English pheasant or possibly a rabbit."

"I hope you are not suggesting that I should trap those bats for your cooking pot," smiled Jenkins.

She giggled and tossed her hair back as she shook her head. The door opened and Flynn emerged.

"It's all right Hayward. We've been granted first class tickets to the show," laughed Flynn. "Ah! I see you've met Doris. Doris, this is Hayward. Hayward, Doris. Doris is a well known, umm, entertainer."

He ushered them into the house before they could shake hands.

They walked past the guards in the front room, along a musty dingy corridor and into a crowded arena. A pit had been dug out in the middle and sweaty men, smoking and swearing, sat in a circle around the pit, eagerly waiting.

"Watch yourself, Hayward. Most of these men have gangland connections and would not hesitate to slit an *Ang Moh*'s throat at the slightest provocation. I'm going to place a bet now but I'll be back soon."

Flynn made his way through the crowd towards a fat man standing behind an elevated table. Numerous bets were already being made and the fat man, who Hayward guessed was the bookie, was stuffing large bundles of cash into a black box and handing out small slips of paper.

Two men jumped into the pit and were immediately cheered. Cradled in their arms was something Jenkins could not make out at first. Then he realised they were cockerels carefully wrapped in dark cloth.

The two men were gently stroking their pet cockerels, circling the pit and showing them to the eager crowd. Jenkins had to stifle a laugh when he noticed one of them talking softly to his cockerel.

"This is it, Hayward. We missed the preliminary fights but everyone's been waiting for this contest. It's a fight between two unbeaten champions. We're just in time for the big one," said Flynn who had returned.

Small groups of men were becoming more animated as the cockerels and their owners passed them. There was much pointing and gesticulating. A short man dressed in a sleeveless T-shirt and what looked like pyjama shorts was shouting at the other men nearby in Hokkien. He stood up suddenly and pulled out a wad of cash. Waving the wad in the air a few times, he suddenly slammed it down dramatically in front of the others.

"*Gor chap ki,*" the man announced.

Jenkins looked enquiringly at Doris.

"He's about to bet all the money his dead grandmother left him," said Doris. "Fifty dollars. He says she has never let him down."

Jenkins felt uneasy. He was not sure whether fighting cockerels was illegal but he knew that gambling was against the law.

"We shouldn't be here, Peter," Jenkins pointed out uneasily. "What if there was a police raid?"

"No chance of that old boy. This place has too many lookouts. Besides I've already made a huge bet."

"Which one have you bet on?" asked Jenkins.

"The favourite, Hayward. The smaller bird with the blue tag tied around his left leg. That's the leg he leads with but he's got a mighty slash with his right. He's strong, vicious and a very experienced bird. He's an attacking bird and lashes out at every opportunity. His opponent's a dodger and a counter slasher. This is going to be an interesting contest, Hayward."

Jenkins felt himself being caught up by Flynn's enthusiasm. Down below in the pit, the two cockerels were still being held tightly by their owners. Sharp metal spurs were now attached to their feet. There was a roar of excitement from the crowd and more bets were hurriedly being made.

"This is even better," whooped Flynn. "Those spurs mean it will be a fight to the finish. Make a bet Hayward."

Jenkins quietly shook his head in refusal.

There was a hush as two men walked into the room. Their arms were tattooed and the crowd parted before them. Jenkins knew at once that they were gangsters.

Heads that were turning out of curiosity, quickly turned back. Few men in Singapore would look directly at gangsters. A stare or even a prolonged look would quickly escalate into a brutal fight.

Doris who had been standing quietly next to Jenkins grabbed his arm apprehensively.

"Do you know who they are, Peter?" asked Jenkins.

"Shh. Not so loud. That's Ah Seng, the Sar Ji triad chief and his right hand man, Seow Kow. I don't know what he's doing here. This isn't his territory."

Both men had stern faces but Hayward noticed that the gang chief had a charismatic aura. He had a carriage which commanded respect and was used to it. His right hand man was big for a Chinese. His body was a tangle of knotted muscles and raw power and he looked capable of the utmost cruelty. An evil face, thought Jenkins.

Ah Seng was placing a bet with the fat bookie while Seow Kow had settled into the far corner. Attention was diverted back into the ring as the judge raised his hand and spoke.

"Prize money worth $100 to the winner," Doris translated.

The judge moved to the middle of the pit. With a quick hand signal, he started the contest.

The two roosters circled each other, their heads craned like vultures. The feathers on their neck were unfurled upwards as a sign of aggression and to make them seem bigger. They were both magnificent-looking creatures, large birds although one was slightly smaller than the other. Their wing feathers had a healthy sheen of dark blue and red. Their beaks had been honed and their claws similarly polished and manicured.

They moved cautiously as they kept away from each other's striking distance at first. Then like a boxer, the smaller cockerel feigned one way and then attacked from the underside. A quick flurry of claws, croaks and feathers and then they parted. A section of the crowd cheered.

"See, I told you he's good," Flynn shouted at Jenkins.

"*Tah Say Ah, Tah Say Ah,*" Flynn shouted in his pidgin Chinese dialect, much to Jenkins' surprise.

Several onlookers started to laugh at the *Ang Moh* who was mixing up the Cantonese and Hokkien dialects.

Once again, the smaller cockerel made a quick move forward. This time the larger bird managed to side step the attack. As the small cockerel charged past, it lashed out. Both birds were flapping their wings, slashing with their feet and dodging at the same time. When the two birds disengaged there was a trickle of blood on the larger rooster's side.

Flynn screamed in delight. The crowd pushed forward slightly screaming encouragement.

Encouraged by drawing first blood the smaller rooster rushed forward slashing with his metal spurs. Claws clashed again as the cockerels lashed out at each other. Then the smaller cockerel made the mistake of trying to disengage too early. Seizing the opportunity the large rooster kicked upwards into the unguarded belly of his opponent.

Twisting in mid air, the smaller rooster managed to partially parry the blow. When it landed on its feet, Jenkins could see a small gash under its wing filling up with blood.

Flynn groaned and cursed.

All eyes were now riveted on the two contestants. Jenkins could sense that this was a crucial moment. Both cockerels had minor cuts and circled each other again. The smaller cockerel was moving faster and feinting left and right.

"This is it. He's preparing for the death blow. I've seen it before," Flynn cried out excitedly.

As Jenkins straightened himself up to get a better view, something at the edge of his vision caught his attention. Ah Seng had moved closer to the fat bookie.

His stance looked awkward and Jenkins sensed that he was somewhat out of place. Then Jenkins noticed that Ah Seng was not looking at the cockerels but across the room.

He followed Ah Seng's line of sight and saw Seow Kow, the right hand man, on the far side of the room. There was an almost imperceptible nod by Ah Seng. Seow Kow immediately moved towards the door.

A signal, Jenkins realised but for what?

He watched Seow Kow open the door and then an irresistible urge caught Jenkins. He had to find out what Seow Kow was up to. Quickly, Jenkins got up and moved to the door, keeping low. No one else had noticed him. All eyes were still riveted on the arena. Still stooping, he pushed the door open carefully. Seow Kow was standing next to another man by an open fuse box.

Quickly Jenkins turned to check on Ah Seng. He was standing right next to the bookie. Turning around, Jenkins saw Seow Kow coming out of the door, staring straight at Jenkins. Seow Kow's eyes were smouldering with rage. It was a look that screamed death.

Suddenly the lights went out. Jenkins reacted

immediately, rolling away from Seow Kow's position. No one else moved for a few moments. Then there were angry shouts as people began to push each other in the darkness. Someone next to him fell heavily but Jenkins pushed on towards Flynn.

"Peter, Peter!" Doris was screaming for Captain Flynn.

Then a cigarette lighter illuminated the room. It was held by Ah Seng. Everyone stopped moving, momentarily transfixed by the light. Then in an almost synchronised move, they turned to look at the pit.

Two cockerels lay in a pool of blood in the middle. They were both clearly dead. It took some moments for the crowd to gather themselves as the bookie shouted something in Chinese and then everyone started to shout at the same time. Jenkins saw Flynn push his way to the front of the crowd towards the bookie. Angry words were being exchanged and the crowd was clearly agitated. Jenkins turned questioningly to Doris standing by his side.

"Someone has stolen the betting money," said Doris. Her voice was strained and frightened. "This could be highly dangerous. I think we should leave."

"I don't think we can," replied Jenkins. He had noticed that two men were now standing by the door effectively preventing anyone from leaving.

"They're indirectly accusing Ah Seng. There could be a fight, Hayward."

Ah Seng had now moved into view. Although he was faced by overwhelming numbers, everyone feared him and kept a respectful distance away. Ah Seng smirked and stared defiantly back at the crowd. None of them dared look back.

Then Jenkins noticed the bulge in Ah Seng's pocket. It was conspicuous enough for everyone in the room to be aware of. It was clear that the crowd suspected that their stolen money was concealed within that bulge.

"He's got our money. That thief has got our money but no one here has the guts to get it back from him," said Flynn returning.

"Why not?" asked Jenkins slightly amused that Flynn himself had not dared to approach Ah Seng.

"No one here wants to cause any trouble," interrupted Doris. "Ah Seng is a guest here. He's from the Sar Ji triad but this is Kong Puek territory. The two triads have only recently patched up their differences. This has to be resolved quickly without anyone losing face."

Jenkins knew that losing face was an important facet of Chinese culture.

Instead of moving to the door, Ah Seng took a step closer towards the crowd in front of him. Jenkins was amazed to see them take a step back.

Someone at the back of the crowd shouted out.

"*Aiyah!*" Doris exclaimed. "He's accused Ah Seng. If Ah Seng retaliates, there could be gang warfare."

Ah Seng was talking now and the crowd hushed to hear him.

"He's saying a guest does not bite the hand that offers him food. Even a dog is brought into a house only because he's trusted."

"Meaning?" asked Jenkins.

"He is indirectly accusing the Kong Puek man, that's the one with a beard, of treating him worse than a dog."

"Maybe Ah Seng engineered this whole charade to create conflict between the two triads," Flynn chimed in. "The Sar Ji triad is extremely strong now and feared. If the bearded man gives in it will mean that his triad has publicly acknowledged their allegiance to the Sar Ji triad."

Jenkins looked at the two men and then noticed Seow Kow behind them, close to the door. Then he realised what had really happened.

"Doris. Tell them that Ah Seng has not got the money."

"What?" cried Doris and Flynn almost in unison.

"What makes you say that, Hayward?" asked Flynn.

Before Jenkins could reply, Doris hushed them both.

"Ah Seng has agreed to empty his pockets. He says he wants to keep the peace but he won't forget this insult."

All eyes were now fixed on Ah Seng's hand as it rummaged his bulging pocket. He withdrew it slowly looking angrily at the bearded man. Then, quiet unexpectedly he paused and turned to the two men guarding the door. It looked as if he was considering a quick escape but there were far too many men blocking his way. Then he pulled his hand out of his pocket to reveal a brown paper bag. In an over dramatic slow manner he let the bag fall on the floor. Bits of paper tumbled out of it.

Someone in the crowd moved forward and stopped. Then the crowd realised that the bits of paper were betting slips. The crowd looked up from the bits of paper to Ah Seng and then noticed a gun in his hand. The front part of the crowd rushed back expecting him to shoot but Ah Seng ignored them and calmly walked to the door.

The guards were still standing in front of it uncertain and baffled. Then one of them keeled over with a knife sticking out of his back. The other rushed towards Ah Seng but he was caught by a blow to his throat and then was picked up and smashed against the wall. S e o w Kow, Ah Seng's right hand man had killed the two men before anyone could even flinch.

The crowd now withdrew in fear of their lives as Ah Seng and Seow Kow stepped out of the door. No one moved for a few minutes and then one by one the shocked spectators of the cock fight left.

A shaken Flynn, Doris and Jenkins made their way to a nearby coffee shop.

"Bad business," mumbled Flynn. "That's the last fight I'll ever attend. It cleaned me right out."

"How much did you lose?" asked Jenkins.

"Almost half a week's wages, Hayward, but tell me how did you know that Ah Seng did not steal the money."

"He did, Peter, but it was not on him. The bulge in his pocket was just too obvious and took the attention away from the place where the money was hidden."

"And where was that?"

"In his killer friend's shirt. They probably planned it all along. At the most exciting part of the fight, I saw Seow Kow fiddling with the fuse box. He must have switched off the main switch.

Ah Seng must have grabbed hold of the money and passed it on to Seow Kow. At the same time he filled his pocket with the useless betting slips and his gun to create a suspicious looking bulge. All suspicion would be turned on him and no one would even consider his partner. Once he emptied his pockets and was found to be innocent, it would be difficult to accuse him or his partner again. They could then walk away scot-free.

I think Ah Seng wanted to make a point that he could have taken the crowd on by disposing the two guards."

"Very astute, Hayward, but what made you think that Seow Kow had the money."

"Well, when they came in, I noticed that his shirt was undone quite a way down his chest. After the lights came on again it was buttoned up. It could only mean he was concealing something."

"That's very perceptive, Hayward. You're probably right but it still doesn't change the fact that I've lost all my betting money," sighed Flynn. "I promised to take Doris home. She lives practically around the corner but after this evening's events I think it's necessary to walk her home. I'll be back for you in a few minutes."

With that Flynn walked away with Doris, leaving Jenkins conspicuously alone as the only Englishman in the coffee shop. He ignored the occasional curious stare and continued to sip his drink. A man at the next table cleared his throat and spat into the spittoon only a few feet away from Jenkins while another picked his teeth and chewed on the toothpick.

"Why you English sitting in Chinese coffee shop?"

Jenkins looked up and saw Ah Seng standing over him.

"I don't exactly frequent coffee shops. I'm simply waiting for a friend." Jenkins felt strangely uncomfortable in Ah Seng's presence but still managed to sound reasonably courteous.

"You bet in cock fight? I think I see your face just now."

Jenkins just shook his head. He knew how dangerous Ah Seng was.

"You waiting for friend or for girls? I know many girls if you have money," Ah Seng asked. His lips twirled into a grin but his fiery eyes were as menacing as ever.

Even the way he smiled looked dangerous, thought Jenkins.

"I've got no money but I know you have lots," replied Jenkins and immediately bit his lip.

There was a brief uneasy silence and Jenkins thought that maybe he had over stepped the mark as Ah Seng looked directly into his eyes. Then Ah Seng laughed.

"You brave, Captain. You alone here among strangers and yet you speak your mind." Ah Seng pulled up a chair and sat opposite Jenkins.

"You English not very polite. You should have offered me seat."

"I would have asked you to sit down but seeing you already have, that would be superfluous."

Ah Seng's shirt was partly rolled up to reveal the dragon tattoos on his forearms, the typical mark of the gangster. There was a long scar over one of the tattoos probably from a knife slash. His face was smooth, almost unblemished and had a babyish charm to it when he smiled. The pleasantness ended there. The undeniable malevolence he exuded came through when he was serious. He stared at Jenkins through the corner of his cold dark eyes.

Jenkins felt troubled and threatened. He knew he had to choose his words carefully or he might not walk out of the coffee shop alive.

"Those men by the bar seem to be watching you,"

Jenkins observed. "Surely you're not trying to avoid them by sitting next to me."

"They not watching me. They watching you," Ah Seng replied, without deigning to turn around. "They think same question as me. Same question on my mind all night."

Ah Seng paused and leaned back. His actions seemed relaxed but Jenkins saw that they had been carefully calculated to reveal a revolver and a knife tucked in his belt. Jenkins shifted in his chair uneasily.

The soft murmur of friendly voices in the coffee shop now sounded hostile. He could see half a dozen faces glaring at him threateningly as he fought to remain calm. He was in mortal danger and had to act soon to save himself. The coffee shop was crowded and he could possibly escape from Ah Seng by dodging in between the little groups but what if some of them tried to stop him. What if they were Ah Seng's men? He could not be absolutely sure. Ah Seng's face had cracked into a half sneering smile. He probably derived pleasure from watching his victims squirm but I am not going to satisfy him, thought Jenkins.

"I don't think the men in this coffee shop are really concerned about my presence. They're still wondering about the fight and I've overheard a few disgruntled murmurings. Some people are decidedly unhappy. In fact if I were you I think some reparations might be in order."

"Lepalations? You talk what *Ang Moh*. You *Chow lang*. You be careful what you say to me," said Ah Seng, hissing through his teeth.

"All I'm saying is that the people in this coffee shop

seem to be looking at you and talking. They must be friends of yours."

"They nothing. Just like chicken shit. They frighten of me."

Good, thought Jenkins as he leaned back in relief, most of the men in the coffee shop are not with Ah Seng.

"These people will crawl for me if I want. They know I master. If they please me, I reward them and if they annoy me, well, I'll reward them better." Ah Seng's hand brushed past his revolver as he continued.

"You better respect me *Ang Moh*."

Once more Jenkins became aware of how dangerous his situation had become. The coffee shop was crowded but he felt increasingly isolated. No one would stop Ah Seng if he shot him. He could picture himself lying in a pool of blood on the floor of the coffee shop. Not a single hand would be raised to help him and when the police finally arrived they would be met by a blank wall of denial and feigned ignorance. It was important for him to maintain his composure. If Ah Seng wanted to kill him he would have already done so. There must be a purpose to this conversation.

"Mr Ah Seng I believe you to be an intelligent man and not a savage who simply lashes out in anger. We both know that this is your territory and that you could do anything you wish. There is no need to try to impress me. If you have a question to ask me please do so."

Ah Seng sneered again as he answered. "No. No question but if you sit here you must pay, Captain."

He paused and then suddenly pulled out his opened pack of cigarettes and thrust it close to Jenkins' face.

"No, thank you, I don't smoke," said Jenkins but Ah Seng's hand was still extended towards him clutching the pack of cigarettes.

He looked up to see Ah Seng's cold cruel eyes staring hard at him. He obviously had to respond in some way to this strange ritual but he did not know what was expected of him. He was about to speak when a man walked across the coffee shop and slipped a piece of paper into Ah Seng's hand. Ah Seng read the paper, crushed it and swearing angrily, he got up and walked out of the coffee shop.

Jenkins straightened his hair in relief. He had only just escaped what could have been a fatal confrontation, but why did Ah Seng approach him? There was something strange in the gang chief's manner. His eyes were too watchful, almost probing. He was testing me somehow, waiting for a certain response, thought Jenkins. It wasn't the stolen money from the cock fight. Ah Seng was probing for something more.

The piece of paper that summoned him away must be important. Jenkins could still see it lying crumpled on the floor. He was nearly overcome by the urge to pick it up immediately. That would attract too much attention but the paper must contain some information. At least it would shed some light on Ah Seng's strange behaviour.

Jenkins was still sitting pensively by his table when Flynn returned.

"Time to go, old boy. Sorry to have kept you waiting," said Flynn.

As he started to walk out Jenkins seized his opportunity. He bent down to tie his shoelaces carefully turning his back so that it shielded him from prying eyes.

Then as he finished tying his laces, he slipped the piece of paper into his shoe. When he got up he felt sure no one had noticed what he had done. He would read the note later but first he had to get out.

The arrangement of the tables and the unusually large crowd meant there was no unobstructed path through the front entrance and Jenkins was only too aware that at any moment a restraining hand could be laid on his shoulder or worse a knife thrust into his back. No one would notice. Even if they did, they would claim ignorance. He had to remain calm and suppress the urge to run. That would only attract attention or possibly worse. He felt unfriendly looks burning into them as they made their way through the dangerous crowd.

Flynn was chattering away as usual. Although he scarcely paid any attention Jenkins was glad. Flynn's monologue helped him to steady his nerves as they brushed past groups of tattooed men.

They finally came out of the coffee shop on to the street. Flynn's Vauxhall Humber was parked on the other side of the road. A group of street urchins were playing little games and annoying a trishaw rider who was trying to rest after a hard day's work. Next to them a street hawker was serving Chinese noodles from his mobile stall and Jenkins recognised the distinct smell of soya sauce pervading the street.

Then two faces popped out of the far end of the street. It was Ah Seng and Seow Kow. Seow Kow had turned to look down the road. His eyes locked onto Jenkins. Then he abruptly turned to speak to Ah Seng. At that moment Jenkins turned cold. Seow Kow must have related to Ah

Seng about seeing Jenkins while he was by the fuse box. Jenkins was a witness to their diabolical schemes.

There was very little time to make a decision. Ah Seng was less than thirty paces from the side of the coffee shop. They had only seconds to act.

"Run," grunted Jenkins and before Flynn could answer he grabbed his arm and pulled him across the street. They crossed it with total disregard to the traffic causing a car to screech to a halt. Jenkins knew that everyone's attention was now on them, including Ah Seng's. He wrenched the car keys from Flynn and jumped into the driver's seat. Flynn followed open mouthed and stupefied. Behind them there were shouts of anger and Jenkins could see Ah Seng running towards them in his rear view mirror.

The car sped off along the narrow street but had to brake suddenly as a trishaw lazily wheeled past. Then to Jenkins horror, instead of crossing the street, the trishaw stopped in the middle. The irate rider gestured and shouted at Jenkins in Chinese.

"*Hakin ki, hakin ki*," shouted Flynn out of the window, trying to hurry the rider but this only provoked him into more aggressive shouting.

Jenkins turned around to see Ah Seng and his men still running towards them. He put his foot down and gently rammed the trishaw.

"What are you doing? Have you gone mad?" screamed Flynn.

The two passengers sitting in the trishaw only just managed to jump out in time but one of Ah Seng's men was nearly upon them. Jenkins felt palpitations booming in his ears. His clothes were drenched in sweat and his wet hands found it hard to grip the steering wheel firmly. If they jumped out of the car they could try to lose their pursuers in the busy streets under cover of darkness but Ah Seng knew this area far better than he did. He hurriedly reversed the car into the man. The glancing impact threw him on to the pavement. He swerved the car around the trishaw and sped off.

It was quite a few minutes before either man spoke.

"I'll drive now, Hayward. I know these roads better than you do and besides this is my car which you have dented so blatantly."

Jenkins apologised and stopped the car.

"What happened back there, Hayward?"

Jenkins related his conversation with Ah Seng to Flynn.

"Tough customer, Ah Seng. Someone you don't want to bump into in the dark. He must have taken umbrage at your presence or something you did," commented Flynn.

"I didn't do anything offensive and what was that little charade with the cigarettes? Why did he thrust them at me like that?"

"It's an old triad test. Normally when two members of rival gangs meet especially to establish a truce after a gang war, one of them will offer the other a cigarette from an opened pack. If that person removes the longest cigarette jutting out of the pack, it means he is asserting his dominance. Usually a fight ensues when that happens. It's strange that he should try that on you. He can't be thinking that you are in any way connected with a rival gang. You're not, are you, Hayward?" chuckled Flynn but Jenkins' mind was already deep in thought.

He had remembered that Ah Seng had addressed him as Captain. Someone had told him that. Their meeting in the coffee shop was not a chance conversation. Ah Seng knew he was a military man and was probably aware that he worked in RAF Changi. Jenkins had a disconcerting feeling that he would meet the evil man again.

When he arrived home, he removed the crunched piece of paper in his sock half expecting a coded message to be scrawled on it but there was no coded message. Not even a few words. Instead, there was a symbol written on it. He examined it closely and then realised it was a Chinese character.

He turned over the paper again and again, examining it thoroughly and was finally satisfied that nothing but the Chinese character was written on it but what was its significance and why did it upset the gangster so much?

7: The Regatta

Melanie adjusted her dress carefully as she stepped up to the podium. The loud clapping and wolf whistles that followed hardly ruffled her. Most wives would have blushed either in embarrassment or mock modesty but not her. She expected it.

There was a time when the lustful stares of men did not fail to kindle a curious excitement in her. No more. After years in Soho, she had come to realise it was not the sexual admiration of men that she enjoyed but the power she had over them. They were weak without realising it, their strength and resolution crumbling in the face of overwhelming desire. It was easy to manipulate them. Sometimes too easy.

The regatta had been a success. Once again Changi had defeated both the rival air bases of Seletar and Tengah comprehensively and won most of the honours.

As she gave out the prizes to the winners, Melanie caught sight of her husband, Giles, talking to the Commander of another air base. Now that her husband was the Manpower officer, she was glad to see that he fitted in quite easily with the field officers of the three air bases in Singapore.

She mingled with the officers of the other air bases after the presentation. Most of them remembered her from the previous year when she created quite a sensation by sunbathing in a skimpy bikini during the regatta. As usual they were respectfully complimentary as they chatted to her about the events of the day. Melanie had other things on her mind.

She had received a disturbing phone call only hours ago. At first she had wanted to slam the phone receiver down when the caller refused to identify himself but it took just one word from the stranger to change her mind.

Churchill's!

Churchill's after all these years, a chilling reminder of her past, a past she had so desperately wanted to be dissociated from. It was a time when hunger and the necessity of money forced her into prostitution. She had been young and naive not realising how easily she could manipulate men without having to sell herself but gradually she learnt and became aware of her innate powers to control and dominate. Soon she had found employment at an exclusive men's club. She was still a prostitute in the club but now her clients were mainly from the upper middle class and extremely wealthy. It was in Churchill's that she had first met her husband. When they were finally married, she thought the secret of her past would be buried forever as she made her way up the exclusive social circles of fashionable London. Now this stranger had called and had subtly threatened to reveal her dark past.

He had not mentioned money so what could he be after? They had arranged a special code. The stranger would identify himself by talking about orchids and she should then lead him to a place where their privacy would be assured. It was an unusual arrangement and although she had been with many strange men in Soho, she could not help feeling apprehensive.

"Hello, Mrs. Hartson. I hope you're having a pleasant evening."

Melanie turned to see the CO, Air Marshall Collins standing by her elbow.

"Why, hello Marshall." Melanie smiled sweetly. "I see you haven't brought your wife with you."

The CO turned a bright scarlet but maintained his composure as he replied. "No, I'm afraid Cathy was slightly under the weather and has to rest. It has been such a splendid regatta, a resounding success."

"I'm not surprised. Changi Air Base won so many prizes because its rowers seem to be able to find the time to train nearly every day," replied Melanie.

"Yes, quite," mumbled the Air Marshall but his attention had drifted on to something else.

"You seem to be a little preoccupied, Marshall."

"Yes. It's that new chap over by the bar. Don't quite know how one should take him. Charming fellow and all that but a little too loud around the women. Maybe he's had a little too much to drink."

The Air Marshall waved to Jenkins who was walking past. Discreetly he instructed Jenkins to caution the officer at the bar.

"Seems like a reasonable officer. Damn good

credentials, Sandhurst and all that," said the Air Marshall.

"Oh, he must be very good if he was trained in Sandhurst. Probably got carried away by the occasion. I've seen officers from Changi behaving worse," Melanie quickly added.

"Was he reasonable, Jenkins?" the CO asked when Jenkins returned.

"Well I don't know sir," replied Jenkins. "There was some measure of insubordination in his replies but he obviously had been drinking heavily so I chose to ignore his strong words."

"Strong words, Jenkins? You mean he swore at you?" the CO grunted.

"He is a young officer, sir, and I prefer to overlook these petty indiscretions. If you'll excuse me, sir, I have a friend who's waiting." Jenkins turned and walked away abruptly.

"Well, I suppose I'll just have to have a word with young Lt. James Smith tomorrow. Can't have any insubordination in this air base, you know," said the CO.

Melanie laughed.

"Why are you laughing, Mrs Hartson?"

"It's just that I'm surprised to see you were totally taken in by Captain Jenkins."

"Taken in?"

"Oh I'm sure you're able to see through Captain Jenkins. He did a wonderful job in discrediting that young officer."

"But he did say he thought that the incident should be overlooked."

"Yes, he did, but not before he mentioned insubordination. You see, it was Captain Jenkins intention to create an impression that he thought the behaviour of the officer could be ignored. He knew that you were watching him and could see some angry words being exchanged. He calculated that your reaction would be to castigate and punish the officer even more severely."

"Hmm. I see your point, Mrs Hartson, but I've never thought Jenkins to be a devious person."

"Oh no, of course he isn't or rather wasn't."

"Wasn't?" The CO looked perplexed.

"I suppose you might as well know, Air Marshall. Ever since my husband was promoted, Captain Jenkins has become a bitter man. He still maintains his outward charm when I've talked to him but Mrs Crabtree, his neighbour, told me he is ambitious and felt slighted by the air base when he was not promoted."

"That's rather interesting, Mrs Hartson, because I have noticed a change in Jenkins recently. He seems distracted."

There was a lull in the conversation as they watched a few couples gathering around the floor for the evening's dance. Melanie could see that the CO was about to ask her but before he could do so she quickly turned and made her way around the dance area. She was looking for her husband, Giles, when she bumped into Jenkins.

"Beg your pardon, Mrs Hartson."

"Hello, Captain Jenkins. What are you doing standing by the veranda? Aren't you dancing?" She found it difficult not to respond to the physical attraction he exuded.

"I'm afraid I'm not much of a dancer, Mrs Hartson. I

came out here for some fresh air. Don't you find the smell of fresh flowers exhilarating?"

"Flowers?" Melanie was aghast. She remembered the strange phone call. Surely it could not be Jenkins.

"What flowers?" she asked, dreading the answer.

"Don't you know? Frangipani."

"Frangipani? What do you mean?" Was he toying with her?

"Yes frangipani. They are small white flowers and they have this beautiful scent at night. It's really quite captivating."

Melanie considered Jenkins for a while and decided he was quite sincere. It had been merely a coincidence that flowers were mentioned.

"I like some local flowers," Melanie commented, but I do miss the lovely seasonal English flowers. Daffodils, roses. They are really lovely."

"Oh yes, I miss them too," replied Jenkins.

They spoke for a while about England. Melanie was conscious all the time of Jenkins masculinity. As she listened, she had to remind herself constantly that she was married. A thought ran through her mind, a strange feeling and response to the physical proximity of Jenkins. She was not sure of it at first but as the conversation progressed it dawned on her what that strange feeling was. He possessed something which most men she knew lacked. Jenkins was sexy! Their conversation was interrupted when a young Chinese girl came through the doors.

"Oh, hello, Doris." Jenkins introduced Doris to Melanie. "I've promised to drive Doris home, Mrs Hartson. It's been very pleasant talking to you."

Melanie watched them walk towards the car park. So that's why the women from the RAF had no success with Jenkins. He obviously preferred local women. The conversation she had with Jenkins left her slightly confused. He had been pleasant, interesting and had made her feel like a woman but...

Melanie was about to return to the dance when a man crept out of the shadows. He was Chinese or possibly Malay for his complexion was a dark tan. Melanie realised with disdain from the way he dressed that he was a guest at the party. She thought it was bad etiquette to invite the locals to RAF parties. After all as their masters, the British should not be fraternising with them.

"Hello," the man smiled politely nodding his head.

"Hello and good-bye," Melanie replied scornfully.

"Wait, don't you want to see the orchids?" the man shouted after her as she was about to pass through the open door.

"Orchids?" The code word of her telephone call.

"You?" Melanie looked at the man with suspicion. How did a Singaporean get to know the secret of her past?

The man simply nodded his head and smiled. She studied him closely. His accent was clearly Singaporean but the voice on the phone had been distinctly British. Maybe he was simply a manservant sent on an errand.

"Have you got a message for me?" she asked.

"There is no need to speak slowly. I understand you perfectly. Can we talk here? Do you think this veranda is private enough?"

"You weren't the person I spoke to on the phone. How many of you are there?"

"I don't think that really matters, Mrs Hartson. You still haven't answered my question. I personally feel this verandah is safe enough for both of us but are you comfortable with that?"

The man was too confident, she thought and therefore more dangerous than she anticipated.

"Who told you about Churchill's and why did you mention it to me?" she asked.

"No one will know about Churchill's and you Mrs Hartson, if you co-operate. All I ask is a simple favour and in return I can guarantee the silence of my colleague and me. Your secret will be safe." He paused to light a cigarette.

"Secret?" Melanie laughed. "Surely you're not so naive as to believe I have any secrets."

"You're forgetting Churchill's, Mrs Hartson. I'm sure you don't want your past association with Churchill's to surface in this society."

"Churchill's is not only a very respectable place but also highly regarded. It attracts not only the aristocracy but the cream of London society. Its location in Mayfair alone commands respect."

Melanie could see the man was floundering.

"You can't fool me, Mrs Hartson. If there are no skeletons in your cupboard then you would not have kept this illicit rendezvous. You and I know the truth. The truth that will tarnish your name."

Melanie was sure now that the stranger had never been to Churchill's and probably not even London. Churchill's was in Soho and not in Mayfair but the man had not spotted that deliberate mistake. She walked up to the door and opened it wide. Turning quickly she saw the man looking at her in open-mouthed surprise.

"Now listen to me you silly little man," she hissed, "I don't know who put this pathetic idea into your head but you've chosen the wrong victim this time. There is a law against blackmail in this country and it carries a severe penalty. I came here not because I had anything to hide or fear but to reveal you to the police."

"The police?" the man spluttered.

"Yes. That was my signal to them. In a moment they will be here to arrest you."

Melanie had calculated that the open door would attract someone's attention and sure enough someone was walking towards it. Melanie had expected the man to flee but he remained where he was. She considered screaming at the man but was stopped by a voice behind her.

"I think we have to listen to what this man has to say, Mel." Giles Hartson closed the door behind him.

"Giles. What's going on? You sound as if you're in league with this... this ... creature."

"He's spoken to me, Mel, and he knows about your past but fortunately I know something about him as well. I think we can settle this matter together amicably."

"He tried to blackmail me, Giles," said Melanie.

"Not blackmail, madam. I just want to come to an agreement which will be mutually beneficial to all of us," the man replied.

After a long deliberation, Melanie hesitantly agreed to listen.

Jenkins poured out the drinks and handed one

to Doris. He had seen her walking in with Flight Lieutenant Flynn at the party and had soon engaged her in conversation. They had spoken for some time about their past meeting and about Ah Seng. Doris sounded concerned and frightened when Jenkins mentioned how they had only just managed to escape but she was just as perplexed as to why Ah Seng had an interest in Jenkins.

When Jenkins mentioned the character scrawled on the piece of paper, Doris told Jenkins that she could read and write in Chinese. She agreed to accompany Jenkins back home to translate the message.

Doris stretched herself on the settee in Jenkins' lounge, folding her legs so that the slit in her skirt revealed as much of her legs as possible. Jenkins chose to ignore the advance and handed her the piece of paper.

"What do you think?"

"There's only one character on it." Doris turned the paper back and forth expecting to see more writing.

"Do you know what it means."

"Well it's a little more difficult to interpret a single character. It usually depends on the context it is written. I'm not an expert but a single character could have many different meanings."

"What's the most common word associated with that character?"

"Oh that's easy. A sword."

A sword!

The word hit Jenkins with a jolt. It had been only a fortnight ago when someone had mentioned a sword to him. It was the Inspector. Had he accidentally stumbled on Major Hughes' murderer?

Then he remembered something else. He went back into the bedroom and picked up the diary that Mrs Hughes had given to him. He looked at it carefully this time and closed the book in shock. Was it possible that Major Hughes knew his murderer or did he share a common secret with Ah Seng? In any case Jenkins had some evidence that the two people were somehow linked.

He went back to the lounge and phoned Thomson. The phone rang for a long time but there was no reply. Maybe he should send a telegram to London. They might be able to shed more light on the matter.

He was still thinking when a hand crept up his thigh. Looking down he saw Doris kneeling on the floor completely naked.

"You're beautiful, he said as he pulled her up. Then he carried her into the bedroom. They made love for what seemed like hours to Jenkins. She was eager and aggressive but Jenkins was preoccupied. He simply followed her lead perfunctorily. There were other things he wanted from Doris. Doris moaned softly as Jenkins put on his clothes as soon as they finally finished.

"Come back to bed," she purred seductively, "I haven't had enough of your sexy body."

She slowly sat up allowing the sheets to gently slip off her firm breasts. Jenkins pulled her up.

"We have to go now. It's nearly nine o' clock."

"Go? What for? I want to sleep with you."

Jenkins handed her clothes. "I want you to take me somewhere."

"Now? Can't it wait till the morning? Where do you want me to take you?"

"To Ah Seng."

"What? But why do you want to see him? He nearly killed you and besides I don't know where he lives."

Jenkins grabbed Doris' arm roughly. He had only a suspicion that she was hiding something. Reading the diary had triggered a distant memory. There were too many coincidences for his liking. He could not be absolutely sure but he dared not take any unnecessary risks.

"You know Ah Seng far better than you've pretended. What did he tell you?"

"No, no. You're hurting me," cried Doris but Jenkins simply tightened his grip.

"Tell me the truth. You know Ah Seng personally, don't you"

"Yes, I do, but so does every one in Geylang. He's well known and controls everything from Geylang to Chai Chee."

"Why did he send you to me? What did he want you to do? Poison me or were you sent here to find out something else." Jenkins shook her.

"No you've got it all wrong, Hayward. He didn't send me here." Doris was sobbing now.

"Tell me the truth. You told him who I was, didn't you?"

"Yes... He spotted you and wondered what you were doing there. He's very suspicious of any new faces and would have unscrupulously killed you. I protected you by assuring him you were simply a curious onlooker from the RAF, nothing more. I didn't do any harm, Hayward. Why are you angry with me?"

"Why did he try to kill me after you left with Flynn?"

"Tried to kill you?" Doris looked surprised. "I don't know why, Hayward. There's no reason why he should and if he did I had nothing to do with it. Please believe me, Hayward."

Jenkins let go of Doris and thought for a long while. It was possible that Doris was telling the truth but he was not absolutely certain. Then he phoned for a taxi. He had decided to find out more about Ah Seng

Within an hour they were in Chai Chee, a Chinese kampong not far from Changi. This was where Ah Seng lived, according to Doris. Jenkins had ordered the taxi to wait by the main road as they walked up the mud path leading into the kampong. Ah Seng's house was tucked slightly away from the rest of the houses jutting out incongruously from the surrounding jungle. They waited under the shadows of the trees amidst the incessant hum of beetles and crickets. Presently a man appeared on the verandah. It was Ah Seng. Jenkins immediately sent Doris back to the taxi.

8. Pursuit through the jungle

Jenkins stared pensively at the kampong around him. The undergrowth had not been cut and there were only a handful of houses nestled amongst the trees. From afar no one would be aware of the houses. They would be perfectly camouflaged by the jungle.

He had not expected Doris to lead him to Ah Seng so easily. Had he been led into a trap? Was Ah Seng lying in wait? As he watched he detected a movement. Keeping behind the bushes, he circled round to the back of the house. He crouched in the darkness and watched. A window slowly moved outwards. Something resembling a huge sack stuck out of the window. Thud! It fell to the ground and rolled. Then what had appeared to be a sack changed form and revealed itself.

It was a man.

His hands were tied behind his back. He was taken aback when he spotted Jenkins. He opened his mouth to speak and then stopped. Jenkins moved closer as he tried to assess the situation. The man was short and stocky and was probably a captive of Ah Seng. He could have been another gangster, a policeman or an unfortunate victim of a crime but he seemed aware of every movement that Jenkins made. The man stood still. His face was expressionless but his jaw was locked and resolute. Even though he was bound, he faced Jenkins defiantly and returned Jenkins studied gaze. Jenkins sensed that this was not an ordinary man but why was he bound? He must have been tied up by Ah Seng but for what, he wondered.

There were angry shouts in the house. They must have discovered the man's escape. His dark eyes stared at Jenkins and communicated one word — danger.

Jenkins reacted instantly. This man would know something about Ah Seng. He cut through the ropes with his penknife. The man pushed aside the ropes, hurriedly bowed and plunged into the jungle, signalling Jenkins to follow. Without hesitating Jenkins complied.

The door flung open and men emerged from the house.

Even with his torch Jenkins found the terrain to be extremely difficult. He stumbled and fell several times as he tried to make his way through the tiny path that was sometimes abruptly obstructed by low branches and bushes. It was a struggle to keep up with the man in front of him. At every turn he was going further and further away.

Then he disappeared.

Jenkins had only covered a few hundred yards but there was silence in front of him. He was alone and lost. He switched off his torchlight and sat by a tree. The jungle was unusually dark. All around him were dark shapes on a background of inky black. No discernible landmarks.

Nothing could be seen. Which way had he gone? After less than a minute of running through the jungle he was hopelessly lost.

His eyes were beginning to adjust to the darkness and he could see a few gaps in the bushes. Which one? He had to choose soon. Ah Seng could not be very far away. The thought of wandering aimlessly in circles through the jungle until he fell into the hands of Ah Seng's men terrified him. He could wait until the morning but it was unlikely that Ah Seng would not find him before then. He searched the ground carefully on all fours trying to retrace his steps.

Crack! A twig broke. There was someone behind the trees among the eerie shadows. Jenkins got up and backed away.

A voice whispered hoarsely. "*Chi tao*. This way."

If he moved in the opposite direction he would at least be increasing his distance from Ah Seng. He treaded carefully, making sure that each step could not be heard. Through thickets of bamboo, thorny bushes and long grass, he threaded his way slowly through the jungle. The sounds behind him gradually grew fainter but he maintained the same slow careful pace. After a few minutes the undergrowth abruptly cleared into an area of tall trees. There was a suggestion of flickering light through the foliage in the distance. This must be the edge of the jungle, he thought, and broke into a trot.

Suddenly, strong arms grabbed him and pinned him against a tree. A torch shone into his face.

"Captain Jenkins! Nice surprise."

It was Ah Seng pointing a gun at his cheek.

"You should not come here." Ah Seng spat at his face and savagely kicked him in the midriff.

Jenkins could not ward off the blow fast enough and was winded. He coughed and spluttered and sank to the ground.

"Where is Sato?" barked Ah Seng.

Jenkins did not reply and was kicked again.

"Get up," commanded Ah Seng, "you coming with us."

Ah Seng led the way as they walked through the jungle. There were three men behind Jenkins and two more walking abreast with Ah Seng. They were all armed with guns. He had no chance against such overwhelming odds.

As the party made their way, Jenkins realised how foolish he had been in thinking he could escape from Ah Seng. The confidence and swiftness, with which Ah Seng found his way, showed his familiarity with the jungle. He had obviously walked through these paths many times.

They had only covered a short distance when Jenkins saw a strange light less than fifty yards ahead of them. It had a dim blue haze and not the shiny penetrating beam of a torch.

The party stopped as Ah Seng consulted one of his men. They spoke in Hokkien but Jenkins heard the word gore uttered a number of times.

Gore meant five in Chinese, thought Jenkins. Was he referring to the five men that accompanied Ah Seng? Jenkins studied Ah Seng's face. He certainly was not expecting to see the light that was still flickering further ahead. One of Ah Seng's men withdrew his gun from his holster and quietly slipped into the bushes. Jenkins could see him slowly glide from one tree to the next as he made his way through a wide arc towards the light.

Ah Seng was sending him on as a scout. Why was Ah Seng being cautious in his own territory? Then Ah Seng signalled the party to move. As they drew near the light, Jenkin's hopes faded. There was no one on the path. It ended in a small area where the bushes and undergrowth had been cleared. Large acacia trees fringed the clearing. Hanging from a branch of a tree, gently rocking in the breeze was a lantern. It stood eerily almost in the centre of the clearing and seemed to beckon them on. For a moment they hesitated. Then Ah Seng barked an order and they walked into the clearing. Ah Seng examined the lantern and laughed. It was a child's lantern.

"I'm glad you find my lantern amusing" a voice said.

Nearly everyone jumped at the sound of that voice.

Jenkins could faintly discern a man standing in the shadows not more than twenty paces away. He spoke in clear English. A distinct accent but not Singaporean.

Ah Seng took a step towards the stranger.

"Please remain where you are. You owe me an apology."

"Apology? This my territory," laughed Ah Seng. One of his men walked up to him and whispered in Ah Seng's ear. Jenkins could see that Ah Seng's men seemed afraid.

This was a chance to escape. Slowly he nudged and crawled towards the bushes.

"Stop," shouted Ah Seng turning to face Jenkins.

"Let him go," the stranger replied. "I want an apology or my honour will demand satisfaction."

"You just one man and you dare threaten me," shouted Ah Seng.

Ah Seng turned and withdrew his revolver in one smooth movement but he was not as fast as the stranger. There was a rustle and a whooshing sound and Ah Seng cried out as the revolver was flung out of his hand by a projectile. His men fired almost immediately but the stranger was gone.

"Put out the lantern," shouted one of the men but Ah Seng stopped him.

Jenkins could see that the stranger had a strategic advantage. He was hidden by the darkness while Ah Seng was clearly visible in the light. If he put the lantern out now it would take several seconds for their eyes to adjust to the darkness and by that time they could all be killed.

Ah Seng and his men were now moving away from the lantern silently waiting.

Jenkins knew that his only chance of survival lay with the stranger and he had to help him somehow. He picked up a rock and hurled it at a nearby bush.

Three shots rang out almost simultaneously and suddenly the stranger was upon Ah Seng. The men turned quickly to face him but he was faster. In a blur of movement two men fell with two swift strokes of a sword. A third slash caught Ah Seng on the shoulder. Before they could respond he had disappeared into the darkness.

"Leave the Englishman with me and I'll let you go," a voice rang out.

Ah Seng replied in a flurry of curses. There were still four of them armed with guns against one man but Jenkins could see that except for Ah Seng they all looked terrified as they stared at the surrounding jungle.

Jenkins had slowly rolled his way towards the trees. Just a few more yards and he would be out of the clearing. Then one of the men caught sight of Jenkins and moved towards him. A second man followed close behind. They had obviously decided to use Jenkins as a human shield. There was a rustle of leaves above him and a whistling sound. The man closest to Jenkins fell with a knife buried in his throat. Jenkins stayed low as a volley of gunshots was fired into a tree above him.

Three men were left and they all slowly approached Jenkins looking anxiously at the trees behind him. They were less than five paces away when there was another whistle. The knife had been hurled from the opposite direction and another gangster slumped to the ground.

The two survivors fired wildly and ran into the jungle cursing.

"Come with me quickly," a voice spoke behind him.

He could vaguely trace out the outline of the man in the darkness as they hurried through the jungle. The stranger jogged briskly and at times Jenkins found it difficult to keep up with him.

They had only covered a hundred yards when Jenkins stepped on something slippery and immediately felt a sharp pain in his left calf. He screamed as he fell. The stranger was next to him almost immediately and slashed at the ground twice. Jenkins could vaguely see a dark cable twisting in the air. Then he realised he had been bitten by a snake.

The stranger hurriedly applied a tourniquet.

"Can you walk?" he asked Jenkins but Jenkins shook

his head. He was already beginning to feel the effects of the poison.

The stranger squatted down, hooked his arm under Jenkins leg and lifted him.

"It's not very far," he said. "Try to hold on."

Jenkins was beginning to feel dizzy and held on as tightly as he could. His calf throbbed in a painful rhythm with the stranger's heavy footsteps as he trudged through the jungle. On and on the footsteps pushed forwards, now turning left, now right, cracking little twigs and squelching through bits of mud but always persisting onwards. Jenkins in a whirling swoon trying to hold back the delirium, clutched hard and wondered how the little man could bear his weight so far without rest. Through thorny shrubs and silken ferns he marched, the thudding crunch of his feet merging with the incessant chirps of crickets. On and on through the dark jungle. Through the tortured branches casting gnarled shadows and silhouettes of frightful skeletal claws, through wafts of sickeningly sweet frangipani flowers. On they marched, now in darkness now in the soft moonlight. Jenkins' head swayed in rhythm with the pain as the man trudged on.

They stopped for a short rest by a giant *Angsana* tree, silently listening and hoping that Ah Seng had given up the pursuit. Then once more with surprising ease Jenkins was flung on to strong shoulders and they plunged through a thicket of sharp *lalang* grass. The serrated edges of the grass slashed across his dangling arms but he welcomed the incisive pain, which helped him maintain consciousness. There were no visible landmarks and the undergrowth sometimes thickened into an impenetrable wall. The man hardly faltered or paused.

The stifling stench of the jungle suddenly cleared. They had reached some kind of clearing.

Jenkins lifted his head and caught sight of a large white cross hovering in the air. An omen or the first sign of impending death? He did not have the strength to determine which. He looked up again and there it remained. A huge white cross floating in mid-air. Is this the start of death he thought? His endurance was spent and he slipped into unconsciousness.

He awoke, breathing a mustiness that suggested he was within four walls once more. His eyes took some time to accustom themselves to the flickering light. Was it morning?

Turning his head slightly he could see two figures talking by candlelight. One was hooded and got up to leave as he looked. It glided over the ground and disappeared into the dark in the wall. Was that a monk he had just seen? Here in Singapore? Or was this death?

Confused and disorientated he looked about him searching for reality and some sense. There appeared to be some bricks in the walls and the earthen roof was propped by stout timbers. This was not a room, he decided, but some sort of cavern, a secret dwelling or a hideout. It was not more than twelve feet in length and just wide enough to fit the hard bed he was sleeping on. It was strangely clean with shelves on one wall and boxes at the far end.

Then he remembered the white cross that he had seen before. Was it real or was it a hallucination, a remnant of his Christian past resurfacing?

The man had noticed him stirring and was moving towards the bed with a bowl. He was dressed in what appeared to be a thin floral dressing gown tied with a large sash in the middle. The bowl was held out to Jenkins.

"Drink this. It will do you good."

Jenkins took a sip and immediately spat out the vile taste.

"Drink. This contains herbs that will flush out the poison of the snakebite."

Jenkins complied. Studying the man carefully he realised that he was not Chinese, as he had thought but Japanese. Jenkins sat up and shook the dizziness out of his head.

"You are Japanese?" Jenkins asked.

"Yes," the man replied bowing in the traditional Japanese manner and then in an after thought held out his hand. "I am Japanese. Shun-Ichi Sato and you are Captain Jenkins."

"Yes, Hayward Jenkins," said Jenkins in surprise as they shook hands, "but how did you know my name."

"Ah yes. I know many things. Too many maybe."

"I'm very grateful to you for helping me escape from the triad."

"And I am grateful to you for saving my life. I've given you an anti-venom injection while you were asleep. The pain and swelling in your leg will ease and you should be all right soon."

A Japanese doctor with gangland connections? In a cavern? If this was an elaborate ploy designed to confuse, it had certainly succeeded.

He noticed a tattoo on both of Sato's forearms, two strange black designs on taut muscles. There was something in the Sato's tattoo and his manner which were oddly familiar and tugged at Jenkins' memory.

In response to Jenkins' confused expression, Sato explained.

"We are underground and safe from Ah Seng. This is where I sometimes live, close to the Lord in repentance for the sins I have committed and will have to commit. Our paths it seems are inexorably entwined by Providence and I think it is appropriate that we become acquainted in His presence."

"It wasn't providence but Ah Seng, our common enemy that brought us together. Did he tell you who I was or have we met before?"

Again his gaze drifted towards the strange tattoos.

Sato had noticed the direction of Jenkins' gaze and lifted up his arm.

"The folly of youth," said Sato. "I was a *yakuza* in Japan, a gangster but that part of me is now dead and buried."

"Yes, we have met but not under happy circumstances, Jenkins *San* . We were aware of each other but that was all. I don't think either of us could have anticipated a second meeting but these matters are sometimes decided by higher powers and we are manipulated for reasons and ends that are beyond our comprehension."

The inscrutable Oriental, thought Jenkins. Sato in his roundabout way was trying to convey something to Jenkins, something subtle, a delicate matter but one of importance. He had to indulge this enigmatic man without upsetting his sensitivities and at the same time glean any important piece of information.

"There was someone else in this room." Jenkins paused and knew from the concerned look on Sato's face that the other person was not meant to have been seen.

"Yes, she brought me the anti-venom. She saved you from possible death," Sato replied.

She! Not a monk but a nurse. Seeing Sato's unease Jenkins decided to pursue his curiosity in a different direction. He looked around him slowly gathering his thoughts. Then he saw a uniform. It was a military uniform, a Japanese military uniform from World War 2. Turning in shock he realised that Sato knew what he had seen. There was a long awkward pause. Jenkins struggled to find the right words and Sato looked on with a sad expression. When the silence was finally broken, it was Sato who spoke.

"Some things are best left unknown and not mentioned too glibly, Jenkins *San*. What you have seen I hope you will treat with the same honourable respect I have shown you. We all deal with our purpose in life in different ways. Mine is not ended yet and it is possible you may stumble across my path as I might across yours. If you do, do not judge too quickly and don't forget we perceive honour in different ways."

Another pause, then Sato continued.

"I have to go now and you are free to leave when you wish but this place must remain our secret, the same secret as Beethoven 96. Ah Seng especially must never be allowed to know it even exists."

Jenkins watched Sato retreat to the far end of the cavern. Daylight streaked through as Sato removed a stone and crawled out of the small opening he had made. Jenkins did not stir for quite sometime but just lay on his back reflecting on past events.

Here in this vault in the jungle, he had found a stray Japanese soldier, a forgotten living relic from a war that ended years ago. Why was he here? What single minded strange purpose could compel a man to stay through all these years? An evil purpose possibly? No. Sato certainly did not sound anything like an evil person.

Jenkins had heard of stories of Japanese soldiers who had refused to surrender and who still fought on in the jungles of Guam. They persisted for years but not more than a decade. Sato did not appear to be insane or a fanatic. Sato had sounded decidedly religious and placid but obviously was still fighting an imagined crusade, but against what and what did he mean by the secret of Beethoven 96?

His limbs were sore when he finally got up but the strength in his legs had returned. Curiosity drew him towards the uniform. It was ironed as if in preparation for an important parade and had corporal stripes, a brigade insignia and some sort of military decoration. Next to the uniform hanging from rusted nails were two scabbards, one containing a short sword. He unsheathed the sword and it caught the light as he held it up. At that moment he was almost overcome by a terrifying recollection. It was the same gleam he had seen on the dreadful night at the air base and he realised then what Sato had tried to indirectly confess.

Sato was Major Hughes' murderer.

Jenkins dropped the sword as he recalled the cold-blooded nonchalance with which Sato had deposed of Ah Seng's henchman. Sato was a killer! It might have been self-defence against Ah Seng but there would have been no mercy in the killing of the four men at the base.

Sato was a killer, a cool, detached and ruthless killer!

Jenkins hurried to the opening. His only thought was

to flee from this dreadful cavern. Climbing out he found himself in a tunnel. It forked to the left but straight ahead he could see daylight. He scrambled on all fours to the end of the tunnel but paused before he crawled out. Sato could be waiting outside to chop through his neck if he peered out. He hurriedly pushed the large boulders that blocked the bottom of the entrance aside, expecting at any moment to hear the fearful swish of Sato's blade.

With a leap Jenkins was through. The ground sloped downwards and he struggled uncertainly to stay on his feet. There was a dirt track and some houses just ahead. He ran onwards and did not pause until he had covered more than fifty paces down the track.

Sato had not given chase and the track was deserted. Beyond the houses he could see the jungle they had come through that night. Behind him the track rose steeply upwards, past some houses and disappeared behind the trees. He was lost. His present course down the sloping track offered the best choice. It skirted past the jungle towards a cluster of houses. Hopefully it would lead to safety.

He slowed to a brisk walk but still looked back expectantly. At the bottom of the slope, he turned back and stopped in surprise. He saw a chilling reminder of the previous night, the white cross. There it was on the side of a grey building at the top of the hill, boldly defying the evil of the jungle which it faced. Jenkins calculated that Sato's underground hideout was somewhere underneath that building. A church was providing sanctuary for a killer.

He was nearing the end of the dirt track and there were a few people now in the streets further on. The smell of a hot morning, a mixture of tar, grass and dust, rose in gusts through the humid air. Jenkins was already bathed in sweat and quite lost. There was a junction to his right and to his relief he spotted a street sign.

Swan Lake Avenue. This was Opera Estate, home to many from the RAF and the British army. The track was flanked on both sides by railings separating it from two small canals that carried flood waters during heavy rains. The dry weather had reduced the muddy water to a slow trickle and there were some children running and playing games in the canal. Two hawkers had their carts parked close to the shops to the right. A group of road workers had paused for a rest in the shade of the large trees which lined the dirt track. There could be no danger here. If he could get to the end of Swan Lake Avenue, he would be on the main road and be able to hail a taxi back home.

He turned into Swan Lake and then several peculiar things happened at once.

A man sitting on the railings, by the small canal leisurely smoking, threw his cigarette up in the air. The street had been quietly lazing in the morning sun till then. The people on it were relatively static but suddenly there was movement. The group of workmen at the opposite end of the track dropped their tools and crossed to the other side. The men were less than sixty paces away and were moving towards him steadily.

To turn back now would be disastrous, so Jenkins walked on making sure he did not look at the approaching men but carefully considering his next move.

He had been slowly edging towards the railings when he first spotted the men. Some of them had tattoos and their collars were all turned up in typical gangster fashion.

Ah Seng's men thought Jenkins. They must have combed the jungle and were now sealing off his possible exits.

There were men ahead of him on the dirt track and he imagined there must be men behind him. On either side were two canals. He could neither move forward or back. He was trapped.

The distance between them had nearly halved when Jenkins vaulted over the railings and into the canal on the left. The little boys in them started to giggle in amusement but this was not a time for pride or embarrassment. He ran down the almost dry canal and realised he had calculated correctly. The canal ran past the back of some houses and on the other side was a small alley separating the houses. A few steps took him over to the other side and he climbed onto the back alley between two rows of houses.

Without looking back he ran and could hear the angry shouts of his pursuers behind him. They would have paused long enough, hesitated before making a decision and then split up to cut him off.

He knew he had to jump into a garden at some time cut across to the front of the house and into the adjacent street. If he could do this before any of the men reached the back alley, it would confuse them further but the row of terrace houses remained unbroken. He ran on realising that they could cut him off at the far end of the alley. Then suddenly he saw another opportunity, an open back door. Climbing over the fence, he was through the door in seconds. A Chinese woman, preparing food at a table stared at him in open-mouthed disbelief as he strode through her kitchen.

"Pardon me, madam, I think I've got the wrong house."

He hurried past the lounge, opened the front door and was out into another dirt track. There were no signs of men running. He had gained some respite but the danger still lurked somewhere beyond.

While he had been running he had kept his sense of direction. Although he was not familiar with the area, he knew it was relatively new and the streets were probably laid out in a grid. A left turn down this street would take him further away from the chasing men and then a right turn would bring him straight towards the main road.

There were fewer people on this street but they all stared at his dishevelled appearance and wet trousers in surprise. He contemplated approaching an English couple walking in the opposite direction but they seemed to be trying to avoid him thinking that he was either drunk or had been in a fight. Surrounded by law-abiding people, some of whom were English, he still felt unsafe. The assumed guise of security in a quiet rural suburb had all but vanished. Even if he could reach the main road he could still be killed in the open, in broad daylight and the terror of the triads would ensure a blanket of denials from all witnesses.

He straightened his shirt and flattened his hair and walked casually on. There were no sounds of pursuit behind him but to turn his head back might give him away to anyone who had reached the bottom of the street. He turned right and could see that the dusty track he was on, merging with a tarred road. The main road could not be far away. A man with an upturned collar was watching him closely as he walked past. A watcher possibly, thought Jenkins, and walked up to him.

"Have you got the time, please," asked Jenkins.

"Uh. 10 o' clock," the man stammered, looking slightly confused.

How many men did Ah Seng have at his disposal? There were half a dozen behind him. How many more further on? A car had turned into the next junction and stopped. Jenkins could see that the driver was English. He hurriedly crossed the road but as he approached the junction he noticed a young boy looking eagerly at him.

There was a loud whistle and a shout behind him. Jenkins ran. The car was only a short distance from him but the driver had got out and was walking away. Ahead, two men were running towards him and Jenkins could see they would reach the car before he did. He turned back pushed past the boy who stood in his way sending him sprawling and cursing to the ground.

A man stood in the middle of the street barring his way to the right turn at the junction. Turning left would bring him back the way he came. Jenkins charged him in a rugby tackle and they both tumbled over. As he got up he could hear a police siren in the distance.

The main road. He had to get to the main road. It could only be less than a half a minute's sprint away.

A car came screaming down the street and Jenkins had to jump out of the way, forcing him to turn right towards Swan Lake Avenue. A menacing knot of men stood at the end of the street. He was hemmed in between the car and the group but the siren was getting louder. The police car was somewhere just beyond the men and his best chance. He rushed towards them. They stood strangely still as he approached and then suddenly parted as a car drove through them, screeching to a halt as Jenkins crashed on to the bumper and over the bonnet. He slid down to the road as two men stepped out of the car.

"Hello, Captain Jenkins."

It was Inspector Prem.

9. Communists

Inspector Prem and Sergeant Lee had agonised over the four murders after inspecting the fence at Changi Air Base.

The communist connection intrigued Inspector Prem. He knew about the communists under Chin Peng based somewhere in the jungles of the Federation of Malaya. Where were they in Singapore?

He needed further advice from reliable expert sources. Nigel Morris, the ex-Commissioner of police, had dealt with various communist subversive activities. Prem decided that Nigel would be able to assist with their enquiries.

"Why Nigel Morris?" Sergeant Lee asked.

"He's my ex-boss and a friend," replied Inspector Prem.

"But he's retired. How would he be able to help?"

"He knows the communists. He broke up the bus riots a few years ago. Do you remember or were you too young then?"

Sergeant Lee did indeed remember the riots. The militant students. The charred body of his colleague burnt to death. Days of rioting and violence after a strike got out of hand.

The strikers were from the union of a bus company. Their strike had paralysed the transportation system but some among the general public openly supported them. Chinese middle school students donated money and brought the strikers food. Many believed that these students were communists but Sergeant Lee knew that this was merely a rumour.

He also knew that Nigel Morris' inept handling of the riots led to several deaths. Sergeant Lee decided that it was best not to mention this to the inspector.

They drove to Morris' plush residence on the east coast, off Mountbatten Road. The driveway wound through a garden of neat rose bushes and orchids, dotted around the shade of majestic palm trees. Morris was in the veranda lounging on the soft batik cushions which covered the rattan furniture.

"Hello, Prem. Nice to see you again, although I must say you have thickened around your torso a little bit. They're feeding you well at the CID," Morris laughed.

"Too well and too much of the soft stuff, Nigel. This is my colleague and partner, Sergeant Peter Lee."

They sat down and waited patiently as Morris' maid poured out the tea and served them.

Inspector Prem got to the point immediately.

"I need an update on the communists in Singapore, Nigel."

"Communists? The Emergency ended last year Prem. Officially the British government are not fighting the communists in Malaya."

"Yes, officially but the Malayan Communist Party still exists. I'm sure they're planning something."

"Well at the moment, there's more activity in mainland Malaya. Chin Peng is still top dog with the MCP but here in Singapore, there is a new communist threat. Barisan Socialis."

"The new party? What makes you think it's communist? Have you got proof?" Sergeant Lee blurted out.

Inspector Prem raised his hand to stop Sergeant Lee.

"We're not here to discuss politics," Inspector Prem remarked calmly.

Turning back to Morris, he explained, "The communists might be involved in two or more murders. You know something about their methods, Nigel. Do you think they would murder for political reasons?"

"Most certainly. They've already committed many atrocities in the jungles of Malaya. They would do anything to gain power. "

"What about here in Singapore?" Prem asked. "Can you think of someone they would employ here?"

"Well Prem, I know someone who can help you there. This is strictly between us and nothing leaves this room."

Nigel Morris turned to look at Sergeant Lee who immediately got up and walked out into the garden below.

"John Thomson. You'll find him at the British High Commission. You must give me your word that my name is not mentioned in any of this."

"On my word of honour, Nigel, nothing leaves this room."

"Good man. I know I can trust you."

Inspector Prem got up to leave but Nigel's hand reached out to stop him.

"One more thing," whispered Nigel Morris. "There is someone in the MCP Politburo who organises their dirty work. Fong Chong Pek. He has a criminal record and he is here in Singapore. Arrived just a few weeks ago if my sources are correct."

"You think that he plotted these murders?"

"I don't really know but if the MCP is involved in any criminal activity, then Chong Pek will be the brains behind it."

"If he is, we'll get him."

"That would be near impossible. Fong covers his tracks well. Nothing can be traced back to him. You won't find any evidence to convict him."

Nigel looked at the inspector with genuine concern.

"Be careful, Prem. Fong Chong Pek has dangerous friends."

Nigel's view of Fong was confirmed when Inspector Prem studied his records later that day at CID headquarters. Fong had been arrested several times but never brought to court.

"I want you to place a partial points bulletin for Fong Chong Pek to these CID squads only. Stress confidentiality. No one else should know, we're looking for him."

"Why not an APB," Sergeant Lee asked.

"Just in case, Peter. Just in case."

Sergeant Lee looked up at Inspector Prem.

"You think there are communists here in CID headquarters? Did Nigel Morris suggest that?"

"No, but I'm not taking any chances. We'll use only the men we can absolutely trust. Fong has a brother in Singapore. We'll arrange a stake out. He might be there."

The CID spent several days of surveillance at Fong' brother's address without success. Inspector Prem's attempts to arrange a meeting with John Thomson proved to be even more frustrating. The British High Commission initially refused to allow their personnel to be interviewed. They even denied the existence of John Thomson. It was only at the insistence of the Governor's office that Inspector finally managed to secure an interview.

Inspector Prem kept details of the meeting quiet. On that morning he had quite suddenly announced to Sergeant Lee that they had to leave immediately.

"Who are we meeting?" asked Sergeant Lee.

"A Mr John Thomson. He liases with the police and the army on security matters. A not too clever front for an MI5 spy."

"MI5! How did you guess that MI5 is involved," asked a surprised Sergeant Lee.

"I don't know the extent of their involvement or even if they are involved," answered Inspector Prem, "but MI5 cropped up when I enquired about the murdered Major Hughes. MI5 is largely run by civilians but has always been involved in military matters since the war. They deciphered the Nazi codes in Europe during the war. They also provided munitions for the communist guerrillas fighting the Japanese in the jungles of Malaya."

"Are you saying that they are on the communists' side and not ours?" asked Sergeant Lee.

"They are on their side and no one else's. They have their own agenda. They make allies with those whose interests mirror their own. We are not unique here in Singapore. The same double-dealing has occurred in India, the Palestine and South Africa. The MI5 uses all embryonic political organisations in these budding new nations for self gain and then disposes of them when they cease to be beneficial."

John Thomson ushered them into his large air-conditioned office at the British High Commission. Sergeant Lee plumped himself into the largest settee. The Inspector moved to the opposite side of the office so that Thomson had to move his head from side to side as he spoke to them. The mild discomfort would make it more difficult for the MI5 man to dominate proceedings.

"Thank you for seeing us at such short notice, Mr Thomson," said Inspector Prem.

"A pleasure, Inspector. Her Majesty's Foreign Service is always glad to be of some assistance," replied Thomson.

"The murders in Changi Air Base are a terrible tragedy and the CID is determined to bring the perpetrators of this horrendous crime to justice," said Inspector Prem.

"Oh yes, indeed. I certainly welcome the help of the CID," said Thomson.

Not quite challenging us on the question of jurisdiction, thought Inspector Prem but nevertheless he saw an opening.

"So where have your investigations led you so far?" the Inspector asked, nonchalantly.

"Investigations? I'm afraid we haven't done any. As you know jurisdiction was taken out of our hands," said Thomson. There was no mistaking the trace of bitterness in his voice.

So Thomson had been overruled but by whom? His own department or...?

"Well the CID is always willing to work in tandem with your department. We value your long experience and resources," said the Inspector.

"Oh, really. I've heard that before," Thomson murmured.

Not the British. His trace of disdain is directed towards the locals. Someone from the government or maybe the police must have overruled him, Prem realised.

"You told me on the phone that Major Hughes was here on holiday but perhaps his wife had some work or business to complete in Singapore. Some investment deals possibly?"

"No, the Hughes family was quite devastated by the war. I don't think overseas investment could be accommodated in their limited budget," said Thomson.

"Yes, I'm sure you're quite right because the Foreign Office funded their air fare here," said Inspector Prem quietly.

His piercing eyes studied Thomson carefully. He was pleased to note Thomson's hesitation and slight unease which was quickly masked. The concealment itself was more important than the actual discomfort. It confirmed one of Inspector Prem's suspicions. Major Hughes was an important person in Her Majesty's government and probably still worked for them. He was not a retired gentleman on holiday in Singapore.

"It was actually funded by the RAF. A generous act in return for the Major's long service with the RAF."

Inspector Prem paused and nodded in agreement. He touched his collar. It was time for Sergeant Lee to ask their rehearsed questions while he looked on.

"But the good Major was in the British army and not the RAF wasn't he?" asked Sergeant Lee. The Inspector could see Sergeant Lee smile as they both noticed Thomson wincing.

"Yes, but we were all comrades in arms during the war."

Sergeant Lee continued.

"He wasn't captured during the Japanese invasion, was he?"

"No, that came later. He was one of those fighting in Batam Island or Borneo. I'm not sure which. He served as a POW for only a year before the war was over."

"He is acquainted with Captain Jenkins, of course, who was at the party," said Inspector Prem. Thomson's head swivelled quickly back to him.

"No, two different generations. I doubt whether they have even heard of each other."

That confirms one thing thought the inspector. Jenkins did not murder Major Hughes. He decided to shift the subject slightly.

"The Changi murders are very similar to another murder years ago."

"Oh?"

"We strongly suspect a communist involvement."

Thomson looked hard at the CID men. Inspector Prem could see that his curiosity was aroused.

"The Changi murders were probably carried out by the same person who murdered a suspected MCP member years ago. Was Major Hughes in any way involved in intelligence work against the communists during the Emergency?"

A tiny flicker in Thomson's eyebrows but he did not reply. The inspector already strongly suspected that Major Hughes worked for MI5. He pressed on.

"Was Major Hughes a double agent?"

Thomson visibly jerked in his chair and almost stood up.

"Preposterous!" Thomson exclaimed. "There are no double agents in Her Majesty's government. James Hughes was unquestionably loyal."

"But you've acknowledged that he is an agent. An agent for MI5," Prem replied calmly.

Thomson leaned back and a slow smile crept over his face.

"If you say so, inspector. I wouldn't know anything about MI5."

Inspector Prem leaned forward.

"Mr. Thomson. I understand perfectly the secret and confidential nature of Major Hughes' assignment. I'm not asking you to divulge any of it."

Prem paused and acknowledged Thomson's almost imperceptible nod.

"I'm here to investigate his murder. Your co-operation would help in bringing his killer to justice."

"I accept that inspector but I'm certain that Major Hughes' duties had nothing to do with his murder."

"How can you be sure, Mr Thomson?"

Thomson sighed. "Because Major Hughes more or less said so. He found out something during his short visit here. Something disturbing from his past. He mentioned it to me but flatly refused to reveal anything. He said it was personal and not connected to his duties."

Inspector Prem looked at Sergeant Lee. Thomson had corroborated Mrs Hughes version of events. A significant step but it took them no closer to the killer.

"His past in Batam Island?" asked Inspector Prem referring to his notes.

"No. He said he had found something here in Singapore. Something linked to his past. That was all he was willing to say."

Inspector Prem raised his hands in mock disappointment.

"All right, let's leave Major Hughes for the moment. What do you know about Fong Chong Pek?" Prem asked.

"Fong, from the MCP? Is he a suspect?"

"No. We're just trying to eliminate him from our investigations but we haven't found him yet."

"He was spotted at his brother's house, a few days ago. I think that was when he arrived. He has a favourite communist hideout that he uses at the Changi Road and Jalan Eunos cross roads. "

Inspector Prem carefully wrote the location down in his notes.

Two roads met the main Changi Road at the Jalan Eunos crossroads. Jalan Eunos, a long dirt track from the North met Still Road, only recently paved, from the

South entrance. There were a few shops on the western end of the main road; a taxi and trishaw stand at the eastern end and a clinic on Still Road. The only building of significance was the headquarters of UMNO, a political party, opposite the clinic.

It was mid morning but traffic was heavy as usual, churning up swirls of dust. The morning heat was oppressive and humid. A few hawker stalls had taken advantage of the morning crowd and had set up at the Jalan Eunos, Changi Road junction. Not far from them, by the doorway of a small shop, an inconspicuous tramp sat quite motionless.

Dirt and grime caked his clothes and skin and his hair was long and matted. His collection tin which he held up to every one who looked his way, had already accumulated quite a few coins. He did not really care for the money. That was not his purpose here today.

For more than an hour, his darting eyes scanned through the crowd.

Every person that passed through the crossroads was registered in his mind, nearly every incident and almost every movement. Occasionally he would get up and cross over to another corner of the junction. Even as he walked, seemingly slow painful steps, his eyes watched carefully.

Next to the UMNO building two men had exchanged something surreptitiously. Quickly the tramp doubled back. This might be an important incident. The men walked towards a taxi where a girl was waiting. No, the tramp realised, the man had merely paid for the services of a *joget* girl.

A shop assistant arrived late for work at the clothes shop opposite. A street urchin trying to steal some cigarettes had just been caught red handed by a hawker. Nothing escaped the tramp's attention. He studied the faces of every passer by carefully.

No, none of them was the person he was looking for. He got up again and crossed over to the UMNO building. As he sat by the doorway, he noticed a tall Indian sitting on the short bench of a hawker stall. The man nodded at a trishaw rider, lounging in his trishaw further down Changi Road.

The tramp knew who they were. Detectives from the CID.

Inspector Prem sat by the hawker stall sipping his coffee. Parked just a few yards from him was the police car which had been carefully modified to resemble a taxi.

Prem could see both his men clearly from where he sat. Detective Razli spread-eagled in his trishaw and Sergeant Lee disguised as a tramp. So far there had been no signals from either of them and in a couple of hours they would have to change shifts. Prem knew that patience was needed for this task. He had been in several stakeouts before. The suspects always seemed to show up at the least expected moment.

It was the same that day.

Sergeant Lee stood up to stretch himself. He was careful not to reveal the revolver concealed deep beneath his tramp disguise. It was a signal that there had been no sightings yet and that the Sergeant had decided to move to another spot. Prem similarly stood up to acknowledge the signal but as he sat down someone moved swiftly behind him. It was the nature of the movement that aroused his suspicion. Sudden, swift and with unmistakable stealth.

Turning around he briefly caught a glimpse of a dragon tattoo on an arm.

A gangster!

Prem slowly sat down and picked up his almost empty cup of coffee. Through the corner of his eyes he could see the tattooed arm had moved closer. Then to his surprise the gangster sat next to him and ordered coffee.

"*Kopi oh,*" a gruff voice said.

Inspector Prem sensed rather than saw eyes burning into him. It was important to show total indifference. He looked up at the hawker and ordered another cup but the hawker simply stared back at him and shook his head.

The hawker appeared to be angry.

Then a hand grabbed his coffee cup. It was the gangster. Prem could feel his cold eyes glaring threateningly but he did not turn. Quickly Prem released his cup and took a step back. There was no need for confrontation especially since he was in a middle of an important operation. He made sure that he did not look directly at the gangster but kept his averted gaze downwards.

"You go," muttered the gangster.

Prem turned to the hawker. The hawker's facial expression also seemed intent at wanting him to leave. This was strange behaviour thought Prem. They obviously were about to communicate in secret. Was this a worthless distraction, he asked himself. He had to focus on the other two men and the stakeout. On the other hand, this could be important.

Prem relied heavily on instinct and it told him that the gangster and hawker's behaviour were extremely suspicious. He really did not want to leave. His irrepressible curiosity urged him to find out what was going on.

He took another step back, expertly feigning a stumble over the short bench he was sitting on. The act proved to be too good as he tripped himself and fell heavily on the dusty pavement. As he picked himself up he could hear two voices chuckling and laughing.

Rolling up his trouser leg, he noticed he had bruised his shin. There was no need to pretend he was in pain. The bruise was throbbing. He dabbed it gently. Nothing serious. With slow deliberate motions he dusted himself and started to hobble away. He could sense two pair of eyes turning away as they lost interest in the clumsy and apparently easily frightened man.

They had started to whisper, he noticed.

Prem took a step forward and then as if he had forgotten where he was supposed to go, turned and hobbled back past the hawker stall. He strained his ears. Their voices were barely audible. He just managed to catch fragments of the conversation.

'*Lai loh*' and '*Chap it tiam*' were the only phrases he picked up. His Hokkien was very basic but he knew that the phrases translated to 'He's here' and '11 o'clock'. He walked a few yards up Jalan Eunos until he was out of sight of the hawker stall. The time on his watch showed 10.55 a.m.

Five minutes to go but for what he wondered. He checked that he was within sight of the other two CID men. Razli was still in position near the trishaw stand but staring at the crossroads with obvious interest.

Then he heard the loud rattle of coins in a tin. Sergeant Lee's signal!

Something important had happened. Looking across the junction he saw Sergeant Lee staring hard at him.

Fong Chong Pek had been spotted.

Quickly Prem acknowledge the Sergeant's signal and started walking briskly towards him. As he crossed the junction he noticed that Razli had also noticed and acknowledged the Sergeant's signal.

"Red shirt. Changi Road. Towards the trishaw stand," whispered Sergeant Lee as Inspector Prem kneeled to tie his shoe laces by the tramp.

Inspector Prem scanned the road and sure enough there was Fong. Razli, the third CID man was already in his trishaw and was pushing it towards Fong.

"Back in the car," whispered Prem to Sergeant Lee.

The Inspector could see Razli accosting Fong offering him a trishaw ride. It would be easy to track Fong while he was in the trishaw.

Razli was still talking to Fong but a few other trishaw riders were similarly clamouring for Fong's custom. Which trishaw would Fong pick?

Let it be Razli, the inspector quietly hoped. Then to his consternation Fong doubled back. He was walking straight towards the hawker stall where Prem had sat earlier.

The gangster was still there. Prem had not had the opportunity to observe the gangster previously. Now he was shocked to see who it was.

Seow Kow! The notorious Sar Ji Red Cudgel.

What was he doing here, Prem asked himself?

Prem hurriedly bought a newspaper from the street vendor next to him. Using the newspaper to shield him, Prem looked at both men. They were not looking at each other but Fong was gradually getting closer to the hawker stall.

Further down the road, the inspector noticed Razli peddling furiously as he crossed the road in his trishaw. He obviously had some information to pass on. Prem crossed the junction. They had to act fast and keep each other informed.

Then quite suddenly Seow Kow got up and walked down Jalan Eunos. Fong was still more than ten paces away. Had his instincts been wrong Prem wondered? It appeared that the two men were not connected. Fong paused by the hawker stall. Prem could see that he was buying a packet of cigarettes.

Seow Kow had already disappeared from view. The inspector concentrated his attention on Fong. There was something in his manner which did not seem right.

Razli parked his trishaw next to Prem, got out and examined his wheels

"Keep track of him but keep on this side of Changi Road, " Prem whispered. "If he goes down Jalan Eunos, Sergeant Lee will take over in the police car, parked there. Have you still got the walkie-talkie?

Razli nodded.

"Switch it on but don't transmit and keep it hidden. Wait for Sergeant Lee's instructions."

Looking back, Prem saw Fong poised to cross Jalan Eunos, his packet of cigarettes still clutched in one hand. At that moment, he realised what he had missed about Fong.

He had bought the cigarettes without paying for them. Was it significant? He was uncertain. He had to get closer to Fong to find out. The traffic lights at the junction had just turned red. This was his chance. Weaving skilfully behind the traffic he got to the other side to only a few feet from Fong.

He watched Fong from behind. Fong was about to light a cigarette. Then Prem saw it. A small piece of paper in Fong's palm. A message! Prem was too far away to see it. Fong was tapping a cigarette on the piece of paper and then slipped the paper into his shirt pocket. The cigarette hung in his mouth unlit. He walked a few steps down Changi road and then quite unexpectedly turned. To Prem's horror, Fong was coming straight towards him.

There was nothing he could do. Prem dared not turn but kept his head down as his pace slowed down to almost a crawl. He stopped, turned to face the road and opened the newspaper, tracing his finger over the paper in mock reading. His gaze was locked on the newspaper but his total attention was focused on the approaching Fong.

Just as Fong passed him, Prem turned and bumped into Fong's side. The newspaper he was holding hit Fong squarely on the chest and was scattered all over the pavement.

"Sorry, sorry," yelped Prem. Without waiting for a reply he bent over to pick the strewn pieces of newspaper.

Fong paused and looked about him angrily. Then he pushed Prem away and kicked out at a loose sheet of paper, swearing under his breath. Prem allowed himself to stumble. He was not going to retaliate. He watched Fong's retreating form merge with the crowd. It did not matter.

He had got what he wanted!

As he gathered the bits of newspaper, Prem carefully looked at the paper he had pick-pocketed from Fong. There were three words.

Blue. Opel. Still.

It was a message and an important one. He had to get to Sergeant Lee quickly or they would loose Fong. He left the remnants of the newspaper and made his way back to Jalan Eunos. The crowd frustratingly got in his way a few times. He could not run as that would attract too much attention. He knew where Fong was going and only the police car could keep track of him.

Razli would have seen Fong turn back and would be following from a safe distance but the trishaw would be useless if Fong got to his destination.

He had reached the junction now and could see the police car parked on the other side. Sergeant Lee was already in his driving seat but was not looking his way. He seemed to be partially covering his face with his hand. Prem was about to wave wildly when a shadow stepped from behind the police car.

At that moment Prem froze. He could see in plain sight who Sergeant Lee was covering his face from.

Seow Kow was walking past the police car. He walked so quickly that he almost broke out into a jog. Prem waited a few moments to allow Seow Kow to get to the crossroads. Then he ran across the road to the police car.

"Radio Razli now," Prem almost shouted.

"Fong is getting into a car," Prem explained to Sergeant Lee.

"The communist hideout isn't in a building as we thought but the hawker stall where I sat. They use it to pass messages. Here it is."

He passed the piece of paper to Sergeant Lee who simply looked at it non-plussed.

He snatched the walkie-talkie from Sergeant Lee as soon as Razli voice came on.

"Find and track a blue Opel Rekord on Still road. Maintain your distance from it but keep on the south side. It will probably head south and turn to the city. Over."

"What now?" asked Sergeant Lee.

"We wait."

A crackle from the walkie-talkie then Razli's voice was heard.

"Target spotted entering the car. Hold on."

Another crackle.

"Someone else is entering the car. It is the target's brother. Repeat target's brother. Over."

Prem and Sergeant Lee looked at each other. They had not expected Fong's brother to be here.

"Keep track. Do not lose them. Over."

Turning to Sergeant Lee, Prem asked, "Do you know what Fong's brother looks like?"

"No, he has no records and we've got no photographs. Razli was in the other stakeout and must have recognised him"

A short pause and Razli came on the speaker again.

"Headed north to the junction. Repeat north towards you."

"On our way. Over and out."

Sergeant Lee immediately started the car.

"Slowly," said Prem.

The unmarked police car stopped and parked right by the junction.

"We don't know which way it will turn. Did you alert the second car?"

"Yes, a few minutes ago they are about a mile away on the city side of Changi road."

Prem picked up the microphone for the car's radio.

"Car two? Make your way to the junction but be prepared to turn. Target is a blue Opel Rekord. Driver and one passenger. Target will probably be coming your way in a few minutes."

The lights were green when they saw the Opel Rekord approaching from the other side of the junction. It slowed down and stopped. A horn from the car behind started to blare but the blue car did not move. Just as the lights turned red, the Opel Rekord screeched and turned right.

At that moment, Inspector Prem and Sergeant Lee had a clear view of the driver. Both turned to each other and were speechless. It was someone they least expected. Prem shook his head. It was clear to him now. It all made sense. How could he have missed the obvious?

The Opel Rekord was already speeding away and he could only see the back of the driver's head. There was no mistaking who it was.

Seow Kow, the Sar Ji triad's Red Cudgel!

"You saw the driver inspector?" asked Sergeant Lee.

Prem nodded but he was deep in thought. If they lost Fong now one of their leads could be lost forever. The blue Opel Rekord was obviously taking Fong somewhere. A place where Seow Kow and Fong could speak freely.

"Do you think he's spotted us?" the Sergeant asked as the police car began to turn.

"No, Seow Kow was looking at the lights all the time. I think he was just being cautious."

Prem picked up the microphone again.

"Car 2. Target is heading down Changi Road to Upper Changi Road. Proceed as fast as you can. No siren and get to Siglap junction as fast as you can. Station yourself at the bus terminus there."

Sergeant Lee was weaving through the traffic.

"Why Siglap?" asked Sergeant Lee. "There are three other places he could turn off."

"Because I have a strong suspicion Sergeant. A very strong suspicion."

"Razli said that Fong's brother got into the car but there were only two men in the car," Sergeant Lee observed. "What happened to Fong's brother?"

"Seow Kow is Fong's brother, Peter."

The inspector allowed Sergeant to ruminate on the facts for a while. He could see Car 2 catching up and overtaking them. Further away the distinct blue of the Opel Rekord was just about to move through the next junction.

"That's why you chose Siglap junction," Sergeant Lee realised. "Seow Kow is headed for Chai Chee, the Sar Ji stronghold."

"Yes and there are two routes to Chai Chee from the Siglap junction. The traffic will be heavy up to that point and then it is a free run to Chai Chee."

Prem could see that the Opel Rekord was speeding up. It would soon disappear from their sight. Car 2 however, was not far behind. Prem made a quick calculation and for the first time began to feel optimistic. Car 2 would catch up with Fong and Seow Kow before Siglap junction.

A few minutes later, on a quiet lay-by on the dirt track, Inspector Prem and Sergeant Lee were huddled in conversation with the detective from Car 2. The jungle was thick all around them and easily hid their cars.

"They took the second turning on the left. It leads straight into some kampong houses but I don't think you can enter," the detective explained.

"Why not?" asked Sergeant Lee.

"I think it is guarded. Lots of gangsters milling around. I saw a group of them cutting through in that direction," said the detective pointing with his thumb.

"That's towards Opera Estate," said Sergeant Lee. "Was Seow Kow or Fong with them?"

"No, the Opel Rekord turned into the narrow track. These gangsters were already there. Probably the Sar Ji triad"

"End of the stakeout," remarked Sergeant Lee.

"Yes but at least we've established one fact of the murder."

Sergeant Lee turned to the inspector questioningly.

"If one or more of the Changi murders were planned by the communists, then it is probable that Fong masterminded it and Seow Kow and his men are the murderers."

"Probable?"

"That's as far as we can go."

The police radio suddenly came on.

"Disturbance involving an Englishman in Opera Estate." The voice on the radio chirped.

The Inspector turned. He looked with deep concern at Sergeant Lee and blurted, "Hurry, we can get there in less than five minutes. Hurry, Peter. I fear there is great danger."

Within seconds they were in the police car speeding

towards Opera Estate. Sergeant Lee pushed hard on the accelerator and switched on the police siren as they entered Opera Estate's main road.

"Shall I turn left into Swan Lake or right?" asked Sergeant Lee.

"Slow down and stay on this road. I can't see anything suspicious." The kampong is on the right thought the Inspector. Could it be there? He could not be certain and staying on the main road kept their options open for the moment. Sergeant Lee stopped the car at the junction.

"There's a gangster over there Inspector."

They could see the man crossing in front of them making his way into the kampong while casting furtive glances at them.

"I think he's trying to draw us away. Into Swan Lake, Peter," said Inspector Prem, "unless you think otherwise." Sergeant Lee turned the car sharply as the wheels spun and screeched into Swan Lake Avenue.

"Nothing so far. Group of men on the right. Shall we stop by them, Inspector?"

"No, no drive through them Peter. They might be hiding something."

The men parted as the police car approached and then there was a loud bump. Sergeant Lee cursed as he realised he had driven into someone.

"It was an accident, Inspector..." spluttered Sergeant Lee.

"Not an accident, Sergeant. It's Captain Jenkins."

10. The Diary revealed

Sergeant Lee held up his CID badge as he ordered the crowd to disperse. He subtly allowed his revolver to protrude out of his shirt as they walked away muttering angrily.

"You seem alright, Captain Jenkins. No severe injuries?" asked Inspector Prem.

"No, no I'm quite alright. Just a few bruises but I'm fine."

"We'll drive you home, then."

During the drive to Changi, Jenkins related all the events of the past night leading to his chase in Opera Estate. Sergeant Lee was delighted and amused at seeing the Inspector writing the notes for once. The Inspector often stumbled and had to repeat himself as the Sergeant intentionally allowed the car to lurch on many occasions.

"It is advisable that we enter your house first, Captain," said the Inspector when they arrived. "Just in case Ah Seng's men are lying in wait."

Beautiful, thought Sergeant Lee. A search without a warrant as Jenkins nodded in agreement. The house was simply furnished. Sergeant Lee covered the lounge. Finding nothing of importance, he joined Inspector Prem in one of the two bedrooms. The Inspector was carefully putting a little book down as he entered.

"Bring Jenkins in, Sergeant," said the Inspector.

"The man you met in the jungle, Captain," began Inspector Prem. "Are you sure he was Japanese and not Chinese?"

"Absolutely. I've seen many Chinese and quite a few Japanese in Singapore and I can distinguish between the two. He wore a kimono, had a Japanese army uniform. His name, Sato is definitely Japanese."

"Was he in his forties or older?" asked Inspector Prem.

"Not older than forty. He appeared to be in his late thirties but I could be wrong. His physique definitely was that of a man just past his prime but not above forty I think."

"That makes him a soldier in his very early twenties during the war," commented Sergeant Lee.

"You said there were two swords in the cavern. Was he carrying the other one when he left?" asked Inspector Prem.

"I don't know. He could have but I wasn't looking very carefully and it was dark."

"But you are quite sure that the second sword is the one you saw on the night of Major Hughes murder," said Inspector Prem.

"Very similar. I can't be absolutely sure of course but when I held the sword up, the glint and curvature of the blade was reminiscent of the one the murderer used in Changi. The descent of that blade towards one's neck is not something that is easily forgotten," Jenkins replied, shaking his head at the frightful memory.

"I'm sure you're not mistaken, Captain but a Japanese soldier wandering around the jungle in Kampong Chai Chee is very hard to believe," said Inspector Prem.

"No one has heard or mentioned him through the many years since the Japanese surrender. Not a single rumour that I know of," added Sergeant Lee.

"There may be one other possibility," said Inspector Prem. "Did Sato, if that is truly his name, appear to be a trifle excessive in proving that he was Japanese?"

"No, in fact I had to ask him if he was Japanese. He didn't tell me he was," Jenkins answered.

"During the whole time he was with you do you think he acted normally?" asked Sergeant Lee as he grasped the reason for Inspector Prem's question.

"I don't think a killer can ever act normally," replied Jenkins.

"So he was aggressive?" interrupted Sergeant Lee.

"No, not at all. He was placid and almost amiable. He behaved almost like a friend whom I was visiting and was courteous and hospitable."

"Putting aside the fact that he was a killer, would you say he was sane and not a lunatic who was obsessed with being Japanese? I'm sure you must have met with various people who were unable to cope with the traumas of the war. Do you think he was suffering from a similar mental condition?" Inspector Prem asked, stressing the important words and looking directly at Captain Jenkins all the time.

"To be honest that hadn't occurred to me but I'm

still satisfied that he was Japanese. I'm sure you're right in thinking that the war must have unhinged him."

The Inspector looked at the ceiling mimicking deliberation and then quite suddenly turned to Jenkins.

"We spoke to Mrs Hughes before rescuing you in Opera Estate. She mentioned a diary."

A diary? That must be what he was reading in the bedroom, thought Sergeant Lee. He watched in silent amusement as Jenkins shifted uneasily in his seat.

"A diary?" Jenkins responded with innocence.

"Important evidence, Captain which I'm sure you don't want to withhold. Have you got it with you?" The Inspector's quiet tone had a threatening edge to it.

Jenkins sat quietly in awkward silence and Sergeant Lee could see he was struggling within himself. Privacy, he knew was very important to the British. Inspector Prem was looking on like a hawk. In spite of Jenkins' previous ordeal, Sergeant Lee knew that the Inspector would press on unrelentingly. Presently Jenkins got up, walked into the bedroom and came back with a small black book.

"Mrs. Hughes gave me this on assumption that I treat it with the respect due to a dead man's possessions. I've read it myself, Inspector and can't find anything which might help your investigation. Before I hand it to you, will you give me your word as a gentleman that it will be afforded the same respect?"

"I will treat it with the same respect that you have, Captain," said Inspector Prem reaching out for the diary which was still held away from him. "I give you my word."

Inspector Prem flicked through the pages and studied

the single written page carefully. Sergeant Lee had moved over to his side to read the diary.

Basking in the sun, the city has changed so much since we left after the war ended and peace began. Elegant buildings and a few landmarks still stand but none of the peaceful colonial atmosphere that we all loved exists anymore. Everyone here seems to have forgotten the war but the scars remain. There are still quite a number of colonials who chose to stay behind, unable to part with a lifetime's habit of tiffin and tea in spite of this island's looming independence. Hours frittered away in the blazing sunshine. Opulence and extravagance still dominate their pretentious activities. Very few would gladly embrace the changes that are sweeping through this island and accept that they are no longer masters of this nation. Even the churches and convents face an up hill task in coping with progress and crime. No longer can they provide the spiritual comfort for people who work from 9 to 6.

"Did you scribble this bit at the bottom, Captain," asked Inspector Prem.

Jenkins moved to the Inspector and stepped back suddenly.

"What's the matter?" asked Sergeant Lee. Jenkins' face seemed frozen in horror.

"That's Sato's tattoo," Jenkins croaked.

Both Inspector Prem and Sergeant Lee turned to look at the mark at the bottom of the page.

"It could be a Japanese character," said Inspector Prem looking enquiringly at Sergeant Lee.

"Japanese and Chinese, Inspector. The written form

of both Mandarin and Japanese are almost identical. The character in the diary is too straight and badly written but I think we've stumbled on something which is important," said Sergeant Lee.

Inspector Prem was deep in thought concentrating on the diary. "You wouldn't happen to know what it means in Japanese do you."

"It bears some resemblance to *tao*. That character is pronounced dow in Mandarin. It means knife or sword and probably represents the same in Japanese," said Sergeant Lee.

"That's why Sato had it tattooed on his forearm. He was deadly with the sword," said Jenkins. "It also explains Major Hughes' murder. The major knew that Sato was still hiding in the jungle and Sato killed him to keep his existence secret."

"Major Hughes was here for only a few days before he was killed. He couldn't have found out about Sato in such a short time," countered Sergeant Lee.

"Captain Jenkins could be right, Sergeant," said Inspector Prem. He noticed a strange expression come over Jenkins face and remarked, "You've seen something, Captain."

"No, there is something else I must show you," said Jenkins and then he quickly left the room.

Sergeant Lee looked at the Inspector. "It all points to this Sato person, doesn't it? Do you think he killed Major Hughes?"

"Maybe, but that does not solve the case. It complicates it," said Inspector Prem.

Jenkins came back excitedly handing a torn piece of paper to the Inspector. "I thought that 'sword character' was familiar. Ah Seng was given this piece of paper at a coffee shop and was absolutely livid. The character is identical to Sato's tattoo. The meeting in the jungle can't be coincidence. Sato and Ah Seng must have known each other for quite some time."

Inspector Prem compared the two characters and noticed the similarity.

He handed the paper to Sergeant Lee and looked up at Jenkins. It was the same piercing look that Sergeant Lee knew well. "You met Ah Seng at a coffee shop?" he asked slowly.

Jenkins narrated his first meeting with Ah Seng in Geylang.

"It was Flight Lieutenant Flynn's idea you say?" asked Sergeant Lee as he exchanged glances with Inspector Prem.

Jenkins nodded.

"Do you have his address?" asked Inspector Prem.

"I'm afraid I don't know where he lives," said Jenkins. "Whenever we do meet after work, it's usually at some insalubrious haunt that Flight Lieutenant Flynn frequents," he added remembering the cockfight. "I can let you have his telephone number though."

"That's all right, Captain, we'll get it from the air base. Just one more thing. The church you mentioned, the building with a large white cross," said Inspector Prem. "It's not a church. It is a convent. The convent on the hill mentioned in the diary. I'll make an appointment to visit it in the next few days. I'm sure you'll like to come."

"Yes, definitely," said Jenkins.

Inspector Prem was about to slip the diary into his pocket when Jenkins stopped him.

"I'm sorry, Inspector, you'll have to ask Mrs Hughes permission before I can let you have the diary."

"I suppose we'll manage for the moment without it," sighed the Inspector.

Sergeant hurriedly copied the contents of the page and then led the way to the car as they left a tired Jenkins.

"Case solved, Inspector?" remarked Sergeant Lee.

"Explain," smiled the Inspector.

"We have found the Changi murderer. It is Sato."

"We have confirmed one of the murderers, Peter. Remember there were four murders and two murderers. Sato is one of them, the sword murderer. He is linked to Ah Seng who in turn is Seow Kow's boss. Fong Chong Pek is linked to Seow Kow. I still feel the gangsters of Sar Ji are in this somehow but we lack the evidence."

"In that case, we've still got both murderers. Sato is one of them and the other could be one of Ah Seng's men. I think Ah Seng hired Sato to kill Major Hughes and used some of his men to help Sato cover his tracks by killing the guards. We just need to find proof but we're getting close at least."

"Far from it, Sergeant. There is also a suspected link within the air base personnel themselves. Someone who corroborated with one or more of the murderers. Someone told them about Major Hughes' visit and someone stopped Captain Jenkins."

"Yes, you're right. We need evidence to pin Ah Seng and find out the RAF inside man."

"We also have to find out a little more about this mysterious jungle man, Sato. A visit to the Japanese Consulate tomorrow will help us verify Sato's existence."

Jenkins watched them drive away in the police car. Then he sat at the table and opened the diary. He was close to exhaustion but what he had to do could not wait. How did he fail to spot it the first time? The Japanese character and the convent were clear indicators that the diary was coded. He was sure of it. A word based code hidden in the single page of writing. There had to be a key somewhere which would unravel the diary's secrets. He searched through the blank pages carefully, checked the spine and the binding to satisfy himself that the key was not hidden somewhere other than the written page.

The word convent could be the key. C could represent the third word, O the fifteenth. No that was not it. He tried a few other combinations using convent as the key but could not construct a meaningful sentence or phrase from the chosen words. He tried one key after another and failed. His leaden eyes kept closing in protest but he was determined to unlock the mystery that night.

He tried to recall what he had learnt during his initial training at Leconfield House in London. A code always has a key. It could be an important word, a phrase or a set of numbers. The only way that the key would not become confused or forgotten was to incorporate it into the coded message itself. Somewhere in Major Hughes' diary there had to be an important word. That word would then be used to scramble the message. Find the key and you will be on the first step into unravelling the secrets of a code. That was what his superiors had said but there were no obvious keys here. No word that was incongruous or was written differently to suggest its importance. This message was not a jumble of letters but written in English in the same hand and style throughout. Nothing emphasised or underlined.

Mrs. Hughes had said that her husband had spent a long time writing his diary and had mentioned that the diary was important. She had also said that her husband did not like to divulge anything until the very last. Whatever the code was, it had to be simple if it was to be recalled in the distant future. A code simple enough for Major Hughes to reveal his hidden message without any elaborate calculation. Simple enough for him to read instantly by choosing the words in a predetermined sequence.

That must be the key. Not a single word but a rearrangement of the words or sentences in some kind of order. But what order? It could be the first word in the first sentence, followed by the second word in the second sentence. No, that did not make any sense. The first letter of the first line followed by the second letter. That was too obvious. He had to approach this systematically. That is how a trained MI5 or MI6 man would do it.

Carefully he rewrote all the sentences, one below the other placing each word in neat columns. As he tried to unscramble those words it did not produce a sensible message. He re-wrote the first words in a column and the last words in another. Basking, Elegant, Everyone, There How, Opulence, Very, Even, No.

Then he saw it.

He had broken the code. His temples throbbed in a flood of excitement as he stared at Major Hughes' posthumous message. His throat felt dry as he checked the diary again. It was crystal clear.

The first letter of the first word of each sentence spelt Beethoven. Beethoven 96. Sato had mentioned it. The secret of Beethoven 96 he had said. Could there be more he wondered? The last letter of the last word. No, that was gibberish. To his amazement another word popped out of the diary. The first letter of the last word produced BARISANC. The new party suspected to have communist support was called Barisan Socialis. The C must be superfluous. No, he concluded there were two words. Barisan Communists? No, that would be a repetition. Barisan crime? Barisan Conspiracy? Yes, that seemed likely. Major Hughes' hidden message became clear. Beethoven 96 was a Barisan crime or conspiracy. Major Hughes had somehow stumbled on a plot by the communists. A crime was about to be committed. Jenkins sat back on the settee, stunned and too tired to consider moving. He had to pass this message to the proper authorities but whom could he trust? The communist organisation was a powerful force. Its tentacles of influence penetrated deep into the fabric of the Malayan and Singapore societies. He fell asleep with the diary still in his hand before he could make up his mind.

11. Joo Chiat

The next day Sergeant Lee and Inspector Prem decided to call on their favourite police informer. He would be able to give them an insight into the situation with the triads at that moment. A forty-minute drive took them to the scenic East Coast Road and then to the busy Katong area where even in the early hours after dawn, groups of youths were strutting about Roxy cinema trying to impress the opposite sex. Inspector Prem could see that Sergeant Lee was momentarily distracted by a petite Chinese girl. She pouted and smiled at the Sergeant as she crossed in front of the car.

A left turn took them into the ethnic melting pot of Joo Chiat and finally to Freddy's bar. It was a popular bar and well known for its attractive *joget* girls but tainted like so many bars with a gangland presence. Their contact had chosen this bar mainly because policemen, usually those who were corrupt were known to frequent it. The early hour would also ensure privacy from prying eyes.

They walked through the bar past several dance hostesses and Inspector Prem noticed that Sergeant Lee looked at a couple of them with approval. The bar's owner, Freddy, ushered them through two doors and up the stairs into a small darkened room. At one end was a bed covered in red, shiny floral sheets, its purpose only too well known to the policemen. Three chairs had been provided for them and their contact. They had to wait for a long time before the door opened and to their surprise a scantily dressed girl walked in and spread herself on the bed.

"Where's David?" asked Inspector trying his best not to look at the mound of pubic hair as the girl crossed her legs. Sergeant Lee had no such qualms and eyed her greedily.

The girl's voice was low and husky as she spoke.

"David will be here. I entertain you good?" She tossed her head back and then turned seductively to Sergeant Lee.

"Perhaps some other time," said Inspector Prem looking at Sergeant Lee.

The girl shrugged and rang a little bell by the bed. The door opened quietly and a huge man walked in.

"Hello Inspector, welcome to the tiger show," he laughed.

Inspector Prem smiled pleasantly and introduced Sergeant Lee.

"David is Freddy Toh's brother, Sergeant. You've probably heard of the two Toh brothers seeing you live in this district."

Sergeant Lee gestured towards the girl who was still sprawled on the bed.

"Oh sorry. This here Mimi Wong. Our very popular girl. Freddy say, it is good idea if she here too. You two watching me having sex with her. No one suspect."

Seeing the Inspector's frown, David added," She is safe, Inspector, She can answer some of your questions better than me."

The Inspector shrugged and began. "Do you know of any triad Red Cudgels active in the Changi area especially one whose favourite weapon is a knife?"

"Most triad members use knives or meat cleavers, not just Red Cudgel," said David.

"Yes, but killing four in one night quickly and silently requires someone special even by gangland standards," said Inspector Prem.

"You right! Red Cudgel would be responsible for that. I can't think of one who is knife specialist."

"What about the type of knife, a sword say?" asked Sergeant Lee.

"Definitely no. Too bulky. Cannot hide weapon." replied David.

There was a knock at the door and Freddy, the bar owner, entered with a tray of glasses.

"Compliments of Freddy's bar, Inspector," said Freddy winking at them and then quietly leaving.

"Is it the Sar Ji triad that controls Changi?" asked Sergeant Lee.

"Yes Sar Ji, Ah Seng's triad," David answered. "He covers whole area now from Changi, Bedok, down to Geylang, part of Joo Chiat and most of Katong. Practically half eastern Singapore."

Inspector Prem sat back in surprise.

"All that? Are you sure? I thought he was based in Kampong Chai Chee and was named successor to the Sar Ji triad after his sister married their biggest Red Cudgel. That was only last year."

"Last year and two deaths ago. He killed Sar Ji chief. Brutally killed. He blamed Kong Puek people in Joo Chiat at the same time. Kong Puek triad weak at that time. Power struggle inside. Leader killed.

Ah Seng moved his men in. Take over weakened extortion rackets and bars in this area. Other triads too shocked. Failed to react. Once he had Joo Chiat, Geylang was next target. He was too strong for smaller gangs in Geylang. He won control. No big fight, no big bloodshed," explained David.

"He must be the triad Dragon Overlord they are talking about at the Organised Crime Division," said Sergeant Lee.

"Not yet. He still has long way to go before he Overlord. But he in the best position to be Dragon Overlord in Singapore, compared to the other chiefs," said David.

"A frightening proposition," mumbled Inspector Prem. "Well, just one more thing, David. I've got a photograph here. I wonder if you have ever seen the third person from the left."

Sergeant Lee handed the group photograph of Captain Jenkins to David who shook his head and passed the photograph to Mimi who had been quietly listening.

"No. Never seen him. I don't know many *Ang Mohs*," said David.

"I know him. I had date with him before," said Mimi to everyone's surprise.

"The third one from the left? Can you tell us his name?" Sergeant Lee eagerly enquired.

"No, not third one. The one at end. I can't remember his name but he been out with my friend Doris quite often. We visit his house in Opera Estate once and randy bugger wanted both of us at the same time. He was perfect gentleman though. These *Ang Mohs*, tend to be. Not like our miserly locals. He gave us big tip," said Mimi.

Inspector Prem reached out for the photograph, held it up so that Sergeant Lee could see it too and looked at it carefully. Both men exchanged surprised glances as they recognised the RAF man at the far end. It was Flight Lieutenant Flynn.

"Have you ever seen him talk to anyone else, with any triad members in particular?" asked Inspector Prem.

"He more friendly towards the Chinese than most *Ang Mohs* but I quite sure he never spoken to a triad member. Gangster and *Ang Moh* don't mix," said Mimi.

Inspector Prem stood up to leave thanking Mimi and David for their hospitality. As they walked downstairs there was a loud crash. Everyone rushed to the door. A large Mercedes had crashed into a night soil carrier. There was hardly any damage to the car but the night soil carrier was crouched on the road, breathing heavily in agony. The two large containers he was carrying had toppled over and smashed against a lamppost. There was excrement strewn all over the road and a ghastly smell that forced the on-lookers to cover their mouths. Inspector Prem took a step forward but David held out a hand to restrain him as the driver got out of the car.

"That Seow Kow, Ah Seng's Red Cudgel," whispered David.

Inspector Prem and Sergeant Lee stopped. To announce their presence as policemen would be a betrayal of Freddy's faith and loyalty.

Inspector Prem looked at the shifting ripples of muscles on Seow Kow's tattooed forearms, his scarred brown face and bull inflated chest. He could imagine cruel eyes looking through the fashionable sunglasses at the man lying on the road.

The night soil carrier was bleeding from cuts and gashes on his legs, arms and face. Writhing in pain, he looked pathetically upwards at the approaching Seow Kow. Seow Kow kicked him in the stomach and the night soil carrier yelped like a beaten dog. Another kick and the carrier rolled over, squashing the excrement on the road onto his face. Two women who were watching intently, jumped backed to avoid him, pinching their noses in disgust. Swearing and shouting Seow Kow kicked the man again before glaring defiantly at the crowd. Everyone, it seemed, knew who Seow Kow was and turned away from his challenging stare. Even the night soil carrier, who was piteously sobbing, looked downwards. Satisfied that the crowd was sufficiently cowed, Seow Kow drove off.

Sergeant Lee started to move towards the car but Inspector Prem quickly stopped him, pinning his arm. The Sergeant had reached for his revolver. No one moved to help the night soil carrier as he abjectly got up and placed the two large bins onto each end of his carrying pole. Inspector Prem moved away from the Sergeant and nodded good-bye to the Toh brothers. Behind him he glimpsed Sergeant Lee, in a tearful rage following. As they passed the night soil carrier, Sergeant Lee slipped a few dollars into the pocket of the carrier's shirt. Tears rolled down the man's cheek as he nodded gratefully.

"Scum. Just Scum," said Sergeant Lee and then thinking that the Inspector had misunderstood him added, "Seow Kow, not him. You know Seow Kow means mad dog, don't you, Inspector? One of these days that's exactly how I'm going to treat him. I'm going shoot his balls off like a mad dog."

12. The Japanese Consulate

Jenkins had a difficult time explaining his absence to the Commanding Officer of Changi Air Base, Air Marshall Collins. He gave a truncated version of events that had occurred the previous day. Sato and Doris were completely omitted and he simply repeated the police report which stated he had been chased by gangsters for an unknown reason. The CO's indignation was aggravated when Jenkins explained he had an important appointment that afternoon. He strongly berated Jenkins for abandoning his duties at RAF Changi. Jenkins' mind was too preoccupied with Major Hughes diary for him to pay heed to the Air Marshall's strong words. He listened passively until the CO finally dismissed him. They both knew that there was little the CO could do. As liaison officer he was almost a civilian and was not compelled to adhere to the strict regulations of the RAF.

He should have studied the diary more carefully when he first received it. Major Hughes had left an obvious message which was not even in code. Decrypting had never been one of his strengths during MI5 training.

Beethoven 96 was a code-name of something vital. Important enough for Major Hughes to be killed. The major must have passed on some information before he died. Someone in MI5 would be familiar with Beethoven 96. Was it possible that Major Hughes told John Thomson of the Foreign Office what he knew? It would be futile to call on Thomson. The man was too secretive and suspected his own colleagues. There was one other person who could help him. Jenkins picked up the telephone and dialled the code for Kuala Lumpur.

A few minutes later he was sitting at the back of a Hillman Hunter, being driven into the city. The Transport Officer who had heard about Jenkins' misfortune was sympathetic and had offered Jenkins a staff car. Throughout the drive Jenkins was working out how he should broach the subject of Sato. The Japanese officials would flatly deny Sato's existence even if they knew he was lurking in the jungle. He wished he had taken Sato's uniform or an article that would expose his identity. He was so deep in his thoughts that he failed to notice the blue car that had been following them. It was the driver who brought it to his attention as they passed the huge gas works and the putrid stench of Kallang river.

"Blue car at the back, sir. It might just be a coincidence but I think it's tailing us."

Jenkins resisted the urge to turn around and checked the mirrors instead.

"I can see it, driver. Do you think you can try to speed up or at least shake him off?"

"If you'll take full responsibility sir, I'd love to have a go."

Jenkins agreed and the car suddenly shot forward

towards the traffic lights. Skilfully, the driver squeezed the car into a gap in the right lane. There was no time for the blue car to respond.

"Well done, driver, but I think he's waving his arms and signalling he wants to switch to the right lane. He's definitely following us."

The lights were turning amber and Jenkins, looking at the side mirror could see that the blue car had succeeded and was only three cars behind them.

"Don't worry sir. I've still got another trick to play."

The driver pressed hard on the accelerator and instead of turning right weaved in an arc and drove straight. There was a screeching of brakes from the car to their left and angry shouts and curses. For a moment Jenkins thought there was going to be a nasty accident but the driver swerved past and they were through.

"We've lost him sir. He's turning right into North Bridge Road," chuckled the driver. "Why was he following us?"

"I think it's someone who owes me money and is eager to pay me back," smiled Jenkins.

The realisation that Ah Seng had not given up the chase chilled Jenkins. The gangsters were still after him, he thought. But how did they know when he would emerge from Changi air base. How did they even know that he worked there? He had to watch his back from now on. He knew that Ah Seng would kill without a second thought.

"Is it possible for him to turn into this road further up?"

"This is Beach Road, sir. It runs parallel with North Bridge Road where they turned into. If I beat the car to the next junction, it will take him a full minute to turn into a side street and come up behind us. Keep a look out as we pass the next junction on the right."

Sure enough, just as they passed the junction, Jenkins could see the blue car at the other end of the side street.

"He's just turned left. He will be out into this road in less than a minute."

Beach Road was particularly crowded that day and carts of vegetables and dried fish were being wheeled across the road disregarding the traffic as usual. The vendors converged at the huge market at the top of the road. Sticking his head out of the window, Jenkins screamed at the crowd to move out of their way. As they turned right back towards North Bridge Road, Jenkins looked back anxiously. Was that a hint of blue coming out of the side street?

As they sped through the side street Jenkins kept a close watch of their rear.

"No sign of the blue car. One more turn and we've given him the slip. He'll be on Beach Road and we'll be on North Bridge Road."

They weaved through the hawker stalls that lined the end of the street. Jenkins had been struck by their ubiquitous presence and had sometimes wondered whether the Singaporeans preferred not to eat indoors or at home. They emerged into North Bridge Road with still no sign of the blue car behind them. Jenkins sat back in relief.

"Pity he's not there, sir. I was just beginning to enjoy myself," said the driver.

Jenkins, perspiring from anxiety, smiled weakly.

He had just narrowly escaped the clutches of the triads again.

The Japanese Consulate was situated at the far end of Orchard Road not far from the Botanic Gardens. The growing urban sprawl of the city ended quite abruptly here. Tucked to one side of a dirt track that joined Orchard Road, a farmer was busy watering his vegetables with two large watering cans hanging from the ends of a wooden pole carried over his shoulder. Beyond that, Jenkins could see the jungle. Did Sato regularly visit the Consulate through the jungle he wondered?

"Mr Jenkins? I am Hideki Kamishima, a representative of the ambassador. Please sit down and I'll try my best to answer your enquiries."

"Thank you," said Jenkins. "You might need to refer to some of your records dating as far as ten to twenty years ago. Do you keep such records on the premises?"

"We do have some very old records but it all depends on which particular subject."

"The number of Japanese workers in Singapore."

Jenkins thought it was unwise to reveal the main intention for his visit too quickly.

"In addition to the Consulate staff, the number of Japanese working in Singapore is not more than a few hundred at the most. I could provide you with a better estimate if needed."

"I'm more interested in the type of jobs they perform."

"Most of them are in banking or the commercial sector and the rest occupy a variety of positions in shipping."

Kamishima was brief and direct, unwilling to

comment or elaborate. Now is as good a moment as any other, thought Jenkins.

"Those in shipping. Is that the Japanese Navy?"

"No. As you know, Japan is not allowed to deploy any armed forces overseas after the Japanese surrender."

Jenkins noted a slight change in tone in Kamishima's voice. This was a sensitive subject.

"None at all?" he asked. Although he was fully conversant with the terms of the Japanese surrender it was preferable to show ignorance but once again Kamishima was brief and to the point.

"None at all."

"What about Japanese owned industries in Singapore? Could they be related in some way to the military?"

"There are no Japanese industries in Singapore." Kamishima was slightly more animated and the inert facade appeared to be slipping.

"I know the Japanese government would not dream of having a military presence overseas but is it possible that individuals might defy this rule."

Kamishima reacted visibly to the question and almost stood up.

"Are you with the police because..." Kamishima stopped suddenly and changed his mind in mid-sentence. "Are you from the British Military Police."

"Why do you ask?"

Kamishima was evidently unsure of himself and finally excused himself and left the room.

The police? Inspector Prem must have already been here. It did not matter. Kamishima knows. He knows about Sato.

Kamishima was soon back accompanied by an important looking man.

Kamishima introduced himself as Mori *San*, the personal secretary to the ambassador.

"I have checked with the British Foreign Office, Mr Jenkins and they have assured me that you would not breach the confidentiality of this meeting. Please tell me what you want to know and I will do my best to oblige."

"The same thing you told the police, Mr Mori."

"You have to be more specific, I'm afraid. I cannot recall a police interview."

"The subject of my enquiries is Shun-Ichi Sato. I have spoken to him and some of the things he mentioned might prove to be very damaging to Japanese overseas interests."

Mori shook his head and appeared to be genuinely sad.

"The terrible effects of war, Mr Jenkins. Sato is an embarrassment to us and we regret his persistence in wanting to stay. It is the strict Bushido code you see."

"Yes, when I spoke to him he was proud of being a warrior and still carried the ceremonial samurai swords. He also had a strange tattoo on his arm."

"Ka-ta-na. It is a Japanese character which represents the short sword of a samurai. You actually saw these swords?"

"Sato used them with a terrible expertise. What is he doing in the jungle after all these years and why has he not been sent back to Japan?

"A Japanese samurai cannot surrender without losing honour and shaming himself. Sato is one of the few who does not believe that Emperor Hirohito ordered the surrender years ago. In time we'll be able to convince him to return."

"In time?" Jenkins' voice was raised slightly in irritation. "It's been years. How much longer will it take?"

"We only found out about his presence this year and so far we have been unable to get in touch with him. Messages have been left for him in the jungle and I am optimistic that we will be able to meet and persuade him to leave within the year."

"And in the meantime he would have taken a few more innocent lives."

Mori's eyebrows were raised in bewilderment making his beady slit eyes even smaller.

"Taken lives? The police did not mention any of this. Are you sure?" Mori was clearly ruffled.

"I personally witnessed him killing two men and I have strong reasons to believe he killed a British subject as well."

Mori looked distressed. His gaze was now fixed on Jenkins searching and carefully assessing their positions.

"Rest assured, Mr Jenkins, if he is guilty we will bring him to justice and make necessary compensations to the victims."

Jenkins decided to take advantage of the situation.

"Can you tell me when he was posted to Singapore and his movements during the war?"

"Yes, of course. Sato was not part of the invasion force of Malaya. He was stationed in the Philippines, then Batam Island and finally was posted to Singapore in 1943."

"With his regiment?"

"No, his regiment remained in the Philippines."

A single posting was unusual during a war. Then Jenkins had an idea but he had to be subtle.

"He told me he was a member of the Kempei Tai."

"He told you that?" Mori staggered in disbelief.

The bluff had worked.

The Kempei Tai was the ruthless and brutal equivalent to the German Gestapo in the Second World War. They butchered numerous civilians, often torturing their victims and spreading fear in their wake. It made sense that Sato did not surrender after the war. He would have been shown no mercy from the British or Singaporeans.

"Can you tell me specifically what his duties were as part of the Kempei Tai?"

"I'm afraid no one can. The activities of the Kempei Tai were not recorded. Any country's secret police would not divulge their records. Whatever records they kept were destroyed immediately after the surrender."

"He must have interrogated quite a few British prisoners while he was here."

"That would have been part of his duties. He would also have kept an eye on the Korean guards that were deployed all over Singapore and monitored the communist resistance forces in the jungles of Malaya. Unfortunately the Consulate does not keep files of these details."

"I'm sure it doesn't," said Jenkins, and saw that the sarcasm was not lost on Mori.

"Are you going to arrest him the next time he visits the Consulate, Mr Mori?"

"He has never visited the Consulate. If he did we would have shipped him home."

"Maybe you were unaware, Mr Mori, but I think he has visited the Consulate to meet someone who is sympathetic with his cause."

"I assure you he has not visited this Consulate. Not to my knowledge and not with the consent of the ambassador. If he has told you this, it is not true."

Jenkins thought for a moment. He found it difficult to assess whether Mori was an honest man. The Japanese were experts in masking their true feelings, almost similar to the British stiff upper lip.

"Sato knows far too much about the outside world for a man who is hiding in the jungle. He has external contacts who obviously must be Japanese. His existence would have been made public if he communicated with the locals or the British. Since as you yourself have admitted there are so few Japanese in Singapore, his best chance of establishing a contact would be this Consulate."

Mori nodded. "A very convincing argument, Mr Jenkins. I cannot account for the movements of all the people at the Consulate, so let me check with my staff." Mori excused himself and left the room looking very disturbed.

Through the door, he could see Mori speaking to several men with vehemence. They were shaking their heads and bowing in customary Japanese fashion. Mori's face was a bright scarlet when he returned.

"No one has admitted to meeting Sato in spite of what you say. If in the future someone comes forward, I will inform you immediately. Is there anything else?"

It was a dismissal but Jenkins was not ready to go.

"Just one more question, Mr Mori. What do you know of Beethoven 96?"

"Beethoven, the German composer? What about him?"

"Beethoven 96. Have you heard anyone mention that phrase?"

Mori shook his head.

"Sato said that Beethoven 96 is an important secret. Perhaps it was a code used by the Kempei Tai during the war."

"A code? Kempei Tai codes are in Japanese, Mr Jenkins," said Mori and then hastily continued, "… during the war. As you know, they have been disbanded."

The Kempei Tai still exists? To what end, Jenkins pondered as he was driven back home. Japanese military interests overseas were non existent. Their covert operations were negligible and the whole Western World hardly gave them a second thought. Could it be that they were wrong or was he assuming too much? Mori could have merely stumbled and inadvertently gave the impression that the Kempei Tai was still operating. Then an idea struck Jenkins. The Kempei Tai's present day operations could be industrial and not military in nature. The organisation could have redirected themselves towards industrial espionage. It was a good possibility considering Japan's mercurial rise in the manufacturing sector.

13. Voices #2

There has been quite a lot of movement recently.

Predictable? In accordance with our forecast schedules?

Not all of them. I'm not sure. We might be chasing our own tail. Maybe even biting it.

Your pessimism is grossly exaggerated. Everything has gone according to plan or don't you think so?

I agree. It has.

So?

First of all. The Japanese Consulate.

They know nothing and have no wish to interfere with Singapore's internal affairs.

How can you be sure?

A Consulate cannot afford not to be diplomatic. That is their function. To pacify, placate, alleviate and reassure is second nature to them. They do it even when it is uncalled for.

Our informant at the Consulate mentioned Jenkins' visit.

Oh?

Jenkins frightened the ambassador's secretary when he

mentioned the Kempei Tai. What did the Inspector find out?

His questions sounded routine and were therefore more circumvent.

You know exactly what he asked?

It's all on tape.

Interesting.

Yes.

The Inspector found out the Consulate's depth of awareness of local politics.

But you just said the Consulate doesn't want to know about local politics.

Awareness but not involvement.

I see.

Did our RAF contact send in a report?

It has to pass through the necessary insulating channels and should reach us soon.

Good.

The operation's code name has reached too many parties and is no longer a secret.

You expected that at this point.

Yes, but we have less than a week left. Someone might discover the meaning of Beethoven 96.

We'll know if anyone finds out.

If that happens do we abandon the operation?

We can't pull out if we are not really in it.

But we are at the controls.

And that is what we should do. Control and manipulate. Even if someone discovers the meaning of Beethoven 96, it will still take him quite some time to figure out the details.

Do you think we could succeed before then?

Yes.

Have we got a contingency plan?

You are being pessimistic again.

Careful and thorough. Not pessimistic.

Good.

Well?

Yes, there is a contingency plan.

Do we switch over to that when someone finds out about Beethoven 96?

No.

I see.

What about Fong Chong Pek?

He's not a problem.

But a clever man. He could deduce that he is being manipulated.

Even if he did, his ego would not accept it.

And the triads?

Ah Seng will get what he wants and, eventually will get what he deserves.

Good.

14. Jenkins, Melanie and the CIA

It was late in the evening when Jenkins arrived home. At the sea-end of Nicholl Drive he could see the beachcombers making their way home, leaving a few Malay fishermen to collect shellfish and mussels as the tide went out. A few cars were parked by the lover's lane tucked under the tall coconut trees as the lengthening shadows of the short tropical twilight gave way to the night. Changi beach was always full of people by day but at night it had an enchanting serenity which attracted courting couples from all over the island. There was privacy here but not desolation, peacefulness but not monotony, unsullied natural surroundings without the anarchy of the jungle.

Jenkins had decided to spend a quiet night reading Somerset Maugham. How very different Singapore was in real life compared to Maugham's colonial romanticism. Feeling weary from the exertions of the day, he slipped under his mosquito net and fell asleep.

It felt as if he had only just fallen asleep when a creaking noise woke him up. The luminous dial of his alarm clock showed eleven thirty. He sat up and slipped into his dressing gown. Was it a dream, his imagination or did he actually hear a creak? Through the window he could see the dark palm trees gently swaying in the breeze. He got up and looked out of the window. It was a clear night, unusually bright with a myriad of stars and a full moon. Gusts of salty air blew in from the sea but all appeared to be still. There was no one in the garden. He turned back toward the bed and then heard it again.

It came from inside the house. Jenkins could not deny that he felt uneasy. He was aware of his racing pulse and his breathing felt strained. Was it footsteps? A shift in the floorboards as the temperature dropped? A movement somewhere, of timber or was it a person? Could it be nothing more than the imaginary sounds of solitude?

He stood still for a long time, unable to decide whether he should act or go back to bed. The chilling realisation that he was alone began to play on his nerves. There was nowhere to go and no one to turn to if he was attacked. He took a moment to compose himself. A clear mind was needed if he had to defend himself.

Finally he decided a quick search would appease him. There was enough moonlight for him to distinguish the objects in the bedroom. It might be safer not to switch the lights on. An intruder would be at a disadvantage in the semi-darkness.

He eased open the bedroom door and looked out. The rush of cool air stunned him and heightened his feeling of apprehension. It was much darker in the lounge and it took his eyes a few minutes to adjust to the darkness. His senses had deceived him. There was no movement in the lounge. He walked into the kitchen. No one. It was just the house creaking and groaning with age.

There was no need for him to look further. As he returned to the lounge, he noticed that the Somerset Maugham book had been moved. A flush of panic almost overwhelmed him. He was sure he had left it on the settee before going to bed.

Then he realised he was not alone. Someone was close by. A person hiding in the lounge, There was a faint odour of roses. Not roses. Perfume.

He whirled around. Melanie Hartson was standing by the bedroom door. He could see her tight fitting dress curving gracefully over her body.

"Mrs. Hartson?" Jenkins started moving towards the door. Without a word, Melanie took a few steps back into the bedroom. There bathed in the moonlight, she stopped and simply stared at Jenkins. Her flaxen hair cascaded over her bare shoulders. Strands of golden blonde fluttering lightly as the breeze blew through the window. He could hear her breathing, almost panting, not saying a word as she stood quite still. He wanted to ask her why and how she came to be in his bedroom but the strange atmosphere stopped him. It was charged with raw sensuous urges, compelling him to silence.

Melanie took a step forward and placed her finger on his lips. Her face was very close to his. Her lips slightly parted in open invitation. He could feel the warmth of her body through her dress. Then very slowly, her finger traced a line downwards to his neck and on to his chest. Jenkins wanted to protest but he could feel his body already responding. He had to stop her now before his impulses engulfed him. Melanie's fingers were too arousing. It reached the sash in his dressing gown.

"No, no don't," Jenkins said suddenly, pushing Melanie away.

"Nothing to be shy about, Hayward. I'm a woman and you're a man. You have your needs," Melanie replied huskily.

"This is inappropriate," Jenkins blurted out. "You're a married woman, Mrs Hartson. I must ask you to leave."

He could see that Melanie did not like being rebuffed. The smile on her face slowly twisted into seething anger as she straightened her dress. Without a word, she turned and walked out.

Jenkins spent many hours lying in bed half awake wondering why Melanie Hartson had suddenly turned up. By the morning he felt drained. He wondered how the CO would respond if he took a day off work.

The huge three-tonners that brought the lower ranking RAF personnel from their homes were already queuing at the RP checkpoint. A group of men were hauling aeroplanes, Shackletons and the almost obsolete Jaguars, out of their hangars to clean them before routine inspection. The parade ground was full of platoons of soldiers being put through their paces by the Regimental Sergeant Major. The whole air base was already hard at work but Jenkins did not have the stomach for the dull routine of the RAF. The small building he worked in was situated well away from the main administration block but it served the purpose of preventing the CO from pestering him with more work. He worked sluggishly all morning in the small office he shared with the Transport Officer. It was a mutual agreement between the RAF that he should work at the air base in the mornings and then perform his other duties with the Foreign Office in the afternoon. No one questioned this arrangement mainly because RAF Changi employed quite a number of non-military personnel whose working hours varied.

Jenkins left early that day. He had an appointment with his old friend, Dan Templeton of the CIA. He was picked up by Dan Templeton at the Britannia and driven in a large Chevrolet to the Turf Club. Templeton, like most Americans he had met, was big not only physically but also in personality. He had dark bluish almost purple eyes, an Errol Flynn moustache, an animated face that could not be missed in a crowd and a low booming voice that demanded to be heard.

"The sun tan's coming on fine, Hayward. A few more years and it will match mine," joked Templeton.

"Except you got yours from Florida and not Malaya," laughed Jenkins.

"Do you want to place some bets or shall we get down to business?" asked Templeton.

"No bets, Dan." Jenkins sipped his drink and cleared his throat. "Can you tell me all about communist activity in Malaya and Singapore?"

"Communists? We've been trying to catch their leader, Chin Peng, since the war but he's an elusive devil. You know of course that it was the Brits that provided him with a power base by shipping him arms."

"That was during the war to fight the Japanese. No one knew he was a communist. "

"We did and so did you from what I've heard. Britain made the mistake of believing that all communists were their allies just because Russia was fighting on their side."

"All that's history, Dan. What about the present day? What are Chin Peng's political aspirations now?"

"None. He wants to overthrow the government through armed struggle but I don't think he has looked beyond that. The guerrilla war of the communists has abated somewhat in these past few years. The Emergency is officially over."

"Is that because they are weakening?"

"No. The CIA believes there is a change in strategy. They are concentrating on infiltration rather than open warfare. First they establish the belief that they are the bastions of traditional Chinese culture. Then slowly, they indoctrinate their recruits with communist ideology. They have a huge following in the Chinese schools and some of the Chinese banks."

"What about the Malays who form the majority in Malaya?"

"There are Malay communists mainly in Indonesia but their antipathy with the Chinese is the same throughout this region. They fear a Chinese take-over or even a Chinese dominated nation. Communism will at some time in the future be an excuse for the Malays to strike out against the Chinese. Of course Singapore has a large Chinese majority and the communist problem takes on a different complexion."

Jenkins nodded in agreement. "I can see that guerrilla warfare is out of the question in Singapore."

"Yes, the communists operate politically and not militarily here. The Barisan Socialis still holds a number of seats in parliament and has a strong voice among the unions. They were the brains behind the Chinese middle school students' protests. If Singapore's economy falters in the near future, they will move in with a vengeance."

"Why don't the authorities simply arrest their leaders?"

"On what grounds. Terrorism? That's difficult to prove. Their leaders are Members of Parliament. It would be unconstitutional to have them arrested."

Templeton jerked his thumb at the pavilion below them. "See that man wearing sunglasses in the middle of that group. He's a communist. I think his name is Fong. Notice he commands a lot of respect and he is admired."

Jenkins could see an imposing Chinese, smiling and chatting. He was obviously the centre of attention and the people around him appeared to be in awe of his presence.

"So we can't dislodge the communists in Singapore," said Jenkins.

"Not at the moment but in time the CIA will succeed where MI5 and Singapore's ISD have failed."

Jenkins smiled. Templeton looked fully relaxed and complacent. "Will they succeed by using Beethoven 96?" he asked.

Templeton's reaction was almost comical. He turned in his chair and spilt his drink on the table in genuine surprise.

"How did you know about Beethoven 96?" spluttered Templeton.

"You have to answer my question first, Dan. What are the CIA's intentions with B96?"

"We only found out about it two weeks ago. Highly classified and top secret. Who told you?"

Beethoven 96 was not a CIA operation but important to them nevertheless.

"All in good time. Tell me what you know about B96 and I'll reveal my sources."

Templeton had recovered his self-assurance. Jenkins waited patiently for Templeton. Both parties would want to divulge as little as possible but at the same time were irresistibly rapt with curiosity. He could dismiss whatever Templeton revealed first as common knowledge and then barter for more information with the one important fact he knew.

"Well, you know I trust you implicitly, Hayward, and we can work to our mutual benefit."

Jenkins nodded. The exchange was tacitly agreed.

"Okay. Since last year we've been trying to compile a list of the communist's 'button men' in the cities. You know the ones who press the button of the explosives. The actual killers. We found that the communists were beginning to sub-contract their 'jobs' to add layers of insulation between themselves and their criminal activities."

This was news to him but Jenkins nodded in mock impatience.

"Last week one of our operatives in Singapore stumbled on the code words Beethoven 96. He was in an opium den in Chinatown and overheard it being mentioned by two triad members. It was mentioned in passing in his weekly report and no one thought it had any importance, regarding it as a gangland operation and of no consequence to the CIA. Then a few days ago, the same operative was found drowned in a *kelong*. The coroner's verdict was death by misadventure and a cardiac arrest but our own autopsy revealed the characteristic spots on the face produced by hydrocyanic acid. Capsules of this poison are a favourite with the KGB. So we knew the communists had killed him but there was nothing to suggest that they wanted him removed. He was a minor operative dealing with routine surveillance and not someone the communists would regard as important. A quick check of his reports showed only mundane routine matters except for two words. Beethoven 96. We had a long discussion with all the agents in the area and concluded that it was probable he was killed because he had found out something important. The baffling aspect of all this is B96 was mentioned by triad members and not the communists."

Communists, the triads and now the CIA thought Jenkins. The mystery was not getting any clearer.

"Surely at least one of the Singapore agents would have heard of B96?"

"No. They have been told to give B96 a high priority. We are considering sending more people to Singapore but that has to be balanced with alerting the enemy."

"Why should the triads allow themselves to be used by the communists?'

"They are not being used. I'm sure they are paid for each job and there is also the promise of security in gambling and prostitution for the triads if the communists gain power. I've told you all I know and much more Hayward. Now you have to answer my questions. How did you find out about B96?"

Jenkins briefly narrated his adventure in the jungle with Ah Seng and Sato and then mentioned how he found Beethoven 96 encrypted in Major Hughes diary.

"We've heard about Major Hughes. A very competent man but how did he find out about Beethoven 96 so quickly and why does he think that it is connected with Barisan Socialis?" asked Templeton.

"You can see the predicament I'm in. Too many unknowns. Someone must have told Major Hughes. One of his contacts in Singapore. After all, he used to live here."

"But if Hughes was murdered because he knew about B96, why wasn't his contact also killed? The only way to trace how B96 was passed on to Hughes was through his contact. If the killers knew that Hughes was aware of B96 then they must have also known about his contact and would have wanted to get rid of both of them."

"I think Major Hughes could have been killed for a different reason. He was captured towards the end of the war and served for a short time as a POW. Sato being a member of the Kempei Tai, probably remembered Hughes when he returned and killed him."

"As an ex-POW, don't you think it is more likely that Hughes would want to kill Sato and not the other way around?"

"Yes but I think Sato suspected that Hughes was about to expose him and so before Hughes could strike, Sato killed him."

"A plausible argument. We won't know until we get hold of this Sato character. CIA will be getting in touch with the Japanese Consulate."

Jenkins smiled to himself. He could picture the overpowering Templeton upsetting the Japanese by reminding them about Pearl Harbour and lightly dismissing Hiroshima.

"Did you manage to talk to Major Hughes before he was murdered?" asked Templeton.

"We met on the night of his murder and exchanged pleasantries. I was told by Thomson that he was from MI6 and not MI5."

"John Thomson?"

"Yes the self appointed leader of this region."

"You're not alone in disliking him. We're investigating him and from what I hear, so is MI5."

"MI6 does that type of work. Thomson is rather concerned about confidentiality and security."

"You mean the leaks."

So that was a well-known fact. Thomson himself must have known he was under suspicion. "What does CIA know about them?"

"Naval strength, army and RAF deployment. Nothing important has been leaked but the military aspect indicates that the source of the leak is British. Another Kim Philby is operating in Singapore and could prove to be an embarrassment to MI5. When Hughes arrived we thought he had been sent here to investigate but then I heard that you were posted to Changi a few months ago."

Templeton stopped suddenly and looked up at Jenkins. CIA had been very thorough as usual but Jenkins was not about to oblige Templeton. Let him make the same assumptions as Thomson.

"I am not too worried about the leaks, Dan. It's B96 that is more important." Jenkins was looking at the pavilion as he spoke. There was a familiar figure walking through the crowd. He had only a glimpse of a profile but the man had caught his attention.

"Seen something?" asked Templeton.

The man turned around and Jenkins recognised him at once. Flight Lieutenant Flynn. What was he doing in the Turf Club? Jenkins was sure that Flynn was meant to be on standby duty at Changi.

"Do you recognise that man talking to the tall Englishman?" he asked Templeton.

"No, do you?"

Templeton was looking from Jenkins to Flynn and back again.

"I thought he was a gangster who was about to have a fight with the Englishman," Jenkins lied.

"Whatever gave you that idea? They seem to be having a friendly conversation."

Templeton carried on talking but Jenkins was now listening with scant attention. Flynn! It must have been Flynn all along. His overt friendliness, his carefree nature and hedonistic attitude. It was all a facade. It seemed incredible that he had not suspected him until now.

Jenkins gratefully accepted when Templeton offered to drive him home. Although he had not been followed on the way to the Turf Club, he kept looking back to make sure that there were no cars following them. Even if there were, it would have been difficult for them to keep up as the Chevrolet sped through the roads towards Changi. Templeton's unbroken monologue during the drive made it easier for him to sort out how Flynn fitted into the picture.

There was only one name that came up in all the important places he had been. At Geylang, at the Turf Club, with Doris at the party and on the night of the murders there was one man always present. Flynn.

It could not have been mere coincidence that both a Barisan man and Flynn were at the Turf Club at the same time. Flynn's love of gambling would be an ideal excuse for him to meet the locals so often and his officer status would enable him to have easy access to confidential files at the air base.

Thomson had suspected that Jenkins was here to investigate the leaks. Flynn would have made the same assumption and therefore would have planned his elimination. Flynn had brought him to Geylang to show him to Ah Seng. Ah Seng could have been hired by Flynn to kill him. Flynn had taken over as duty officer after he had lost consciousness during the night of the murders. He could have helped Sato to escape. They were all only possibilities but fitted comfortably into an overall picture.

When he arrived home there was a message left by his housekeeper next to the telephone. Inspector Prem would pick him up in the morning the day after tomorrow to visit the convent.

15. Dragon Overlord

The storm was near. Dark clouds hovered over the *kampong* in Chai Chee that night. The gusty wind howled through the jungle and then churned up little eddies of debris between the houses that the jungle surrounded. Numerous palm trees that fringed the houses swayed in the wind, their branches quivering like the hairy limbs of tall sceptres. The air was charged with forbidding gloom. The storm was near.

A single dark figure, lurking behind the trees, looked up and thought that the darkness was an apt portent for the dark deeds of the night. He waited patiently, watching a single house in that sinister *kampong*. Something important was about to happen. Something he had to be privy to.

Three cars had just arrived at the house. Three cars parked by the single house he was spying on. It was a gathering of some kind, a gathering of malevolence. That much he was sure of as he watched several figures walking through the front door. They were greeted in hushed tones by the house owner. He knew the owner only too well, a detestable man whom compassion had abandoned, the leader of the Sar Ji triad, Ah Seng.

He had to get closer. Slipping through the trees, he circled a house before emerging by the closest car. No one had spotted him but dressed in black on a dark night, no one would. He weaved his away through the cars and then to the side of the house.

Then through the wooden slats, an orange flicker was seen. It lit up and moved to one side of the house. Another orange light moved in the opposite direction and then paused. Whiffs of smoke filtered out through the cracks in the walls. They were smoking in the front room. That was ideal. He knew he could get really close to listen.

Quickly he crept to a window by the side of the house. He knew from a previous visit that this window could be forced open. Pushing a stiff wire through the gap, he probed for the loose latch. Then with the gentlest tug, he pulled the latch and the window opened. In an instant he rolled through the window head first, landing silently on damp floorboards. The wavering light of a kerosene lamp was sifting through the door of the room and he could clearly hear voices. Stepping lightly, he moved to the door and listened

"... and it won't take long," said a voice which he instantly recognised as Seow Kow.

"But we must time it perfectly. Check watches all the time. We must get this right," replied another voice. It was Ah Seng.

The very two men he had hoped to be in the room were there. Unfortunately so were a number of other gangsters. He was sure they were armed.

"Ah no. Everyone do job right, nothing can stop us, "Seow Kow replied.

"Maybe we should move now. Earlier the better," a voice he did not recognise piped up.

"No!" exclaimed Ah Seng. "Too dangerous if there are too many of us there for long time. We wait the phone call. Also he might change mind. Once we know he's in Freddy's bar, we move. Lots of time. He normally more than two hours."

"You sure he has four guards?" asked Seow Kow.

"Always. Two near the entrance and two upstairs with him. He never change. It is habit with him," Ah Seng explained.

"Yes. Bad habit which will kill him," a voice laughed out.

Then something Seow Kow said made him freeze.

"You checked the house?" Seow Kow asked. "Anyone in bedroom. Girl maybe?"

"Safe. I checked everything before I opened front door. Back door is locked. All windows closed. My house I know," declared Ah Seng.

"No harm. I double check," said Seow Kow and then hurriedly added, "for you."

He could hear footsteps moving towards the door. Maybe, providence had not given him the choice. Maybe he had to strike these sons of Satan now. He unsheathed his sword. The footsteps had almost reached the door. The door knob turned. His muscles tensed in preparation. He was poised to strike.

Then the phone suddenly rang. The door knob stopped moving and the room fell silent. Seow Kow had paused as he started to open the door. He could see the door knob being released but it left the door slightly ajar. Light streamed into the room and the large shadow of Seow Kow was cast on the floor. A moment's pause and then footsteps retreated as Seow Kow moved away. He was flooded with relief and hurriedly sheathed his sword. He could hear muffled voices and then a phone being slammed down.

It was time to leave. Without pausing to look back he moved straight to the window and dived out. Rolling silently in the dirt he quickly got back onto his feet and carefully closed the window. The cars were still parked but the front door was starting to open. Swiftly he darted into the jungle and ran towards the main road. As he ran, he began removing his dark top and mask, wrapping it in a bundle and shoving it into a sack with his sword. There would be taxis plying down the main road. He had to get one immediately.

He had to make it to Freddy's bar before Ah Seng and his gang. Above him he noticed the dark clouds merging. The storm would soon be upon them.

Freddy Toh was pleased with the crowd at his bar. It was only eight p.m. but quite a few people had already turned up. Another good night's takings he calculated with quiet satisfaction. Being rich might be the ultimate goal of many, he thought, but getting there gave him greater pleasure. His doorman signalled him.

"He getting out of car. Do you want to greet him?" asked the doorman.

"Of course I have to. He more important than Sultan of Malaya. Tell Mimi to get girls ready," said Freddy.

He was feeling edgy tonight. Two black shirts burst

through the door followed quickly by three more. In the centre of the group was the triad leader who controlled Joo Chiat, a man in his late fifties, thin, hunched and with hair brushed vigorously back like a porcupine. He looked frail and weak but Freddy knew that he was ruthless and cruel. The slightest offence would result in slow painful torture and maybe death.

Freddy never addressed him by name but called him *Tua Yi,* the Hokkien equivalent of 'sir'. He preferred not to remember the triad leader's name. He wanted no knowledge of the backgrounds of any of his patrons. That had always been his bar's policy. Prima facie acceptance of customers; and service without discrimination.

Tonight this policy was being stretched to the limit but he had no choice. Powerful men were at work that night. Dangerous men who could destroy him at a whim. No, tonight he would have to *kow tow* to the strongest for the strongest was also the most lucrative.

"This way, 'sir'. This way," he crooned. "Our best ladies are waiting for you upstairs," pointing to Mimi standing by the staircase.

The Joo Chiat gang leader nodded his head curtly and allowed Mimi to take his hand and lead him upstairs.

Freddy watched as two bodyguards followed the triad boss upstairs while the other two stationed themselves at the closest table to the entrance. Always the same, he noticed. Everything as expected. He made his way behind the bar into his private office.

It was dark but Freddy did not put on the light. The office had to remain dark for his other special guests. These were the most important guests that night.

The curtains rustled and four figures emerged. Freddy

breathed in deeply to calm his thumping heart. One of the figures spoke.

"Has he gone upstairs?" It was Ah Seng.

"Yes," replied Freddy. "Two men upstairs with him and two downstairs. Exactly as expected."

"Okay. We move now, "said Ah Seng. "Which room is he in?"

"Second door on the right of corridor through the waiting room."

"You distract two guards at entrance," Ah Seng ordered.

Freddy obeyed immediately. He walked tentatively up to the two triad members seated close to the entrance. Normally he would be comfortable despite who they were. He dealt with customers from all walks of life. As long as they paid he did not care who and what they were. This evening was different. He was involved in affairs he had always distanced himself from. He was forced into it but that did not make it any easier.

With his natural congeniality, Freddy quickly engaged the two triad members in conversation. As he filled their beer mugs, he could see Ah Seng and his men creeping up the staircase one at a time. Each step they took matched his thumping pulse.

The storm broke at that moment. Large drops of rain pelted against the window panes. Faster they dropped until the torrent turned into a dull roar. It would drown out the noise of the struggle upstairs, thought Freddy. Mercifully it would end quickly and his precious bar would revert back to normal.

He looked around the bar at his guests. They were in their normal ebullient mood. Other than the occasional nervous glance at the two triad members close to the door, no one seemed the least bit perturbed. If everything went to plan they would be totally unaware of the danger lurking above them. It should be over very soon, thought Freddy looking at his watch.

Then to his dismay, he saw Ah Seng briefly appearing at the top of the stairs and signalling him to join them. Something was not right, Freddy realised with trepidation.

"Go in and see what's keeping my man," said Ah Seng when Freddy reached the landing on the stairs.

"What's wrong?" Freddy asked.

"Never mind!" Ah Seng hissed. "Just go in and check. I sent one man in five minutes ago and he still not back."

Nervously, Freddy pushed open the door. His hand was damp with sweat but it felt cold. As he stepped into the waiting room, he expected to see a girl or two chatting with a client. To his surprise, the waiting room was empty. Pushing the door wide open, he ushered Ah Seng and his two men in.

Seow Kow was the first to notice it.

"There," said Seow Kow pointing.

Freddy followed the direction of Seow Kow's calloused finger and to his horror saw blood on the floor. Streaks, parallel and still wet curving in an arc and ending beneath the door across the room. He stepped back but Seow Kow pushed him towards the bloody door. He cringed as he saw more blood splashed on the door. There were strange dark bits on the floor. Hair? Flesh? Freddy felt sick.

"Open it!" ordered Ah Seng pointing at the door leading into the corridor.

The coward in him nagged him to turn away but Ah Seng's icy stare was more fearful. In a fever of anxiety, Freddy reluctantly opened the door. The corridor was dark and there were strange shapes he could not make out on the floor. He took a step forward and slipped. Quickly he held out a hand to cushion his fall. He felt grease on his hand as he regained his balance. No, it was not grease. His hand was red. It was blood. There was blood everywhere.

An object was pressing against his thigh. Lifting himself up, he looked back and screamed in shock. Two dead but haunting eyes were staring at him. A strange man. No, not a man just a head. It was the decapitated head of one of Ah Seng's men.

Further on he could see two more bodies. Freddy recoiled in terror. He wanted to run, to hide but there were greater terrors awaiting him.

In the corner, was a strange dark smudge fixed to the top of one of the doors along the corridor. As he looked, the dark smudge seemed to become bigger and turned into a dark shadow. Suddenly it moved. Only then did he realise that it was man in black. Behind him, he could hear Seow Kow curse softly. To his surprise Seow Kow's voice was tinged with an emotion he thought Seow Kow was incapable of. Fear!

The shadow moved swiftly towards them. Freddy felt paralysed by fear. He could hear Ah Seng and Seow Kow starting to run. From what he wondered. What was this black demon? The third gangster reacted much slower and was in the act of levelling his gun when the first blow struck him. A single blow and the gangster crumpled to the floor groaning.

Then he heard a series of whooshing noises as missiles shot out of the dark figure. One of the missiles hit the wall not far away from Freddy. He instantly recognised it

Shuriken! The throwing stars of a ninja. This must be the notorious rumoured killer who every triad member he knew, was afraid of. Awe, fascination, abysmal dread. Freddy felt al these emotions as he watched the black demon just a few paces from him.

Suddenly a naked figure burst out of one of the doors and came running past them into the waiting room. The Shuriken stopped. The dark figure paused momentarily as the naked figure went past.

"Help me! Help me!" It was the triad leader of Joo Chiat. He was screaming in fright. The fierce mantle of invincibility that the triad leader always seemed to carry was shattered. He was reduced to a blubbering and whimpering imbecile.

Then two shots rang out and the shouting stopped.

Freddie got up wearily as the dark demon moved towards the waiting room. A voice behind him made him stop.

"You did this Freddy. You *lau sai*." It was the third gangster. He was cursing and crawling towards his gun. Freddy froze and could only watch petrified. An unuttered scream was stuck in his parched throat. He could not react, could not move or speak. Then the flash of a blade whizzed past him. He saw the blade descend with horrifying speed. A single stroke cut the gangster through his right eye, slashing across his face to the left carotid artery. Blood gushed out and some splashed onto Freddy's arm.

It was then that he passed out in wretched terror.

Inspector Prem was still in bed when the phone rang. His insomnia had got worse. It was 9 a.m. but he had slept for only four hours. His head felt heavy. Waves of nausea staggered him as he reached the bathroom and he had to sit down to regain his balance. A complex and long drawn case always had this effect on him. First the inability to stop thinking about work at the end of the day, then tension at the back of his neck and not relaxing and finally insomnia. He simply could not unwind. He spotted the whisky glass in the kitchen. No, not the bottle. He had gone through that last year and nearly died after the coronary. Never again. The cold water on his face refreshed and sobered him. The phone stopped ringing.

The flat was untidy. Newspapers and clothes were strewn everywhere. Spilt drinks and food left large stains on the table. He had never been able to keep the flat tidy since his wife left him. He gulped down two cups of coffee and wrapped the clothes on the floor in a bundle. Must remember to pass it to the woman next door, he said to himself.

The door bell rang. Sergeant Lee and two uniformed policemen were waiting outside.

"Are you ready, Inspector? We have an emergency. A homicide."

Inspector Prem dressed quickly and jumped into the waiting car. Behind him he saw Sergeant Lee taking his laundry to the flat next door.

"I phoned earlier but there was no reply. Has the insomnia come back, Inspector?" asked Sergeant Lee.

"Yes, but I don't want any sleeping pills this time. Thank you for remembering my laundry."

The police car turned into Joo Chiat and stopped by Freddy's bar.

"A homicide here?" asked Inspector Prem.

"Wait till you see the victims, Inspector," said Sergeant Lee.

They walked through the police cordon and were greeted by scenes of blood. Blood on the walls, on the floor, on the cushions. There was so much blood that it seemed that brothel itself had bled. Huddled in one of the larger rooms were a few half-naked prostitutes being comforted by the madam, a stout woman in her fifties who stared at them contemptuously.

"Tough nut, that one," said Sergeant Lee. "She nagged the first policemen on the scene for being late and then demanded a fee for walking into her brothel."

They found the bodies upstairs. Inspector Prem counted three heads, decapitated and one with a huge gash across the face. A single eye was still dangling from an open eye socket of one of the heads. Two forensic men were examining the bloodied bits and taking some photographs. Sergeant Lee showed the tattooed forearms to the Inspector who nodded in recognition. The Inspector signalled to the forensic men to put the butchered corpses into the body bags. He had seen enough.

"Time of death could not have been very long ago," commented Inspector Prem.

"An hour maybe two is the forensic estimate," said Sergeant Lee.

"Are they from a local triad? The tattoos on the bodies do not seem identical."

"No, they are not. Two from the Sar Ji and the other three from the local Joo Chiat Triad. A triad that doesn't exist anymore after today. The one who is shot in the waiting room is Lim who's the biggest gangland chief in Joo Chiat and the other two are his Red Cudgels. Whoever did this has literally chopped off the head of the Joo Chiat triad."

"The girls in the other room must have been witnesses."

"None of them are willing to talk. The madam says she saw one masked man and that's all. Her girls only just managed to get out of the way. She refuses to admit she saw anything else. They are all too frightened."

"A demonstration to all concerned. One name springs to mind."

"Ah Seng?"

"Yes, Freddy and several patrons saw him and Seow Kow running out. They're responsible but no one will dare testify against them."

Moving back downstairs they met De Souza, the pathologist.   The forensic man cleared his throat before he spoke. "The modus operandi seems wrong, Inspector. Three men were shot. Two downstairs and the gang chief upstairs. The other four upstairs were killed by a single knife wound."

De Souza paused and smiled triumphantly at Inspector Prem.

"Very similar to the Changi murders?" asked Prem.

"More than that. Almost identical. The same murder weapons as the Changi murders were used here."

"I can see that the sword wounds could be identical but wouldn't you need a ballistic test to verify which guns were used."

"Oh, the ballistic tests will only confirm what I already know. One of the bullets found could only have been fired from the same gun used in Changi. The bullet is 9 mm and was fired from a Stechkin Pistol. It had the right cartridge size, the inclined stripe and indentation parallel to each other which are typical of bullets fired from a Stechkin Pistol."

"I've never heard of a Stechkin Pistol," said Inspector Prem.

"I'm not surprised," smiled De Souza. "Very few people have. It's a special hand gun made in Russia."

"In Russia!" gasped Sergeant Lee. "How did it get here."

"I don't know but it is very effective at close range and very accurate. A good choice for a..."

Inspector Prem interrupted with a gesture. He spoke slowly and deliberately.

"You seem to know a great deal about an uncommon weapon."

"I found out all about the Stechkin Pistol when they sent me to Kuala Lumpur last year. One of the communist guerrillas was caught with it. The Americans performed the ballistic tests and I observed. Learnt a lot from the Americans. They really know their guns."

Inspector Prem and Sergeant Lee looked at each other. Communist guerrillas! Another link to their present case. Inspector Prem thanked De Souza and drew Sergeant Lee to one side.

"They must have co-ordinated this very well. Five bodies in the space of an hour. I'll wager De Souza and his partner won't be able to find a trace to incriminate anyone," said Sergeant Lee.

"He found the bullet and identified it but let's go back to the car."

"Where are we going?"

"Nowhere in particular but we'll be able to discuss this in greater privacy."

Inspector Prem ordered the uniform policemen to disperse the crowd which had gathered outside the house and was spilling into the street. They drove slowly through the back streets of Katong and then stayed on a course parallel to the beach along Marine Parade and East Coast Road.

"I think you should go home and have a rest, Inspector. You look very tired and weary. What about some Chinese herbs? My mother makes this lovely brew."

"No, thank you, Sergeant." Inspector Prem hastily stopped Sergeant Lee. He had tried Sergeant Lee's herbal remedies once and it had given him the runs all day. The headache had gone as soon as they arrived at the brothel. A crime or an important revelation always galvanised him and made it easy to shake off the lethargic effects of insufficient sleep.

He could see the almost unbroken line of *kelongs* out in the open sea. It never ceased to amaze him that these huts suspended on long rickety poles were capable of surviving the most violent storms. Fishermen along the coast were pulling in their boats. The morning's fishing was over. The rest of the day could be spent mending and checking nets or simply relaxing. He had always wanted to live by the sea and even considered leading the life of a fisherman. It seemed so idyllic and uncomplicated. Yes, that was what attracted him. It was restful.

Sergeant Lee had not spoken as they drove along the road by the beach. Ever considerate, the Sergeant would wait until he was refreshed and ready. There were quite a few young Sergeants who had wanted to be paired with him when his previous partner had died but Inspector Prem had chosen the unassuming fresh-faced and compassionate Peter Lee. It was a good choice.

"The Russian gun is an important piece of evidence," the Inspector said finally.

"It could help us charge Ah Seng with murder if we could trace it back to him," replied Sergeant Lee.

"A big if, Peter. Somehow I doubt whether Ah Seng or his men would still have the Stechkin pistol now. They would have destroyed it. We have only circumstantial evidence. No more."

"You haven't given up on this one just because known criminals were murdered?"

"No, I haven't given up. Today's murders are connected with Beethoven 96 in some way and I think that the communists have repaid Ah Seng for his services helping him to get rid of Lim's triad. Unfortunately there is no proof other than the Stechkin pistol."

"David Toh speculated correctly about Ah Seng's ambitions."

"I can't quite remember what David Toh said. He mentioned something about a dragon."

"Yes he did. The gang chiefs will call a truce shortly somewhere and then I'm sure they will surrender allegiance to Ah Seng."

"Would he then be in total control of the triads in Singapore?"

"Yes, he will be the Dragon Overlord."

16. The convent on the hill

Sergeant Lee called on the Inspector early the next day. They picked up Jenkins from Changi Air Base and were soon in Opera Estate. Sergeant Lee turned off the main road, up a steep dusty track. Children playing at the house in the corner of the junction were laughing and waving and a woman picking flowers in her garden smiled kindly at him. The Sergeant waved back at the children and noticed that Jenkins was doing the same. The Inspector sat with his head hanging down on his chest trying to shake off the fatigue of another long night. The track cut its way uphill to the edge of the jungle and led to the huge gates of the convent. There was no one there to receive them and Sergeant Lee had to forcibly push the gates open.

The convent and the track stood on a plateau that had been cut into the side of a hill. All around them were magnificent views of the lush unbroken green of the jungle. It stretched for miles skirting the edges of Opera Estate and extending to the horizon. Sergeant Lee knew that there must be some kampongs in that vast jungle but there was no hint of human habitation from their vantage point. The greenery enveloped everything ending only where it merged with the sky in the distance.

"That must be Kampong Chai Chee," Inspector Prem gestured to Jenkins.

"It looks like jungle to me," said Jenkins.

"Look closely and you can see the hint of a thatched roof."

Sergeant Lee observed that the Inspector was pointing south east, in the wrong direction. The eroded hill to the east and the smudge of blue of the sea to the south were definitely not part of Kampong Chai Chee. He half opened his mouth to correct Inspector Prem and then held back as he realised that Jenkins was being tested.

"I can't see any thatched roofs but I must say the jungle does look spectacular from this height," said Jenkins.

They walked up to the convent. Jenkins stopped by the huge white cross.

"It looks perfectly normal now but quite eerie from the jungle down there at night." He looked down at the jungle and then turned to Inspector Prem.

"Chai Chee lies in that direction."

Sergeant Lee tried to hide his amusement. The Inspector's ruse had been discovered. Let's see him talk his way out of this one.

"It extends slightly that way." The Inspector coughed and pointed. "You came out of the jungle in the direction you indicated and made your way down there. Shall we go in? I can see Reverend Mother Ventura waiting at the door."

Inspector Prem cordially introduced themselves. Reverend Mother Ventura did not condescend to shake their hands but simply bowed, nodded and showed them into her office.

The convent was ghostly quiet and their footsteps echoed in the corridors. Looking at the white washed walls, Sergeant Lee could tell that the building was quite new.

"It couldn't have been here during the war," he whispered to Inspector Prem, who quietly agreed.

Reverend Mother Ventura sat behind a large desk and waited patiently for them. Her face showed age but was not lined. Her thin lips neither smiled nor puckered but her eyes radiated the kindliness so common among most nuns. When she spoke her voice was soft and matched the Inspector's in deliberation.

"How long ago was this convent built, sister?" asked Inspector Prem.

"Just after the war, Inspector, but surely you're not here for small talk."

Sergeant Lee saw Jenkins raise his eyebrows but Inspector Prem calmly continued.

"No, I'm here to talk about the war, sister."

The Reverend Mother did not reply but simply looked calmly back at the Inspector.

"You were here during the war, sister." Another pause but the Reverend Mother was quiet. Sergeant Lee could see that she was not going to be drawn into any comments. It seems she would only comment if a question was asked directly. This was not going to be an informative interview.

"Did you see any of the fighting?" asked Inspector Prem.

"No."

"There was a small skirmish on the main road at the bottom of this track. Quite a few soldiers were wounded including some Japanese."

Was that a slight twitch? Sergeant Lee could not be sure.

"There would have been many skirmishes close by. It was a war after all. We, at this convent were busy with the Lord's work."

"Of course, sister, of course."

Sergeant Lee saw Inspector Prem straighten his collar. It was time for him to intervene.

"The CID found these bullets close to the fence of the convent. They are Japanese and dated around the time of their occupation. Can you account for them?"

It was not altogether a lie. The bullets were found by workers digging at the bus stop on the main street only a hundred yards away.

How will she react? Sergeant Lee wondered. He waited expectantly but the Reverend Mother was cool and collected. It was Jenkins who craned his neck forward to have a look.

"I've never seen those bullets and wouldn't know whether they are Japanese or not," the Reverend Mother replied in an even tone.

Sergeant Lee replaced the bullets back in a box and sighed. They need not have gone through the trouble of obtaining the Japanese bullets. The Reverend Mother was not easily moved.

Inspector Prem now addressed the Reverend Mother.

"Did you know there was a Kempei Tai headquarters not far from here during the war?"

Was that a slight twitch of her hands? Maybe. Sergeant Lee could not be sure.

"Yes," the Reverend Mother replied.

Sergeant Lee leaned forward. They had expected a denial to this question.

"Some of them must have visited this convent."

"It wasn't a convent then. Just a large hut converted into a church."

"But some Japanese soldiers and the Kempei Tai visited the church."

"Yes. The church does not cast out any who seek to commune with God. That would be un-Christian."

"Of course, I understand that perfectly. Do you know the names of any of these soldiers?" The Inspector casually touched the crucifix on the table as he pushed some photos and a list of names forward.

Sergeant Lee marvelled at the Reverend Mother's serenity and calm as she looked at the papers held in front of her.

"Yes. Shun-Ichi Sato. A very devout Christian."

Another surprise, thought Sergeant Lee. The Inspector straightened his collar once more. It was his turn.

"When did you last see him?" asked Sergeant Lee.

"In this convent?"

"Yes," said Sergeant Lee and immediately regretted his eagerness when the Reverend Mother replied.

"He was here just after the war ended. That was the last time I saw him in the convent."

"But you have seen him elsewhere since," said Sergeant Lee.

"Elsewhere?"

"In the jungle?"

"I've never been in the jungle."

Sergeant Lee felt defeated. He had rushed into the question too quickly.

"Is there a crypt under the convent?" asked Jenkins suddenly.

"No."

"I was in a crypt or cavern underneath this very convent just a few days ago, sister. Surely you remember that?" Jenkins pleaded.

"There is no crypt under this convent."

They were not getting any further. Inspector Prem rose to leave. The Reverend Mother accompanied them to the door. Just before she turned away, Inspector Prem spoke.

"I must warn you, sister, that Sato is a dangerous criminal. He has killed four men if not more and is wanted by the police. I suggest that when you see him next, persuade him to give himself up."

Not a flicker, not even a suggestion of unease. The Reverend Mother was unmoved. If anything, she looked sad as she closed the door of the convent.

"We'll have to look for this cavern ourselves," said Inspector Prem.

They crawled through a hole in the fence, down the grass slope and into the jungle. Jenkins led the way slashing through the thick undergrowth with a machete he had brought with him. Mosquitoes and flies swarmed around them and Sergeant Lee could feel himself being bitten in several places.

"I can't recognise anything," said Jenkins stopping and turning to look back up at the convent. "It's somewhere here. We can't be very far from it."

"Let's walk along that grass verge further up the slope first," suggested Sergeant Lee. "We might find something."

The verge extended all along the perimeter fence of the convent, stopping abruptly by an impenetrable bamboo thicket. They walked up and down, searching carefully for tell tale signs of trampled or cut branches. There were none. Sergeant Lee soon gave up and sat under a tree watching the Inspector and Jenkins discussing various possibilities of lines of sight and angles. The jungle would never reveal its secrets. If it chose to obscure, it would do so completely without a trace.

A cat suddenly jumped out of the bush and ran up the slope towards the convent. Sergeant Lee was startled and jumped up. Then something in the bush caught his attention. There seemed to be a gap just behind the foliage. Walking up to it he saw a hole cleverly hidden by some rocks and bushes.

"Over here," he shouted excitedly.

"Well?" asked Sergeant Lee as Jenkins and Inspector examined the hole.

"I don't know whether it will lead us to the cavern," said Jenkins. "Certainly worth a try."

Jenkins pushed aside the foliage to reveal a gaping hole just large enough for a man to crawl through. Inspector Prem led the way, shining a torch in front of him. Jenkins followed behind the Inspector and a reluctant Sergeant Lee came after. He was conscious of the dankness of the air in the tunnel and crawling through the claustrophobic darkness did not appeal to him.

The tunnel was no more than three feet wide and sloped gently downwards into darkness. The rock through which it had been carved was crumbly at a few places but was quite dry and warm. Every few feet, wooden struts and beams supporting the ceiling ensured that a cave-in would be unlikely.

Down they crawled changing direction abruptly every now and then. Whoever had dug the tunnel had designed it to confuse. Sergeant Lee soon felt disorientated.

Jenkins, holding the torch, now led the way. They had not crawled more then ten yards when Sergeant Lee heard Jenkins shout out in surprise. The torch suddenly went out and there was a loud splash. Sergeant Lee clutched at Inspector Prem's leg as they were swallowed by darkness. The suddenness, with which it enveloped them, froze Sergeant Lee. He could not see the Inspector in front of him, could not see his hands not even the ground. No one spoke for a while and all that he could hear was low hoarse breathing echoing in the tunnel. Then throbbing palpitations of fear urged him to flee but he could not move.

"Jenkins? Are you all right?" Inspector Prem called out.

"Yes. Don't move forward. I've fallen into a shallow well and lost the torch. The walls are too slippery. You'll have to help me get out."

Inspector Prem inched his way towards the top of the well.

"Hold on to my legs Sergeant, while I pull him out," said Inspector Prem.

The Inspector's voice stung Sergeant Lee into motion. Mechanically without being consciously aware of what he was doing, he reached out and held on to the Inspector's ankles. After much heaving and pulling they eventually managed to pull Jenkins out of the well. By that time they were all agreed that it would be too dangerous to carry on and decided to turn back. Sergeant Lee crashed into the walls of the tunnel several times as they crawled back.   There could be snakes in these tunnels. Pythons. He touched the ground carefully, feeling the walls before moving. Then the tunnel abruptly ended. Waves of panic overcame Sergeant Lee as his fingers touched hard stone in front of him. There was no opening. The way forward was blocked.

"The tunnel's closed," cried Sergeant Lee.

He was finding it hard to breathe and could feel a sticky film of perspiration covering him. They were going to die in this wretched tunnel. Buried alive. The thought horrified him.

"What do you mean closed? The entrance should be just in front of you," said Inspector Prem from behind.

Sergeant Lee carefully ran his hands along the walls in front of him again. Maybe he had imagined the obstruction in the tunnel but no, he could not find an opening. All around him was earth and stone.

Not stone, he realised, it was concrete. They were trapped. Sergeant Lee wanted to scream.

"There's a concrete barrier in front of me Inspector," he cried as he desperately tried to push against it. "It won't budge."

Sergeant Lee could feel himself on the verge of passing out. He could hear voices swimming in his head, entreating him to move but they seemed so far away. It was useless, he needed to rest. He wanted to close his eyes to prevent the walls from crushing him.

"Come on, Sergeant. We can't give up. We have to

move the barrier." It was Inspector Prem, tugging and shaking him. The Inspector had moved up next to him squashing them both in the small tunnel.

"It's only half filled the tunnel," said Inspector Prem. "We could crawl over it one at a time."

The inspector was already clambering over the barrier. In a daze, Sergeant Lee followed and then came Jenkins. They emerged from the entrance into the fresh air of the jungle. Sergeant Lee sank to the ground in relief.

Jenkins was wet and caked in mud and the Inspector was dirty and dishevelled. Sergeant Lee knew he probably looked worse.

"I'm not going back into that tunnel ever again," Sergeant Lee announced. "It's riddled with traps."

Looking around him he could see Inspector Prem and Jenkins nodding in agreement. After a short rest they started back up the slope. As they walked back towards the police car and passed the convent, Sergeant Lee saw a face peering at them. It was the Reverend Mother, standing stock still by the doorway. She turned abruptly and closed the door of the convent behind her.

A group of boys had gathered around the police car but ran away when they approached. Inspector Prem told Sergeant Lee to find out if the boys knew about a man living in the jungle. Sergeant Lee waved and smiled as he walked up to them.

"Good day for flying a kite," Sergeant Lee commented, noticing the kite being held by the biggest boy.

"Yes, I flew mine right over the hill. It must have been two hundred feet high," the boy exaggerated.

"Do you play here often?"

"My mum's given me permission and the gate was open," the boy answered guardedly.

"Oh, it's perfectly all right to play here. I'm not saying you can't but I was wondering whether you might have seen an old friend of mine. He lives just beyond that fence."

"In that house?" asked the boy.

"No. Just past that. In the jungle."

The boy giggled, spoke to the others and then turned to Sergeant Lee.

"There's a madman who lives there. He's a witch doctor. A *lok tang*. My mum says he eats young boys like me."

"Have you seen him here in the grounds of the convent?"

"No. He wouldn't dare. The cross frightens him off just like all demons and ghosts. My brother has seen him. He's got this sword made from hell which he waves about. If you look at him, he'll burn you to ashes. Is he your friend?"

"No," said Sergeant Lee, "My friend is Jap... uh, Chinese."

"This man is Chinese as well. A Chinese demon." The boys' eyes were wide open as he spoke and he shuddered slightly every time he mentioned the word 'demon'. Sergeant Lee gave him a ten cent coin and tried to reassure him that the demon did not exist. The boy shouted in delight as he looked at the coin and ran off. The other boys followed enviously close behind.

"The boys know he exists so he must at least come up to the fringe of the jungle but they say they have never

211

seen him within the fence," Sergeant Lee reported to the Inspector.

"Maybe we could try again with more men," said the Inspector as they got into the car.

"I won't be volunteering," said Sergeant Lee. "I like to be able to see a criminal before I arrest him and not be bludgeoned by a falling rock."

None of them noticed a shadow gliding between the trees on the brow of the hill. A pair of eyes watched them disappear from sight and then it too vanished.

They drove down the track towards the main road.

"Stop," said Jenkins, just as the car was about to turn.

Sergeant Lee braked hard expecting another concrete boulder to crash in front of them.

"What is it?" asked Inspector Prem.

"Fidelio Street," murmured Jenkins.

"Yes?" Sergeant Lee looked at Jenkins questioningly. Then he turned the car into the main road and parked by the road sign. Jenkins had seen something but was strangely silent and deep in thought.

"What about Fidelio Street?" asked Inspector Prem.

Jenkins finally spoke. "Do you remember what Sato said just before he left me?"

Sergeant Lee hurriedly referred to his notebook. "He said that the existence of the cavern must remain a secret and he called the secret, Beethoven 96."

"That's right. I've just seen the secret of Beethoven 96," said Jenkins. "It's right here. Beethoven's only opera was called Fidelio. Beethoven 96 must be a reference to this street."

"What about 96?" asked Sergeant Lee.

"I think that's opus 96. Beethoven's 96th composition must be Fidelio."

"I can't see anything special about this street," Sergeant Lee remarked.

"Maybe it's not this street. Maybe it is this area. The place where Sato lives," said Inspector Prem.

As they drove back along Upper Changi Road, Sergeant Lee noticed that Jenkins seemed distracted and distant. Was there something more that Jenkins had seen?

"Beethoven 96 is such an odd term to be used by a Japanese," said Inspector Prem. "If it is a reference to where he was located, why did he mention it?"

"I don't know. It could be a warning of some kind but I'm sure that it refers to Fidelio Street," said Jenkins.

"He must have heard it from someone else. It can't be the British. Someone local probably," said Inspector Prem.

"The Japanese Consulate?" suggested Jenkins but Inspector Prem shook his head.

Then Sergeant Lee remembered the face in the convent window and a thought flashed through his mind. "It could be the Reverend Mother at the convent."

"It can't be," Jenkins began and stopped. "It's not entirely unlikely. A nun certainly provides an excellent cover."

Another idea struck Sergeant Lee. "Maybe she is not a nun. We didn't even check to see whether she was the Reverend Mother she claimed to be."

"An impostor!" laughed Jenkins. "She looked very convincing."

They were interrupted by Inspector Prem.

"She is Reverend Mother Ventura and not an impostor. I checked before we left the station and the large photographs in the corridor showed the same person. You're allowing your imagination to run riot, Sergeant, and confusing everyone. The central question is 'What is Beethoven 96'. We know it refers to Fidelio Street or its immediate vicinity but why is it a secret and who told Sato? That is the question we have yet to resolve. Can we eliminate the RAF and the British armed forces first, Captain Jenkins?"

"Yes, and I think the Japanese Consulate as well," replied Jenkins.

Back at the convent a shadow crept through the jungle just before sunset. It paused at the hole which Sergeant Lee, Prem and Jenkins had explored. A few minutes later the hole was totally obscured and the shadow moved on. Creeping slowly among the lengthening shadows, it reached the walls of the convent. Through the windows, the shadow could see nuns moving quietly to prayer. It moved swiftly to the back of the building. No one noticed the shadow as it moved and then quickly disappeared into the rear entrance.

17. Voices #3

The storm clouds are gathering. Almost time.

Four more days to be precise. Beethoven 96 is looming over the horizon.

Suspicion has fallen on Fidelio Street.

The first connection has been made but the whole picture will remain hazy.

We proceed regardless?

Yes. Everything is going according to plan.

What about the police?

They will be around for security but will suspect nothing. They will be deployed in the right streets.

Fidelio Street?

Yes, and Swan Lake Avenue, along the canal.

The plainclothes detectives will be mingling with the crowd and shouldn't pose a problem.

But they will be armed.

Yes, but unwilling to shoot within a crowd. It will take them twenty seconds at least to react. That will be more than enough time for our purposes.

Twenty seconds in broad daylight. You'll need someone very special to finish the task and get away safely.

He is special. One of a kind. Efficient, detached and ruthless.

I have heard about his reputation but twenty seconds might still not be long enough. Maybe we should assist his escape.

Assist? You mean...

Yes.

Neat and clean. I'll make the necessary arrangements.

Before you go there is one more item on the agenda.

Jenkins and the Inspector?

I anticipated that. They have been poking their noses into everything.

They visited the convent yesterday.

The convent! That's very close. Did they find out anything?

Nothing important but I think they may suspect a great deal.

Jenkins is less dangerous.

You are under estimating Captain Jenkins. He has connections with the CIA.

That shouldn't pose a problem. CIA, MI5 or even Singapore's ISD are inconsequential.

I've heard that the Police Commissioner is working with the ISD. A problem?

No. They'll be totally unaware of the real danger.

No one will.

Yes, until it is too late.

18. CID Headquarters

Inspector Prem picked up the thick wad of loose blank forms and examined them again. They were clean. The dust that had accumulated and settled on them had been shaken off. Someone had gone through his desk at CID Headquarters. It had been done carefully and professionally. All the stationery appeared to be in their proper places but there was no question that someone had rummaged through the drawers.

Anyone opening the drawers would have assumed that the chaotic jumble of papers, leaflets, documents and files in his drawers had been tossed in indiscriminately. Prem however was a creature of habit. He had made a point of keeping the most important documents at the bottom, allowing dust to accumulate on the rubbish at the top. Now he found that the dust had been partially wiped or shaken off. It was not unusual for his colleagues to sometimes look at papers on his table but no one would have the temerity to search through his drawers. Who had done this and what were they looking for?

He looked across at Sergeant Lee's neat table. The 'In' and 'Out' trays clearly labelled, his huge diary and a typewriter in the middle of his desk all appeared to be untouched. It was very likely that the Sergeant's desk had been searched as well.

Sergeant Lee was unusually late that day and there was a note on Inspector Prem's table with an unusual summons. Sergeant Lee and he were told to attend a meeting with the Commissioner of Police and the Director of CID. There was no mention of the nature of the meeting but it was labelled as urgent. He had met the Commissioner only once before in his long career when he was singled out for special praise and given a citation for solving the case of the whistling rapist. The Commissioner was a no- nonsense British colonial who was in favour of strong discipline and a good code of conduct among the ranks of the police. Inspector Prem wondered how he was going to explain the absence of Sergeant Lee to the intolerant Commissioner.

The greetings of his colleagues as he made his way to the office of the Director of the CID were strangely muted and lacking in warmth. They knew something he did not, he thought.

There were two men seated around the far side of the huge table. The Director motioned to him to sit at the other side. This was going to be a hostile meeting. The Director of CID was looking down at the well-polished table and even tried to smile slightly at the Inspector. He did not look happy but somehow he did not appear to be antagonistic. There was some hope of support here. The Commissioner of Police straightened some papers and was the first to speak.

"I have just looked through your files, Inspector, and I can see that you have been working hard since the last time I saw you. These are difficult times as far as crime is concerned. In spite of the gallant efforts of the police and the CID, there has been an increase in the number of violent crimes in these past two years."

Inspector Prem nodded in agreement. So much for the preamble.

"We need the best people in the right places," continued the Commissioner. "We can then stamp out the root cause of crime in this city. I have proposed, and the Director agrees with me, a slight re-shuffle which involves you. It will mean that you have to be taken off your present case and reassigned to Dangerous Drugs division. We'll need your experience in finding out the man behind the rise in new opium dens in Chinatown and breaking the smuggling ring responsible for shipping opium from China to Singapore. It is a big responsibility but the Director and I feel you should be able to shoulder it easily."

Inspector Prem did not reply. There were strong political undercurrents in his current investigations. The ulterior motive for being dropped from the present case could well be political in nature. He looked from the Director to the Commissioner and decided that the decision had been made by the Commissioner.

"What about Sergeant Lee?" asked Inspector Prem.

"Sergeant Lee was briefed before you and he sounded quite enthusiastic about his new assignment. Naturally you'll both be partnered together," said the Commissioner.

Already briefed? Why was he briefed first Inspector Prem wondered. A deal of some kind? No, it was too unlikely. Sergeant Lee was just as keen as he was in wanting to solve this case.

"Well, Inspector?" The Commissioner broke his reverie.

"Is it really necessary to re-delegate my partner and I while we are in the middle of a case?" asked Inspector Prem. "Wouldn't it be better for us to finish it first?"

"I'm afraid the opium problem requires our immediate attention."

The Inspector sighed. "All right. When do we start?"

"I'll be sending you the necessary papers and case histories tomorrow."

Inspector Prem nodded in agreement and got up to leave. When he reached the door he abruptly announced, "We might solve our present case by tomorrow." He had exaggerated, of course, but their astonished faces gave him ample satisfaction.

Sergeant Lee was sitting by his desk when he returned.

"A cover-up," said Sergeant Lee. "They're trying to cover-up something."

Inspector Prem had not forgotten Sergeant Lee's possible involvement. He decided to confront the Sergeant directly.

"Did you go through my drawers?" he asked.

"I didn't go through them," said Sergeant Lee looking slightly hurt, "but they might have been looking for an important file."

"File?"

"Yes, the second file on the old Changi murder. I went back to the archives to verify the details of that murder, the name of the victim, the investigating officer and so on. While the archive's man was looking for the relevant file, I had a look at the register of files which he had left open and found a cross reference marked next to the file he was looking for. The reference had a page number further on in the register. When I turned to that page there was a long list of files marked Secret. One of these Secret files had a reference number of the original file. It gave me quite a shock. I'd never realised there was so much secrecy in the CID. I copied the Secret file number and noted its clearance rating. I didn't want to raise suspicions by asking for a file I wasn't authorised to handle, so I merely collected the file and left. For some reason I was overwhelmed with curiosity about this second file."

"You don't have to tell me how you obtained a secret file, Sergeant. I understand perfectly."

"No, no, I do owe you an explanation, Inspector. I used an old requisition form signed by the Director. I went back a few times to the archives department and waited until the archivist was fairly busy processing requests. Then I passed him the requisition form and pretended to be in a hurry. He naturally didn't check the form carefully and handed me the file."

"But you may have to face a disciplinary hearing as a result."

"I already have Inspector, just a few hours ago but they couldn't prove that I had the file."

"Didn't they find it?"

"No, I saw the Director and a few others walking towards the archives department early this morning. The archivist must have alerted him. I had to hide it somewhere. The postal trolley was doing its early morning rounds and that gave me an idea. I slipped the file into an envelope and posted it."

"Posted it! You posted a secret file!" Inspector Prem cried out in disbelief.

"Either that or I would lose my job. It was internal post," Sergeant Lee answered sheepishly.

"Who did you post it to?"

"To the Director."

Inspector Prem laughed. "I don't know what to say, Sergeant. You've created a shambles but resolved it brilliantly. Did you have a look at the file?"

"Only briefly. It was more or less identical to the other file but the investigating officer was from the Internal Security Department."

"The ISD? Are you sure," asked Inspector Prem. Old memories of his clash with the ISD came flooding back.

"Yes, but that's not all. The murdered victim was not a member of UMNO or the Malayan Communist Party as we were led to believe by the official report but a British soldier, a Warrant Officer Ben Pyke. The investigating officer was John Thomson. The similarities with the present Changi murders are overwhelming. John Thomson must be involved in our present case."

"It can't be the same John Thomson from the Foreign Office? He's with MI5," said Inspector Prem.

"I don't know, Inspector, but I'd certainly like to find out."

Inspector Prem agreed.

The Foreign Office was only a short drive away and they were soon being led by the receptionist into

Thomson's office. When the door was opened they were shocked at what they saw.

There were four men seated in the office, John Thomson, the Commissioner of Police, the Director of CID and a fourth whose back faced them.

"Sit down, both of you," the Commissioner said with some severity.

As he sat down Inspector Prem recognised with growing consternation, the face of the fourth person, a vicious witch-hunter he had clashed with some years ago, Sim from the Internal Security Department. Inspector Prem could recall that years ago he had criticised the ISD's tactics as being similar to the Cheka of Russia whereupon Sim had latched on to that statement and grilled him about his unpatriotic communist inclinations. Sim had demanded to know how he, a Singaporean Inspector of police, could have had any knowledge of the Cheka. It was only the Inspector's superlative record as a detective and the numerous accolades he had publicly received that had averted an all-out onslaught of scathing accusations by Sim.

Tap, tap, tap. Sim was knocking the ash from his cigarette as he stared hard at Inspector Prem. It was a habit Inspector Prem remembered well. Even if he was not smoking a cigarette, Sim would habitually tap on the table and scowl as he spoke. His puffy, slitty eyes on a large round face reminded Inspector Prem of a hooded cobra poised to strike.

It was John Thomson who spoke first.

"Why have you come to see me, Inspector?"

"We wanted to know whether Jenkins had been

in touch with you. As you know Jenkins is still under suspicion for the murders at Changi Air Base."

"Oh, really," said Thomson. He leaned back and motioned to the other two men beside him.

"I told you he wouldn't listen to you, Commissioner," said Sim. He glared at Inspector Prem and Sergeant Lee. "Do you realise your actions amount to gross insubordination?"

Sergeant Lee bit his lip and looked at Inspector Prem who calmly replied, "I don't see how a visit to the Foreign Office could be insubordination."

Sim ignored the Inspector for a moment and swivelled in his chair to face the Commissioner. "I told you he wouldn't listen. This man does not understand the importance of discipline and is a disgrace to the CID."

"His record is exemplary," retaliated the Director of CID but Sim persisted.

"Your case is no longer within the jurisdiction of the CID, Inspector. It is now an internal security matter and I want you to surrender the files."

"What files are you referring to?" asked Inspector Prem. "I'm an Inspector of police and not a clerk. I don't keep files. The CID is too busy and is not a bureaucracy that juggles with files unlike the ISD."

It was not the line of defence that the Inspector had wanted but his dislike of Sim tempted him to belittle the odious man.

The Director chuckled and Thomson smiled but Sim was as stern as ever.

"A confidential file was removed from the archives department and I want it returned immediately."

Inspector Prem could sense Sergeant Lee shifting uneasily in his chair.

"If you have lost a file then it is not up to the CID to find it. We investigate crime and not incompetence," Prem answered in an even tone.

Sim stared hard at Prem who merely shrugged. He waited in silence hoping that the Sergeant would do likewise and not break. After a long wait, Sim produced a file from under the table.

"It is fortunate for both of you that I've got the file with me but I must insist that you drop your investigations as from now. There are other important matters involved here and you are not only putting yourselves in danger but others as well."

"If this is such a confidential matter, why is Mr Thomson here?" asked Inspector Prem.

Thomson leaned forward to reply but Sim interceded. He was apparently running the show. "The intricate nature of this case involves Mr Thomson. Exactly how and why you do not need to know."

"If Mr Thomson here is an accessory to a crime, then I do need to know."

"I am not an accessory to a crime," Thomson shouted out.

The Commissioner whispered to Sim and then addressed Inspector Prem. "I understand your dedication to your job, Inspector and I sometimes wish there were more detectives like yourself but this matter supersedes your duties and can only be handled at the highest level. Mr Thomson is here on an advisory capacity and is not and will not be directly involved in the case."

"What are you covering up?" asked Sergeant Lee unexpectedly.

"This is not a cover up. There are higher levels of security concerned and the police, CID and the ISD cannot act independently. We cannot jeopardise this operation just to satisfy your curiosity."

"Inspector Prem and I already know most of the relevant details of the case and I really fail to envisage how it could affect any of your operations."

The Sergeant's talking too much, thought Inspector Prem. It's a mistake. Sim is more dangerous than he sounds. He straightened his collar hoping that Sergeant Lee would notice.

"Believe me, Sergeant," said Sim, "it does affect the ISD. The Commissioner, the Director and I have discussed this at length and we have come to an agreement. Your investigation must stop."

"It might be better if you include us in your plans. We do know a great deal about the case," said Sergeant Lee. Inspector Prem touched his collar once again and noted to his relief that Sergeant Lee was looking in his direction.

Sim blew a smoke ring in the Sergeant's direction. "You know nothing that will surprise us."

"Not even Beethoven 96," said Inspector Prem.

The Commissioner looked up but Sim remain composed and even smiled. Another smoke ring drifted towards Sergeant Lee who brushed it aside in irritation.

"You can't impress me with mere words, Inspector," said Sim. "You don't know what Beethoven 96 means do you?"

"I know its connection with Opera Estate," said Inspector Prem.

"That does not make any difference," retorted Sim but Inspector Prem could see a slight hint of a frown and tension wrinkles at the corner of his mouth. Tap, tap tap. Sim had finished his cigarette but his fingers were drumming on the table. The Commissioner and Director were both whispering to each other but Thomson was craning his head. Was it possible that the Englishman from MI5 clearly did not know much about Beethoven 96? The others certainly indicated they were familiar with it. Major Hughes' code could not have been a big secret after all.

"I wish you would make up your mind Mr. Sim. First you start off by saying we know too much and now you are saying what we do know is inconsequential. Your indecision matches your lack of integrity."

"What do you mean?" Sim growled. Tap, tap, tap.

"You accuse everyone who challenges you of being a communist. Weren't you educated in a Chinese high school where all the communist cadres are trained?" asked the Inspector.

"Don't you dare make scurrilous accusations Inspector, or I'll have your job," Sim snarled. He was standing and the Commissioner had to pull him back to his seat.

"I think you are underestimating the Inspector, Mr Sim," said Thomson who seemed amused. "Our man has already spoken to him and rates him very highly."

Our man? Jenkins? Inspector Prem looked at the four men carefully. Maybe he was wrong. Maybe it was Thomson and not Sim. Thomson could be creating the illusion of his secondary importance when in reality he sat at the helm and gave the orders. It was conceivable that the British MI5 or some similar organisation was in power. After all Singapore had still not gained full independence and most of the important posts in the civil service were still held by the British. If that was true where did it place Jenkins?

"I think this discussion is at an end now," announced the Commissioner, "unless you have any further questions." He looked at both Inspector Prem and Sergeant Lee who shook their heads.

"All right you are both dismissed and you can start on your new assignments tomorrow afternoon," said the Director.

"I suppose that's the end of the case," said Sergeant Lee as the police car turned towards the city centre.

"No, not quite," replied Inspector Prem. "I want you to check as much as you can about triad activities in Opera Estate and its communist history if there is one."

"I can't do that. We've just been told to drop this case."

"Not until tomorrow afternoon. The Director of CID gave us a lifeline and a last chance."

"You think he did that intentionally?"

"I think he was on our side all along and he deliberately mentioned tomorrow afternoon just to get one back on Thomson and Sim. The Director doesn't like his authority to be challenged."

"Do you think those two are the protagonists in this cover-up?"

"Yes, but I don't think this is simply a cover-up. It is a

very intricate conspiracy and I'm not sure that we are not being manipulated."

"What do you intend to do while I consult with the organised crime division?"

"I'm going to arrange a very important appointment in Opera Estate."

19. Traitor in the RAF

"I can't have this in my air base, Jenkins," snorted Air Marshall Collins," we need every available officer to put on a successful air show. I know you're contracted to be in this air base in the mornings but there have been several mornings lately that I've called on you and found out that you are away somewhere."

"I'm sorry, Air Marshall, but I have very urgent work at the British High Commission."

"You have urgent work here as well, Jenkins. I've put you in charge of public relations for the coming air show."

"That's a huge undertaking sir and I'm not sure I can perform all of it on my own."

"Very well. In that case I'll second you to Major Hartson. You will assist him wherever you can. Can you handle that, Jenkins?"

"Yes, sir, I think that's fair."

"Good. Major Hartson wants you to prepare the VIP invitations."

As Collins left, Jenkins felt it was his intention to delegate the invitations to him all along. The rigmarole of the public relations duties was just a subterfuge to justify his actions.

Jenkins crossed the huge parade ground and walked up the steps of the main administration building.

Eunice, a clerical corporal greeted him cordially. "Can I help you, Captain Jenkins?"

"You certainly can, corporal. You certainly can," replied Jenkins.

Eunice giggled in delight, pushed her chair back and straightened her glasses.

"I need some addresses, Eunice."

"Oh. Aren't you being a little too forward asking for my address?"

"I'd love to pay you a visit, Eunice, but I need a list of addresses of the officers of Changi first."

"Suit yourself," said Eunice, trying to look disappointed.

She pulled out a file from the cabinet next to her table and handed a sheet to Jenkins. "Quite a few of them live in Opera Estate."

"Anyone I know?" Opera Estate. That place again.

"Well Flynn lives in Carmen Terrace and I live there too," she smiled.

"Flight Lieutenant Flynn?" Jenkins quickly ran his finger down the list of addresses. Flight Lieutenant Peter Flynn. 15 Carmen Terrace, Opera Estate. Eunice was still talking but Jenkins ignored her. This was no coincidence he thought. He had suspected Flynn when he saw him at the Turf Club but now he felt sure. Flynn must be the traitor at RAF Changi.

"Eunice, do you know where Flight Lieutenant Flynn is at the moment?"

"Hmm. What? Flight Lieutenant Flynn? He's in 205 Squadron. I think they're flying this morning. Should be finishing anytime now. Do you want...?"

Jenkins did not wait. He ran down the steps, past the barracks, round the ammo dump towards the runway. A few aeroplanes were being pushed back into their hangars. He recognised them as the Shackletons of 205 Squadron. Flynn would be one of the pilots walking out of the hangars. He looked at them as they walked past but Flynn was nowhere to be seen. A mechanic standing by a Shackleton was looking at Jenkins.

"Are you looking for someone, sir?" he asked.

"Yes," replied Jenkins, "Flight Lieutenant Flynn. Have you seen him?"

"Yes, sir. He was called to the CO's office about half an hour ago. I think it was some disciplinary matter because he looked quite put out and nervous and the other pilots were trying to reassure him."

"Is he due to come back here after seeing the CO?"

"No, sir, we've finished for the morning. In fact, we've finished for the day."

Flynn is on his way home, thought Jenkins. Instinctively, Jenkins felt a compulsion to challenge Flynn immediately. The main gate was his best chance. He stopped a passing land rover and ordered the driver to drive him to the main gate. As he approached he saw a car leaving. It was Flynn in his Vauxhall Humber. Jenkins desperately waved at the guard by the sentry box to stop him but the car sped off.

"Was that Flight Lieutenant Flynn?" he asked the MP on duty.

"Yes, sir. In a really bad mood," replied the MP.

Was Flynn running away? He was sure Flynn had noticed him in the land rover and had intentionally ignored him. He would have to wait until tomorrow before he could confront Flynn.

It was already way past lunch time. Jenkins signed himself out and decided to walk home. When he arrived home he promptly went to his bedroom to look for Major Hughes diary. Major Hughes had been sent to Singapore to flush out the security leaks in the RAF. The diary might contain Flynn's name hidden in code. If so Flynn could be the person who employed Sato to murder Major Hughes.

He pulled open his bedside drawers. Empty! The diary had been stolen.

He carefully searched his house. The diary was nowhere to be seen. His housekeeper was laying the table for his lunch. He questioned her. No, she had not moved his books and she was not aware of a diary.

Flynn. Flynn could have stolen it. But when?

"Did anyone call for me while I was away this morning or yesterday," he asked the housekeeper.

"Yes, *tuan*," answered the housekeeper. "A tall officer from the RAF was here this morning. He waited for you for a while in the lounge and then left. He did not tell me his name."

"Did he have dark hair or was he blonde."

"Dark hair and moustache, *tuan*. About your age."

The description fitted Flynn. Whoever Flynn worked for would be able to decipher the diary quite easily and would then become aware of Jenkins' knowledge of Beethoven 96. He had to warn the correct authorities. He picked up the phone and dialled.

"Thomson? It's Jenkins."

"Yes. What can I do for you?" Thomson brusquely replied.

"I just wanted to ask you about corruption in the Singapore police force."

"It exists like so many of our ex-colonies. Why? Are you intending to bribe a policeman? I'd be very careful if I were you."

"No, I don't intend to bribe anyone. I just want to know the extent of corruption in Singapore. Would a police Sergeant, say, accept a bribe?"

"If it was large enough, I don't see why not."

"What about Inspectors? Wouldn't their salaries be high enough for them to resist a bribe?"

"Inspectors? You're not enquiring about that underhanded Inspector Prem, are you?"

"Yes, I am."

"Unfortunately he's clean. A good record from what I've been told."

Jenkins rang off. Inspector Prem was not corrupt but Thomson would prefer it to be otherwise. He knew then to whom he had to pass on his information to. He phoned for a taxi.

20. The Member of Parliament

"Is this the house?" asked Sergeant Lee reaching out for the doorbell.

"Yes. This is where Raymond Isaacs, the MP for Opera Estate, lives," replied Inspector Prem.

"Does he know you personally?"

"We spoke briefly at the Victoria Memorial Hall during the police investiture, years ago. I doubt whether he would remember me. It's a politician's job to be amiable when the occasion demands it. It increases his popularity."

"You sound somewhat cynical. Don't you rate him very highly?"

"On the contrary, I do. He is very approachable and, like his brother, unquestionably honest. That is why I'm hoping he might help us."

"Ah yes, his brother, Jacob. There's speculation that he might be the Governor after the next elections."

The door opened and they were led into a dimly lit lounge. Isaacs was seated at a table busily writing. He stopped as soon as they entered, rose and shook their hands firmly.

"This seems like a quiet residential area," began Inspector Prem," but did you know that recently an RAF man was chased through these streets by a group of gangsters."

"Not this particular street. I would have been told," Isaacs interrupted.

"No. On the other side of Opera Estate. Swan Lake Avenue and the side streets along the canal. The gangsters chasing him were armed and were intent on grievous bodily harm."

"He wasn't hurt I hope."

"Thankfully he wasn't but I was wondering whether any of your constituents might have approached you and voiced their worries about crime in the area."

"Well I have been approached by one or two victims of crime but they asked me for legal advice rather than complain about crime levels. Opera Estate does not have a high crime rate anyway."

It was the answer that Inspector Prem had expected. He had to inch his way towards the main line of his enquiries. Ask a few non-committal questions and try to get Isaacs to talk.

"That's true. It doesn't. There are however a few kampongs fringing it and they are the main source of my worries. It is well known that the triads operate in the Jalan Tua Kong area and in Kampong Chai Chee. There must be some racial tensions between them and the Malay kampongs in Siglap."

"I'm not an expert but triad activities will always plague the Chinese kampongs. It's a problem the CID and the Organised Crime Division will have to come to terms with eventually. As for the racial tensions, I must say they are far more diffused in this area than in other parts of Singapore."

Inspector Prem could see Sergeant Lee scribbling in his notebook, nodding in pretended appreciation to what Isaacs was saying. The Sergeant was learning well.

"I'm glad to hear that sir. However, I still have strong worries about Kampong Chai Chee. It is a very insular kampong with only the main Changi Road running through it. The jungle is very dense in that area and provides perfect concealment for illegal activities."

"That may be true Inspector but Kampong Chai Chee is not in my constituency and I really can't comment about it."

"Aren't you concerned that its problems might overflow into Opera Estate?"

"I am and I would like your department to look into the matter more closely."

Isaacs smiled but Inspector Prem carried on.

"If you consider what happened in mainland Malaya during the Emergency period, the same developments could be occurring here in Singapore." Inspector Prem waited. He was sure that Isaacs would be able to make the necessary connection.

"Malaya during Emergency. Are you referring to communists in the jungle?"

"Yes," replied Inspector Prem. He waited, hoping that Isaacs would speak at length.

Isaacs' reply was laconic.

"There are no communists in the jungles of Singapore."

"So how do the communists operate in Singapore?"

"Why are you interested? Surely the communist threat is not within the jurisdiction of the CID."

"Not quite but terrorism is a crime," said Inspector Prem. He had not been able to entice Isaacs into a lengthy discourse on communists. It was time to gamble on a question they had prepared before hand. He touched his collar and Sergeant Lee responded.

"We are working on a hunch there are communists in this area," said Sergeant Lee.

"There are no communists in my constituency," said Isaacs emphatically.

"I'm sorry," said Sergeant Lee. "I meant to say that we suspect the communists of creating some trouble here."

Raymond Isaacs did not comment but frowned at Sergeant Lee. Inspector Prem could see that Sergeant Lee had stirred something up.

"The communist might want to score a political victory here by creating trouble using the triads," said Inspector Prem. Still no verbal response from Raymond Isaacs but he was beginning to look interested.

"It will affect the security for Opera Estate in the near future," Sergeant Lee improvised.

"I see what you're getting at," said Isaacs. "You're worried about tomorrow."

"Yes, exactly. Everyone is," the Inspector lied. His pulse was racing. Something important was happening tomorrow.

He looked across and saw Sergeant Lee trying hard to contain his excitement. The pen in the Sergeant's hand trembled slightly. This was the breakthrough they had hoped for. The importance of Opera Estate would be revealed if they kept their wits and probed deftly.

"As you know, confidentiality forbids me to mention tomorrow openly. That is why we've approached this in such an oblique way. It's very important to us that we cover all possible angles," said Inspector Prem. He had to maintain the appearance of confidence and somehow assure Isaacs into drawing them into his trust.

"Are you in charge of security? I can't remember your name being mentioned. Inspector Prem, isn't it?"

"No, sir, I'm not the person in charge," said Inspector Prem. Was Isaacs beginning to suspect? They were so close now.

"The Commissioner is the real man in charge but Sergeant Lee and I are part of the security operations. That is why I asked you about the kampongs in this region."

Sergeant Lee intervened. "You remember the Englishman chased through Swan Lake Avenue. I was wondering whether we should be especially careful along that street."

Brilliantly done thought Inspector Prem, as he saw Isaacs relax slightly and leaned back. They were poised on the brink now. Whatever reservations Isaacs had, had vanished. Isaacs must have been wondering all along about the purpose and direction of their questions and Sergeant Lee had provided a convincing explanation.

Inspector Prem impatiently waited through what seemed to him an interminable silence. What would the MP reveal?

"Well, the cavalcade will be moving down Fidelio Street and turning before they reach Swan Lake but I imagine that street is still important and will probably be quite crowded," said Isaacs.

Cavalcade? Crowds? It must be a state visit. At last the political link had fallen in place. This very event must be the culmination of their long search. This state visit must be the focus of Beethoven 96. Was it a visit by the Governor, the Prime Minister or a foreign dignitary? He could find out the details later. It was more important now that he milked as much information from the Member of Parliament as possible.

"I'll be honest with you, Mr Isaacs," said Inspector Prem. "This is my first big assignment and I can't afford to get anything wrong. I know you're a man of intelligence and I'm hoping you could guide me. I've been ordered to assess all the non-obvious security threats and propose counter measures."

"Shouldn't the ISD be doing that?"

"I don't know about the ISD. They have their own arrangements but those are my orders. One of the problem areas could be the kampong behind Fidelio Street but you gave me the impression that it would be quite safe."

"I didn't quite say that. I really can't predict where any threats might be coming from."

"I understand," said Inspector Prem. "Another point I wanted to raise is..." Inspector Prem hesitated and scratched his forehead.

"I must admit I'm not very familiar with the geography of Opera Estate." Inspector Prem took out a pen and paper and untidily sketched on it making some blatant mistakes. "This is Fidelio Street and the cavalcade is coming down here and turning here. This is Swan Lake Avenue."

"No you've made a mistake. Swan Lake Avenue is on the other side and the cavalcade turns left. That's where the school is."

"Right. So that's the school. Is the canal on this side of Swan Lake or the other side?" Inspector Prem had drawn so many lines that the sketch was no longer readable.

The MP picked up his pen and turned over the paper. "Let me draw you a proper sketch." He drew a neat grid of streets, explaining as he went along.

Inspector Prem turned towards Sergeant Lee who was scribbling away in his notebook.

"Down Fidelio Street and left into the school. This is Swan Lake Avenue and this is the kampong along Jalan Tua Kong. The Prime Minister will be making his speech and then leaving shortly. There shouldn't be much of a security problem. The whole route and the school are bordered by houses and I imagine they have been vetted and checked."

"Oh, they have," replied Inspector Prem. "I'm worried about what lies behind those houses."

"A street and more houses," laughed the MP.

Inspector Prem and Sergeant Lee left shortly. As they walked out the Inspector saw the MP shaking his head. They had created the correct impression of being incompetent policemen.

"It's all coming together now," said Sergeant Lee. "Beethoven 96, the communists and Sato." He backed the police car and drove towards Fidelio Street.

"It looks very innocuous," said Sergeant Lee as they passed the school.

The school consisted of two parallel, long three storey blocks with a wide drive-way separating the playing field from the buildings. A six-foot high fence ran all along its perimeter. The police car slowed down as the two men studied the school carefully.

"Lots of wide open spaces. It looks as safe as the MP described it," said Sergeant Lee.

"And yet something dreadful is going to happen tomorrow."

"I think they are planning an assassination."

"They? Who do you think 'they' could be?"

"The communists. Barisan Socialis. Who else?"

"Maybe, Sergeant, but I'm not so sure." Inspector Prem's voiced trailed away as he considered the possibilities.

"Who are we going to report this to?"

"I don't know. That is the question that has been puzzling me. It seems Beethoven 96 is already known by the authorities."

"They know the existence of Beethoven 96 but maybe they still don't know what it means."

"Possibly. I think it would be wise to keep this information to ourselves at least for the moment."

"But we have only twenty-four hours left."

"I know Sergeant and that's why we must act quickly."

"Back to CID HQ."

"Yes."

They were surprised to see Jenkins waiting for them when they arrived.

"How long have you been waiting Captain Jenkins?" asked Sergeant Lee.

"Nearly two hours now," Jenkins replied looking at his watch. "I had to see you. Is there somewhere we could talk in private? I've found out something important."

Inspector Prem and Sergeant Lee took him into their office.

"Someone stole Major Hughes' diary," announced Jenkins.

"The diary is important evidence. You should have given it to us," said Sergeant Lee in mild disapproval.

"More important than you think. Beethoven 96 is not the only code in the diary. I picked out the words Barisan crime."

Inspector Prem whistled and nodded.

"Which means Major Hughes and MI5 knew about Beethoven 96," said Sergeant Lee. "How did you lose the diary, Captain Jenkins?"

"I didn't lose it. It was stolen from my house by Flight Lieutenant Flynn."

"You saw Flynn stealing it?" asked Inspector.

"No, but he must be the one. My housekeeper let an officer into the house who fitted his description and he has a motive for wanting the diary."

"What is this motive?" asked Inspector Prem, slowly and deliberately.

"It will take me a long time to explain, but he lives in Opera Estate."

"In that case, let's pay him a visit," said Inspector Prem.

Inspector Prem opened the door of his office and

stopped suddenly. Standing in front of him was Sim from the ISD.

"I want you to come with me," he hissed.

"All of you," said Sim when Jenkins hesitated.

Once more Inspector Prem and Sergeant Lee walked through the corridors of curious staring faces to the Director's office. Once more they sat at the end of his long conference table facing a hostile group of men at the other end but this time in addition to the Commissioner, the Director and Sim, there were two more, John Thomson from the Foreign Office and Mori from the Japanese Consulate.

"You have disobeyed a direct order, Inspector," said the Commissioner.

"Disobeyed an order, sir?" Inspector Prem replied, "I don't think we have."

"Yes, you have," the Commissioner shouted. "I've just received a telephone call from Raymond Isaacs. He told me that the two of you have been asking questions about tomorrow and deceiving him about your involvement. Do you deny that?"

Tap, tap, tap. Sim was lighting a cigarette and smirked at Inspector Prem.

"No, I don't deny that we had an interview with Raymond Isaacs," Inspector Prem, "but I maintain that we were not disobeying your orders. You said that we were off the present case this afternoon. Therefore we carried on with our investigations in the morning. Seeing that it is now almost twelve o'clock we are ready for the next case."

The Commissioner glared at the Inspector and Sergeant Lee and then turned towards the Director of CID. The Commissioner's face was contorted in suppressed rage but the Director coolly looked at the ceiling and smiled. Inspector Prem nodded reassuringly at Sergeant Lee who looked worried. There was a brief period of tense silence which was broken by Sim.

"Inspector Prem," said Sim. His voice sounded oily sweet. "This may be just another case for you, another game for self-gratification but the nation's welfare is at stake. Your reckless handling of it might cost innocent lives."

Sergeant Lee spoke out. "It's our job as policemen to save lives. Is our integrity being questioned?"

"You're being too bold for your rank. Sergeant," said the Commissioner.

"Appropriate disciplinary measures will be taken." He looked defiantly at the Director who kept his silence.

The Commissioner continued. "Anyway it's impossible to change the past. Since you could not be persuaded to leave the case, I'm now putting you back on it."

Sim turned sharply and started to protest but the Commissioner ignored him.

"You already know of the Prime Minister's visit tomorrow to Opera Estate. You and Sergeant Lee will mingle with the crowds and join the undercover security team. Mr Sim will be there to instruct you tomorrow. This incident will be entered in both your records and the insubordination aspects will not be omitted." He glared at Inspector Prem and then addressed Jenkins.

"As for you Captain Jenkins, Mr Thomson has something to say to you."

Thomson cleared his throat. "Hayward you will have to abide by the wishes of the Commissioner of Police.

This matter is outside your jurisdiction and mine. It is an internal security matter and we must respect and not interfere with any operation of the local police if we are to have future co-operation with them. Can I have your word that you will agree to the Commissioner's terms?"

"My life has been threatened more than once and I have got the right to protect myself regardless of jurisdiction," said Jenkins. He raised a hand to prevent Thomson from rebutting. "However, I give you my word that I will steer clear of this affair unless my life is in jeopardy."

"Fair enough," said the Commissioner. "Twenty four hours is all I ask. Twenty four hours of non interference in a delicate and potentially explosive matter." He then faced Inspector Prem.

"I've been very lenient with you Inspector because of your past record and I've over-ruled my two colleagues against my better judgement but this must never happen again. Are we absolutely clear?" asked the Commissioner.

Inspector Prem nodded.

They were then dismissed and Inspector Prem and Sergeant Lee went back to their office while Thomson offered to drive Jenkins back to Changi.

"There is still Flight Lieutenant Flynn," said Jenkins. "I have reason to believe he is a communist." Jenkins then went on to explain his suspicions of Flynn as they drove down Changi Road.

"Unfortunately you're wrong there, Jenkins, Flynn is a habitual gambler and has been reprimanded by Air Marshall Collins several times but he is definitely not a communist. I've collected a long dossier on him when I first found out that he fraternises with the locals and had similar suspicions. However although he is a man of many vices, he is against the communists. His father who fought in the Malayan emergency died at the hands of the communists. Flynn hates them and I very much doubt whether they can tempt him in any way."

"Even if he is deeply in debt?" enquired Jenkins.

"He may be in debt here but he has a wealthy family back in Berkshire who would easily bail him out. The Flynn estate back in England is considerable and he cannot be a traitor. The system favours a person like him and he has everything to lose and nothing to gain by joining the communists or selling important information."

21. Secret of Beethoven 96

Jenkins was still sceptical about Thomson's view of Flynn and confronted Flynn the next day at the air base.

"Why did you run away from me yesterday, Peter?" Jenkins asked.

"I wasn't running away from you. I was avoiding you. I thought you reported me to the CO?"

"Reported you?"

"Yes. I saw you at the Turf Club a few days ago and yesterday the CO hauled me up for a strong reprimand and a slap on the wrist. I thought you had complained but I found out this morning it was the Manpower Officer. God knows how he found out."

Flynn was looking directly at Jenkins and his story sounded plausible.

"I don't think you've been totally honest with me, Peter."

Flynn looked surprised. "Why do you say that, Hayward? I've always been your mate. I volunteered to take over your post as duty officer on the night of the murders and tried to cheer you up the day after."

"Yes, but didn't you have an ulterior motive? Doris, in particular."

Flynn's reaction took Jenkins by surprise. Flynn laughed and slapped Jenkins on the back.

"Ha ha. That's your problem, Jenkins, you've had too much experience with women. You're right about Doris. It was her idea that you accompany us to the cock-fight. I can't help if every woman I know has got the hots for you, Hayward. You should be flattered."

Doris, of course! Doris could have stolen the diary but the diary was still in his bedside drawer after Doris had left. Jenkins' speculations were interrupted by Flynn.

"Look, Hayward, I know a charming place in Joo Chiat. You'll love it. We can have a drink there tonight and drown our sorrows."

Jenkins declined politely and left Flynn. He had to clarify the identity of the RAF officer who visited him while he was away. Instinctively he felt the need to hurry and jogged to Nicholl Drive. Within minutes he was back home. He undressed quickly, throwing off the thick RAF khaki uniform and putting on a cotton shirt. As he removed the loose change in his pocket and placed it on the bookshelf, he noticed that the books had been moved. They were tilting to one side as if an object had been squeezed in between them. He straightened the books, and then to his surprise saw Major Hughes's diary tucked in the pages of a thick book. The stolen diary had mysteriously reappeared or had it been there all the time? He searched his mind carefully. No he was sure it was stolen. He had never placed the diary on the bookshelf. He opened it quickly and found only blank pages. The coded message had been carefully torn off. Whoever had stolen it had removed Major Hughes carefully constructed code. It must have been the RAF officer who had visited him. He had originally thought the officer was Flynn but now he knew it was someone else. The housekeeper would know. Jenkins found her in the garden hanging out the washing.

"Do you remember the RAF officer who visited me yesterday?" Jenkins asked in Malay.

"Yes, *tuan*," she replied.

"How did you know he was from the RAF?"

"He wore a uniform. A khaki uniform just like the officers at Changi Air Base."

"He could have been from another air base or from the army. Are you sure he was from Changi."

"I don't know, *tuan*. I can't tell the difference but he walked up the road so he probably came from the air base."

Jenkins went into the house and came back with a photo album.

"Do you think you can recognise a photograph of him?"

"Yes. He looks very distinguished. A typical officer."

Jenkins opened the photo album. The housekeeper carefully looked at each photograph and shook her head. He turned a page. In the middle was a large photograph of Flynn. He waited eagerly. At any second the housekeeper would either exonerate Flynn or accuse him.

"Yes."

The reply shook Jenkins.

He followed the housekeeper's finger and was shocked to see the person she was pointing at.

It was not Flynn.

"Are you sure?" asked Jenkins.

"Yes, *tuan*," replied the housekeeper. "That is definitely the officer I saw."

Jenkins closed the photo album in disbelief. It was not whom he had expected.

"Are you sure?" Jenkins said more to himself than to the housekeeper.

"Yes *tuan*." The housekeeper was sensing Jenkins agitation and was beginning to get upset herself. "Did I do wrong in letting him in?" she asked.

"No. Don't worry yourself. I'm perfectly happy with your work around the house," he reassured her.

"I just want to be absolutely sure. I'm going to show you a different page and I would like you to pick out the officer."

Carefully, Jenkins chose a photograph which showed a vague profile of the officer and then showed it to his housekeeper.

"Can you pick him out?"

She tarried for only a short while and then her finger came unerringly down on the same person. There was no mistake. The person who stole the diary must be the traitor in RAF Changi. He went back into the house and rummaged through some papers on his dining table. Finding the list of personnel that the clerk, Eunice had given him, he quickly searched and found the address of the officer his housekeeper had identified.

96 Fidelio Street!

His hands grew cold as he was flooded with a new revelation. 96 was not an opus number as they had surmised but an address. He had discovered the real meaning of Beethoven 96. It was not just Fidelio Street that was important but a particular house on that street. Something was going to happen there today. Something was being plotted within that house at this very minute but how was the officer involved? What was his motive?

He picked up the phone and made two quick calls to the air base. He carefully worded his questions to allay any suspicions. At the end of two short enquiries, all doubts about the officer's involvement had been removed. The evidence was overwhelming and Beethoven 96 became much clearer.

Then he dialled for Dan Templeton in Kuala Lumpur. It was imperative that his information should only be passed on quickly to someone he could trust. There was no reply. He waited and dialled again. Still no reply. It was already late morning. He had to act soon or it might be too late.

After several failed attempts at getting through to Templeton he phoned the CID. Both Inspector Prem and Sergeant Lee were out on duty. He asked the operator at CID whether they could be reached through the police radio. No that was not correct procedure was the terse reply. Jenkins argued that the matter was urgent but the operator persistently refused. He had to leave his name and address with the operator and only then would his message be passed on to the Inspector.

It was futile to argue any further. If he left a message it could get into the wrong hands. Jenkins phoned for a taxi. He had to act himself. While he waited he instructed his housekeeper to stay by the telephone. If an Inspector Prem called, she was to tell him that Jenkins had gone to 96 Fidelio Street. He wrote down the address and emphasised its importance. He then wrote a note briefly explaining his findings and placed it within a sealed envelope, which he addressed to the Head of Directorate E at Leconfield House in London.

If anything should happen to him at least the Director of the Malayan and Commonwealth operations would be informed.

"Now listen carefully," he told the housekeeper. "I want you to keep this letter safe and not show it or mention it to anyone. Not the police, the RAF. No one."

The housekeeper was frightened and nodded.

"How long do I have to keep it for," she asked.

"I will inform you. I should be back sometime this evening but I will phone you by 4 p.m. before you go home. So whatever you're doing make sure you can hear the telephone."

"I will *tuan*, but is *tuan* in some kind of trouble with the police?"

"No, I'm not, but I can't trust any policeman. Many of them are corrupt. The only one I can trust is Inspector Prem."

"Inspector Prem," the housekeeper repeated.

"If I don't phone you or I'm not back tonight, I want you to post this letter for me."

"Is *tuan* going to be all right?" asked the housekeeper.

"Yes, I will, but you must do exactly as I have instructed you."

"I will, *tuan*."

A toot outside signalled the arrival of the taxi. Jenkins reminded the housekeeper of his instructions and jumped into the back of the taxi. She stood at the door and waved worriedly as the car drove off.

Down Upper Changi Road, the taxi drove with Jenkins urging the driver to go faster. Past the runway of Changi Air Base, down towards the army barracks and turning sharply right at the notorious Changi prison with its tall black walls. Jenkins counted the red and white milestones at the edge of the road. Eleven, ten and a half, ten, nine and half, nine. It seemed to take an eternity. The turning to Siglap Road and Opera Estate would be just before the six and a half milestone.

He looked at his watch. It was almost two o'clock. He would get there well before the state visit at 4 p.m. but would it give him enough time to stop the conspirators? They were passing through a thinly inhabited area of Changi. There was thick jungle on either side. For a moment Jenkins was fearful that someone might jump out of the jungle to stop him but the car sped through without incident.

"You are in a hurry to meet someone?" the taxi driver asked.

"Yes," replied Jenkins. He was not in the mood for conversation but the driver persisted.

"A special lady friend," the driver chuckled.

"No, my wife. She just died in Opera Estate," said Jenkins. The driver kept quiet for the rest of the journey. The traffic became heavier as they reached the junction with Bedok and quickly slowed down to a standstill.

"Will it be faster if we turn into Bedok and East Coast Road?"

"No," replied the driver. "There will be less traffic along Changi Road. We should get there within an hour even with this traffic jam."

Jenkins craned his neck and saw that the congestion

extended for nearly a hundred yards right up to the traffic lights. Then he noticed the face of the taxi driver. Although the driver was wearing sunglasses Jenkins recognised with horror who he was.

Seow Kow! Ah Seng's vicious Red Cudgel was driving the taxi. He must have been waiting somewhere in Nicholl Drive for an opportunity and had probably disposed of the taxi driver just before he reached Jenkins' house. Jenkins was caught in a trap.

Doubtless he was being driven to Kampong Chai Chee for a meeting with Ah Seng. He could imagine it to be a brief meeting before he was silenced. Maybe a meeting was not intended. Maybe Seow Kow was driving him to a quiet spot on Changi Road. Jenkins had been careless. He should have phoned for a car from the air base but it was too late now.

For a brief moment he was tempted to jump out of the car and run but he was sure that Seow Kow was armed and would shoot him down without any qualms. He considered screaming and making a fuss to attract the attention of the other cars. No, it would make no difference to a man like Seow Kow who would kill him in full view of the public. His only advantage was that Seow Kow seemed assured that Jenkins thought he was a taxi driver and was not expecting him to act. He had the advantage of surprise but he had only one chance. Then he noticed a taxi rank at the junction. If he could crawl out quietly another taxi would whisk him away through Bedok Road. He had to wait for the right moment.

Jenkins closed his eyes and pretended to sleep, slowly slipping away from the driver's line of sight through the rear view mirror. The taxi crawled forward. He waited until the taxi started to move again and gently pulled down the door handle. The 'click' as the door opened slightly was masked by the revving of the engine. Seow Kow's broad back remained still. He had not seen the slightly open door. They moved closer to the traffic lights. He made a quick calculation. Two more stops would bring them right up to the traffic lights and then they would have to cross the junction into the clear road ahead. Seow Kow was humming to himself still unaware of Jenkins intentions at the back of the car. Good, thought Jenkins, he's distracted.

The taxi was now only four cars away from the traffic lights. A large Mercedes had moved to their left. He carefully planned his route. Behind the Mercedes, up to the pavement and into one of the three taxis on Bedok Road waiting to leave. The traffic lights were just about to turn green. Seow Kow impatiently revved the engine. Jenkins pushed the door open and rolled out. The Mercedes had already moved a few feet leaving a clear gap in front of him. He got to his feet and crossed over to the pavement. A few shocked faces were staring at him. Keeping low he ran over to the taxis and crawled in.

"Opera Estate, quickly," he shouted to the stunned taxi driver and repeated himself when the driver did not respond.

"Quickly," shouted Jenkins and eventually the car started. He looked behind him to see Seow Kow driving across the traffic lights towards Kampong Chai Chee, unaware that his passenger and victim had eluded him. The back door of the taxi shook slightly in the wind but Seow Kow drove on.

"You in a hurry, Johnny," asked the taxi driver.

"Yes," sighed Jenkins.

"Are you going to meet nice girl in Opera Estate?" asked the driver.

Jenkins thought of making the same reply as he did before and then changed his mind.

"Yes, I'm going to meet a girl. A very nice girl."

"She must be very lucky if you desperate."

"Yes, I suppose so," replied Jenkins. Do these taxi drivers have a standard conversation for the *Ang Mohs*, he wondered?

"You be careful, Johnny. Make sure husband is still at work," laughed the taxi driver.

"Oh yes, I will. I will have to be very careful," said Jenkins.

The car turned into East Coast Road. Jenkins looked at his watch which showed 2.20 p.m.

"How long will it take to get to Fidelio Street?" he asked.

"Not long. About half an hour. You are horny man, Johnny," said the driver laughing in a high pitched whine.

Traffic policemen were beginning to take up their positions as they turned down the steep hill at the top of Fidelio Street. Curious onlookers were milling about in the street chatting with the residents of Fidelio Street who stood by the gates of their gardens and stared unabashedly at every passing car.

Jenkins shielded one side of his face with his hand. He did not want to be recognised

"Which number do you want?" asked the driver.

"Just drive slowly. I want to make sure nobody unexpected is in."

The driver smiled and nodded knowingly.

Jenkins counted the numbers of the houses. Number 96 was at the end of a row of bungalows. A storm drain and a small path separated it from the fence of a school. The doors and windows were firmly shut and unlike the other houses there was no one standing outside it.

"Which way now, Johnny?" asked the driver when they reached the canal bordering Swan Lake Avenue.

"Can you go round in a loop and turn the car back the way we came from?"

"Easy," said the driver, "but meter is still running."

The car made its way through the grid of side streets. Jenkins recalled with an abhorrent nostalgia, the chase through these streets. They were unusually crowded. Jenkins kept low in his seat.

"There is a big political rally here today, Johnny," said the driver.

The car turned back into Fidelio Street. Huge banners hung across the road, tied to the lampposts on the pavement and children were making their way into the school. They passed by number 96.

"Is there a street at the back of these houses?" asked Jenkins.

"Yes."

"Do you think you can drive there and stop just before this house?"

"Easy."

The taxi turned right into a track up a steep hill. Jenkins recognised it as the one leading to the convent. The taxi turned right again and stopped.

"The house on Fidelio Street backs on to the last house on this street," said the driver. "There is little path along the fence which takes you to Fidelio Street. Have a nice time, Johnny," smiled the driver.

Jenkins took out a wad of notes and paid the driver, giving him a huge tip. He hurriedly walked up to the end of the street and crossed a makeshift wooden bridge which took him to the path along the fence of the school. A little boy who was playing on the path threw a ball at him. Jenkins caught it just before it fell into the storm drain. The little boy cheered and clapped in delight.

"Good catch," the boy shouted. "Now throw it back."

Jenkins gave him the ball and took a coin out of his pocket.

"How would you like to earn ten cents?" he asked.

The boy's eyes opened wide when he saw the coin. "OK," he replied.

Jenkins handed him the coin.

"I want to play a joke on my friend who lives in that house. I want you to go to the front door and knock until someone opens it."

"What do I tell him when he opens the door?"

"Nothing. Just run away and I'll give you another ten cents."

Jenkins held another coin up temptingly. The little boy did not need further encouragement. He ran down the path towards Fidelio Street. Jenkins waited until he had opened the gate to number 96 and was walking down the garden path. The boy would create a little diversion and distract their attention from the back door.

He jumped over the storm drain and climbed over the fence. Keeping an eye on the windows, he made his way slowly along the side of the house towards the back door. The house looked deserted. He stooped low as he crossed the lawn. The door was only an arm's length away when he spotted the little boy returning. Jenkins hurriedly waved to him to be silent and threw a coin in his direction. He caught it easily but to Jenkins' dismay stood on the path watching him. Jenkins angrily gestured to him to move away but the boy stood firm. Finally in exasperation Jenkins threw another coin further along the path, motioning the boy to keep away. The boy walked unhurriedly to the coin, picked it up and then ran away laughing.

All this time the house remained quiet. With a fluttering sense of anticipation, Jenkins turned the door knob gently. There was a faint click. It was not locked as he had expected. He pushed the door open slightly and peered through the gap. The house was unusually dark. The curtains must have been drawn but Jenkins could see some stools, a table and large pots and pans. He was looking at the kitchen. He straightened himself up and waited. Not a sound. Then he pushed the door wide open and swung back against the wall. Nothing moved. There was no one in the kitchen.

He walked in tentatively. Was he too late? Had they already moved on and was Beethoven 96 already in operation. There was a single door in the kitchen which obviously led to the front of the house. He tip-toed to the door. Leaning over, he pressed an ear against it. He strained and listened for several minutes but could not differentiate the noise from the growing crowd in Fidelio Street from any sound within the house.

If there was anyone in the house they were probably armed. It might be prudent to walk out and then inform the police who must be patrolling all along Fidelio Street. On the other hand the traitor and his accomplices in the house could escape as soon as the police were alerted. Once again he felt he had been too impetuous and not planned his actions judiciously. There was bound to be more than one person in there. Could he take them all on?

The crowds in Fidelio Street were getting louder. Jenkins looked at his watch. It was 3.30 p.m. The visiting dignitaries would be arriving shortly. He had to act now. He would rush through to the front of the house and then attract the attention of the police. Carefully he opened the door. It yielded suddenly and a hand pulled him into the room. Before he could react, his arms were held fast and his mouth covered. A strongly sickly smell assaulted his nostrils and within seconds he collapsed to the ground. As he passed out he recalled that he had smelt the same odour on the night of the murders in Changi.

Sergeant Lee had picked up Inspector Prem early that morning.

"Slept well I hope," said Sergeant Lee.

The Inspector grunted in annoyance. "I want to go to library first. There's one in Katong."

"Why do you want to stop at the library? We might be delayed and I don't want to be late after what happened yesterday," said Sergeant Lee.

"I just want to check something."

The library had just opened when they arrived a few minutes later. A bored librarian ignored them for a long time while they waited behind a counter.

"Have you got a book on the life and works of Beethoven?" asked Inspector Prem.

"You mean a biography of Beethoven," said the librarian haughtily.

"Yes, a biography."

"No we haven't got one," said the librarian.

"What about a book that refers to Beethoven and his works?" asked the Inspector.

"There are thousands of books that refer to Beethoven," replied the librarian turning up his eyes patronizingly. "It might be so much easier for you to refer to the card index over there and look under Beethoven. Then choose the book you want." He pointed to two wooden cabinets.

Sergeant took out his warrant card and showed it to the librarian. "We're from the CID and we are investigating corruption. Allegations of corruption in the National Library service. We are in a hurry and need your assistance and co-operation. Now can you get us a book about Beethoven quickly?"

The librarian hesitated but when Sergeant Lee showed him his gun he knew Sergeant Lee was in earnest.

"Maybe a music encyclopaedia might help," said Inspector Prem.

"Yes. An encyclopaedia. Of course I'll get them immediately sir."

He came back with two large volumes.

"C.P.E. Bach, J.S.Bach. Beethoven. Here it is," said Sergeant Lee as he flicked through the pages. "What are we looking for?"

"Fidelio," said Inspector Prem.

Sergeant Lee read out aloud. "Fidelio, opus 72. Beethoven's only opera. Composed in..."

"Read that again," said Inspector Prem.

"Beethoven's only opera. Composed..."

"No, no. From the start."

"Fidelio, opus 72," said Sergeant Lee. Its significance quickly dawned on him. "It's not 96."

"Precisely. We've been deceived into thinking that Fidelio was opus 96."

Sergeant Lee checked the huge encyclopaedia. "Opus 96 is a sonata. Whatever that is. So Fidelio Street has got nothing to do with Beethoven 96. We are back to square one."

"No, Sergeant. Fidelio Street is definitely connected with Beethoven 96. Sim and the Commissioner both acquiesced in its importance when we spoke to them. It is the 96 that we have misinterpreted. It could be ninety six or nine and six separately or nine minutes to six."

"Or the ninth of June which is next month." said Sergeant Lee.

Inspector Prem felt the numbers had a sinister significance. It was Jenkins who had made the connection between Fidelio Street and Beethoven 96. Was there any significance in the number 96?

"Its meaning must somehow connect today's events with the parties involved and only triads use numbers which have two digits. Ah Seng's has taken over Sar Ji, which is two, three, and Kong Puek which is 08. Do you know whether there is a nine six?" he asked Sergeant Lee.

"There is no nine six triad in Singapore but I've got a brilliant idea, Inspector. Nine six could be the triad number for the communist party."

It was a possibility but too simplistic. Then he

remembered Major Hughes' diary. The convent was mentioned in the diary and so was Sato indirectly. If Sato knew about Beethoven 96 and Major Hughes knew about Sato, then it would be logical that Major Hughes knew about Beethoven 96. If so, the secret of Beethoven 96 could be hidden in the diary.

"I'm not convinced, Sergeant. If Beethoven 96 is simply the triad number for the communists then what has today's state visit got to do with it. I think we should phone Jenkins. He might be able to shed some light on the matter."

Inspector Prem had seen a phone box outside the library. He inserted a coin and dialled Jenkins' number. A few minutes later they were rushing back to the police car. Jenkins had indeed solved the riddle of Beethoven 96, but by doing so, he had placed himself in danger.

"The housekeeper said he left just before two o'clock. We must hurry, Sergeant, otherwise there will be another murder."

By the time they arrived at Opera Estate the whole area had been cordoned off in preparation for the important visit. A policeman stopped them before they could make their way to 96 Fidelio Street and ushered them to a large police riot-van, the feared Black Maria. Standing in the van was Sim.

"You're only just on time," said Sim. "I really don't understand you. You persisted for so long to stay on this case and when this important day arrive you stroll in indifferently."

"We had to find out a few things," said Sergeant Lee and was nudged by the Inspector.

"What things?" asked Sim looking menacingly at the Sergeant.

"We asked the Director of the CID whether he knew at what time we would finish today. You see, my mother wanted to prepare a special meal for the family so we had to tell her whether we would be in time for dinner. As it turned out, the Director said it could take all day so we had to cancel."

Sim glared at Sergeant Lee, his face twisting into ugly shapes and then suddenly roared with laughter. "That's the silliest excuse I've ever heard from a detective."

Inspector Prem still maintained a dead-pan expression but he could see Sergeant Lee smiling uneasily like a schoolboy who had been caught out.

"Now listen. These are your orders," said Sim. "I want you to stay on Fidelio Street and mingle with the crowd. Pick out anyone who looks suspicious or is behaving strangely. Arrest them if necessary. You won't be the only ones in plain-clothes so make sure you have your identification ready if you confront anyone. There shouldn't be any trouble but be vigilant. Are you armed?"

"Yes," said Sergeant Lee.

"In that case I must ask you to surrender your ammunition."

"But that would leave us totally exposed," argued Sergeant Lee.

"I don't think bullets are required. Just the sight of your guns would deter any mischief makers."

"Mischief makers?" Sergeant Lee blurted out, "there are potential killers out there who wouldn't think twice about shooting me in the back."

"I'm in charge of security here, Sergeant. Both of you volunteered to help. If you can't abide by the rules then you can always withdraw your services."

"Our ammunition belongs to the CID, Mr Sim. We can only surrender it to the CID and not to you," said Inspector Prem in his characteristic slow drawl. He knew it was not necessary to surrender their ammunition and that Sim, still smarting from being over-ruled by the Commissioner, was trying to deter them from proceeding to Fidelio Street.

"That doesn't make any difference. I'm still in charge here and I won't have any trigger happy detectives wandering around a crowd like this."

"We are not trigger happy detectives," cried Sergeant Lee.

"The choice is yours. If you want to be involved then surrender your ammunition."

Inspector Prem looked at Sergeant Lee who was crestfallen. The time on his watch showed 3 p.m. Precious time was being wasted with the adamant ISD operative. Jenkins could already be dead.

"I suppose we have to do as Mr Sim says, Sergeant," said Inspector Prem.

"What?" cried Sergeant Lee but Inspector Prem signalled to him to do as he was told.

Inspector Prem took out his revolver and emptied the cartridges.

"I want a proper receipt for these bullets," said Inspector Prem.

"Of course," said Sim in triumph as he collected the bullets.

Sergeant Lee similarly emptied the cartridges and Sim wrote a brief note.

"Good enough?" asked Sim.

"Yes," replied Sergeant Lee tersely but the edges of his lips were curling up in a slight smile.

"Did you guess that he didn't know about the spare ammo?" asked Sergeant Lee as they hurried down Fidelio Street.

"Very few people in the CID know that I always carry some spare," replied Inspector Prem. "Come on. Let's hurry."

Inspector Prem was getting worried. The long delay with Sim could be critical. They pushed their way through the crowds that lined the pavements on each side of Fidelio Street counting the house numbers as they made their way down the hill. At the end of a row of terrace houses Sergeant Lee spotted number 96. It was a small red-brick bungalow with a sheltered porch and an untended front garden. Tyre marks on the wide drive-way showed that the owners had a car which was nowhere in sight.

"It's next to the school. Strategically chosen," said Sergeant Lee.

Inspector Prem noted that all the windows were closed which was very unusual for a hot day. The crowd cheered and Inspector Prem could see movement at the top of Fidelio Street. The Prime Minister was on his way. They had to act fast.

"Jenkins must be right about the address but I can't see him anywhere. I hope he wasn't rash enough to go into the house."

"He's not in this crowd, Inspector. He must be in the house."

The crowd was cheering. Traffic police escorts whizzed by in their motorbikes followed by a large car.

"Come on, Inspector. We have to go into the house."

"Wait; let's get some back-up."

Sergeant Lee ordered two policemen standing by the police cordon to accompany them. The house was strangely silent as they approached the front door.

"What shall I say?" Sergeant Lee asked as he knocked on the door.

"Improvise," replied Inspector Prem.

Sergeant Lee knocked at the door but there was no reply.

"Open it," Inspector Prem ordered the policemen.

They positioned themselves to kick the door open but Sergeant Lee turned the knob and to their surprise the door opened inwards into a dark lounge. As they entered they were struck by a pungent smell.

"Don't touch the lights," shouted Inspector Prem. "It's gas." He rushed down to the end of the lounge pushed open the door and stepped into the kitchen. The smell of gas was almost overpowering. Covering his mouth with his hands, he flung open the windows and the back door. Only then did he realise there was someone else in the kitchen.

22. Grenade and gas

Jenkins still felt dizzy as he regained consciousness. He was lying on a bed with his hands tied behind his back. Two hazy figures standing in front of him slowly came into focus.

Giles and Melanie Hartson.

"Hello, Hayward," said Melanie. "Did you enjoy the chloroform?"

"You won't be gloating for long, Melanie, the police will be here any minute."

Jenkins saw the couple exchange glances and then Giles Hartson laughed.

"The police are already here, old boy. In fact they are everywhere and they can't do a thing. I know you're bluffing. We've been watching the police since you arrived and they don't know you're here. It won't make any difference to our plans anyway."

Giles Hartson sounded confident. They could not be absolutely certain, thought Jenkins. He needed time. Delay them.

"How did you know I was in the house? Did the boy tell you?" Jenkins asked.

"Boy? So that was your doing. We know more than you think. We've watched every move you've made."

The gun was still pointed at Jenkins. Hartson might have been unscrupulous but was he a killer? Would he use the gun?

"I know why you've turned into a traitor, Giles," said Jenkins.

"Traitor? Isn't that a strong word?"

"I know all about your family and the Indonesian government." Giles Hartson merely smiled but Jenkins carried on regardless.

"I know that the Indonesians have been threatening to nationalise your family's oil companies and that they have got you under their thumb. That's why you've run over to the communists. You're the one who's been selling RAF secrets for the past few years. You're a traitor, Giles."

The after effects of chloroform were wearing off. Keep him talking, Jenkins thought. In a minute I should be able to rush him.

"I'm not a traitor. I'm one of those who will be saving Britain. I've kept my oil companies functioning in Indonesia through all these years. Who do you think will provide the British army with petroleum after the Suez Canal debacle? The Arabs now control the Middle East and they regard Britain as the enemy. They can't be trusted anymore. It will be Indonesia who will supply Britain with oil. By establishing ties with the communists I'll be making sure that Britain's oil demand will be met whether Indonesia has a communist government or not. I'm the one Britain will be looking to for salvation," Giles Hartson shouted.

The gun was lowered slightly. If Giles Hartson could be distracted, Jenkins could overpower him. He moved slightly to one side. Hartson did not seem to notice. Jenkins looked at Melanie who pouted and smiled back. He had to shorten the distance between them and then he could reach the gun with a single lunge. His eyes were still fixed on Melanie. At any moment Giles would wander what Jenkins was staring at. That was the right moment. Carefully, slowly, Jenkins tensed his muscles for the move.

Hartson was about to turn his head when another man walked into the kitchen. It was Seow Kow. It was too late. Jenkins knew he had no chance of overpowering both men.

Seow Kow must have driven to the house after Jenkins' escape and warned the Hartsons. It was only then that Jenkins comprehended the extent of operation Beethoven 96. He also realised then that he would be killed.

"That was good trick you played in the taxi but you die anyway," said Seow Kow.

Stall them, thought Jenkins. "And so will you. Major Hartson intends to get rid of you as soon as you've finished your job."

There was a momentary flicker of suspicion as Seow Kow looked at Giles Hartson but it faded as the noise from the crowd outside grew louder.

"I would love to slit your throat right now but Major Hartson come up with better plan. You can die with the knowledge that you created diversion."

Seow Kow held Jenkins in a vice like grip and tied his

arms behind his back while Hartson placed a hard object underneath him.

"Don't move now, Hayward. You're sitting on a grenade which has been activated." Hartson held up the safety pin and then tossed it into the sink behind him.

Melanie bent over, kissed Jenkins hard on the lips and whispered, "I hope you enjoy your blow job."

Seow Kow turned on the gas in the cooker and hurriedly walked out of the back door with Melanie and Giles Hartson.

Jenkins sat very still as the kitchen began to slowly fill with gas. Bending very slowly, he could see the 'pineapple' covering of a grenade nestling between his buttocks. He stretched his arms and found it was impossible to reach the triggering clip of the grenade. The clip was attached to the top of the grenade which faced the front of his body while his arms were behind him.

It would be only a matter of minutes before the gas would render him unconscious. He could see himself falling off the chair detonating the grenade which would then set off a secondary explosion with the gas. The house would be blown to bits. Tiny bits of his body would be splattered all over Fidelio Street. The ensuing fire would burn whatever little evidence of foul play there was and the explosion would be construed as an accident. By the time someone could point the accusing finger at the Hartsons or Seow Kow, they would have escaped.

Jenkins put aside all thoughts of false pride and bravery and screamed for help but no one came to his assistance. No one could hear him above the noise of the crowd outside. After some time he stopped. He was gulping down gas in between screams and was feeling light-headed. There had to be another way. He shifted slightly. If he could move the clip of the grenade against one buttock, he would just be able to reach it with his hands. He twisted and managed to budge the grenade slightly.

Suddenly he felt the clip give way. Looking down he saw that the clip had opened up slightly and was close to triggering the grenade. He sat very still, pushing hard on the clip and trying not to swoon from the fumes. If he could hold out maybe someone out in the street might detect the smell of gas. He pressed his mouth on to his shoulder and tried to use his shirt as a filter.

Death was only a few minutes away. A violent and sordid death when there was so much more life he had yet to experience. He thought of his home in Wales, of the green lush mountains, his parents and their close knit family. He was not going to see them ever again.

The fumes did not seem to be getting any stronger. Maybe some of it was escaping from the kitchen but he had already breathed in quite an amount. It would soon become impossible to prevent himself from collapsing. His eyes were sore and the room was becoming hazy. He felt certain that he was going to die.

Then the door crashed open. Through the dizzy haze he could vaguely see two men rushing through. The windows were flung open. A firm hand held his shoulder and familiar voice was calling out his name.

He tried to shake off the dizzy swoon. Looking up, the two figures became clearer. The door to the kitchen was pushed wide open. A tall silhouetted figure stood by the doorway looking down on him. The figure took a step closer and it was unmistakable who his saviour was.

Inspector Prem, the dogged and determined detective, smiled kindly at him. Inspector Prem's timely intervention had rescued him again.

"Jenkins, are you alright."

"Where are they Jenkins?" asked Sergeant Lee.

He was bathed in cool air rushing back into the kitchen as he fought off the lingering effects of dizziness.

"Grenade," he croaked, "I'm sitting on a grenade

Quickly Sergeant Lee grabbed the grenade and held down the clip.

After a quick clarification of the situation, Inspector Prem left Jenkins with two policemen in the house. He delegated some men to look for the Hartsons while he and Sergeant Lee searched along the path by the school fence. 96 Fidelio Street was conveniently next to the school and owned by the Hartsons but there had to be another reason why it had been chosen instead of the dozen or so houses bordering the school.

"There is a clear line of sight to the school for a sniper on the roof of the house," reflected Sergeant Lee, "but that doesn't appear to be part of their plans. There is a policeman guarding each corner of the perimeter fence. They have assured me that no one has climbed over the fence and the ISD have confirmed that there are no holes cut in it for anyone to crawl through."

"We haven't got much time, Sergeant. Let us assume they've got past the fence somehow. Let's check the school itself."

A policeman opened the school's side-gate to let Inspector Prem and Sergeant Lee into the grounds. He could see several cars stopping by the main school entrance. The cordon on each side of the driveway bulged inwards slightly as the crowd pushed forward but it held.

Inspector Prem knew they had only a few minutes. He had sent word to the detectives and police at the entrance of the school to delay the proceedings and although he had not received confirmation he was sure they would await his all clear signal. He and Sergeant Lee were now joined by a uniformed policeman as they crossed the playground which sloped downwards towards the school. Taking a short cut they jumped over another storm drain, past the back end of the building and ran towards the main entrance.

The building appeared to be deserted. What if he was wrong? What if the conspirators had chosen to approach from the other side of the driveway? He looked back at the house and then to his horror noticed something.

The storm drain!

It ran under the fence and straight into the school from the house. It was as if it was pointing straight as an arrow at the school building. At that instant, he realised why the house had been chosen by the conspirators. The storm drain from the school joined the main drain just in front of 96 Fidelio Street. It was more than four feet deep and provided adequate concealment for a man trying to get into the school.

"The drain, Sergeant! It tunnels under the fence," cried Inspector Prem. "They've crawled through the drain into the school."

Sergeant Lee looked back. "You're right. They could be in the building now."

Sergeant Lee was already opening the door into the school building before the Inspector moved.

Inspector Prem noted with dismay that the locks to the door had been picked.

The building had three similar floors each with classrooms adjacent to a long common corridor, flanked at the ends by staircases. Sergeant Lee and the uniformed policeman ran up the steps while the Inspector stood guard at the ground floor corridor. He checked his revolver and looked across to the main entrance.

Then to his horror he saw the Prime Minister emerging from one of the cars. What were they doing he thought? He had explicitly told them not to go ahead. What was Sim doing? Inspector Prem ran down the corridor shouting at the police at the main gate but he was too far away. He could see the dark wavy hair of the Prime Minister jutting above the crowd, a clear and inviting target.

There was only one thing to do. He pointed his revolver at the ground and fired. In the empty corridor, the shot reverberated and sounded like an explosion. Outside he could see heads turning in his direction and some men beginning to circle the Prime Minister but they were too slow. Two shots rang out in quick succession above him.

Inspector Prem burst out of the door at the end of the corridor running straight towards the Prime Minister's car. The crowd moved away from him as he ran and reached the car easily. Sim and several men from the ISD were standing by the car.

"Put your gun away, Inspector. You're frightening the crowd," said Sim.

"Is the Prime Minister all right?" asked the Inspector, as he complied.

"Yes," replied Sim. "We got him back into the car as soon as the shots were heard."

Inspector Prem peered through the barrier of bodyguards and saw the Prime Minister in the car. The Prime Minister was looking anxiously at the crowd and although he was visibly shaken, he was otherwise unhurt.

Then to his surprise, he saw another figure in the car also in a formal suit. For a moment Inspector Prem felt confused. The two figures looked very alike. Then Sim moved in his way and blocked his view.

"Well done, inspector. We have managed to thwart an assassination attempt. I can see the police are in control at the top of the school building."

Inspector Prem was less confident. The assassination attempt had failed but what were those shots he had heard?

He returned to the school building followed closely by Sim. They found Sergeant Lee on the top floor standing over two bodies.

"They were killed before I got to them," said Sergeant Lee. "One of them has got a bullet wound but they both have... Well look for yourself."

Inspector Prem moved closer and saw Ah Seng and Seow Kow. Their faces, contorted in a mask of surprise, were covered in blood from deep lacerations in their necks. The same lacerations he had seen in Changi.

"PC Hamid here says he saw a third person running through one of the rooms and out through the back of the building. We couldn't stop him but the drops of blood he left behind indicate that he must be wounded. It won't be difficult to find him so I decided to wait here."

Inspector Prem nodded in assent. They both knew who that third person was.

They left Sim to restore order and made their way back to the house on Fidelio street.

It was quite some time after he had replaced the safety pin of the grenade with trembling hands before Jenkins recovered his composure. Only then did he realise that it wasn't a live grenade after all.

Inspector Prem and Sergeant Lee had then immediately left to look for the Hartsons and Seow Kow leaving Jenkins in the little kitchen where he had narrowly confounded death. He phoned his housekeeper who poured forth in a torrent of words, her anguish and concern. Jenkins gently reassured her.

Just as he replaced the hand-set, he heard the gun shots. Rushing to the window he could see a small part of the crowd on Fidelio Street surging through the gates. They were all looking at the school building.

Jenkins was considering going out to the front garden when he noticed movement behind the school building. A man swung down a rope from the top floor of the school to the ground. His left hand was pressed against his side and although he moved quite quickly he appeared to be in pain. He was already jogging unsteadily away from the school before Jenkins could react. The crowd was still murmuring and pushing towards the school unaware of the fleeing man. Didn't they realise that one of the murderers was escaping thought Jenkins?

Jenkins charged out of the back and fleetingly caught sight of a face he knew only too well. Sato! Sato was getting away from yet another murder. Jenkins jumped over the storm drain and landed on the path by the fence. A policeman was giving chase but Sato had disappeared behind some houses. Then Jenkins noticed blood on the ground. If Sato was badly wounded he could catch up with him. At the convent, but he had to be quick!

He caught up with the policeman who fortunately knew who he was. Together they ran down the street, up the steep slope and then through the open gates of the convent. At the top of the hill not more than twenty yards in front of him, he saw Sato staggering into the convent. His movements suggested he was extremely weak but even in that state Sato was still dangerous.

They entered the convent warily. An eerie silence and a foreboding darkness greeted them. The convent was deserted and the corridors rang loudly with their footsteps as they followed a trail of blood on the white tiles of the convent. The trail ended abruptly at a door that was left slightly ajar.   Jenkins could hear whispers and murmured voices. He pushed the door and saw the Reverend Mother Ventura kneeling over the prostrate body of Sato on a table. Two nuns stood serenely next to her. Jenkins could see that one of them was distraught and had been crying. They were just outside the convent's chapel and the Reverend Mother was praying softly.

Jenkins immediately recognised the prayer and chose to wait politely. Even though he was not religious and Sato had committed heinous crimes, he had to respect the solemnity of the occasion. The Reverend Mother had deemed it appropriate to say the last rites for Sato. It would be disrespectful for him to interfere.

Finally the Reverend Mother made the sign of the cross and stood up. Jenkins walked up to them and could see tears in the Reverend Mother's eyes. Sato's arms were neatly folded across his chest with his sword half covered in blood, laid by his side.

"He has gone from us," said the Reverend Mother. "I'll phone for an ambulance and contact the Japanese Consulate." She had recovered and sounded calm.

The policeman waited by the dead body of Sato while the Reverend Mother brought Jenkins back to the entrance. At the door, the Reverend Mother pressed a letter into his hand.

"He told me to give you this. Make sure you do read it and don't judge him too quickly."

He watched the Reverend Mother walk away, her black nun's habit fluttering and then slowly merging with the darkness of the convent. It was quiet. Deathly quiet, he thought as he made his way out.

Jenkins stood still outside the convent and looked at the grounds and the surrounding jungle. They stared back at him in a strange silence. A quiet tranquillity or was it grief? The killer of Major Hughes was dead but he felt no triumph and no exultation. The Reverend Mother seemed to be saddened by the death of a criminal. It looked inappropriate and troubled him. She must have known his evil nature but showed sympathy and was willing to forgive. Wouldn't such forgiveness be excessive, thought Jenkins? He was further perturbed by an admission deep within him that he somehow sympathised with the Reverend Mother.

Perhaps the letter would explain. He turned it over and saw that it was addressed to Jenkins *San*. He read it quickly.

It revealed more about Sato and his exploits than he

had expected. All along he had assumed that Sato was a cold-blooded killer. The murderer of four men in Changi Air Base in one night. The assassin who had tried to kill the Prime Minister. Had he succeeded, Jenkins wondered? After the initial revelations from their investigations, Jenkins firmly believed that Sato was a callous and evil man. He thought that Sato had abused the hospitality and kindness of the convent. Sato, he believed, was a soldier who enjoyed killing and could not stop even after the war.

As he folded the letter and placed it in his pocket, Jenkins knew now that he was wrong.

When he arrived back at the house, Sergeant Lee had returned and was waiting for him.

"Where have you been?" asked Sergeant Lee.

"I'll explain in a moment but I heard shots. Has someone been killed?"

Sergeant Lee nodded and explained what had happened. They were joined shortly by Inspector Prem.

"He's dead," Jenkins announced. They both stared blankly at him.

"Sato's dead," Jenkins repeated. "He's in the convent."

"You saw Sato?" asked a bewildered Sergeant Lee.

"Yes I saw him running from the school and followed him to the convent. He's dead."

"How did he die, Captain Jenkins?" asked Inspector Prem.

"He was mortally wounded and already dead before I reached him. The Reverend Mother from the convent gave me this. Read it, because I think it explains a great deal."

23. A Japanese confession

Jenkins San,

When this letter reaches you, I would be on my way to my people in Japan or to make my peace with God. My obligations to friends would have been served and my long quest ended. If I do live to tell my tale it won't be without considerable remorse for my deeds but I cannot live with honour or dignity if I don't accomplish what I have to. I'm bound by an aged Japanese code, one that does not tolerate excuses or seeks compromise. It compels absolute adherence and I regard it with veneration. Therefore, even if you deem my actions to be wrong, my motives were sincere.

I came to Singapore to rest and recover from my wounds after fighting in the jungles of Batam Island. Our unit had been devastated by the lack of foresight of some of our commanders and we had suffered heavy casualties. Most of the survivors were transported to Okinawa to counter the American threat but the Kempei Tai who had enlisted me wanted me to be stationed in Singapore. I welcomed the opportunity to be united with my dearest brother once again who was part of the occupation force of Singapore.

We were housed in make-shift barracks not far from the convent you visited. It was a small church but even then it exuded a dominant spiritual atmosphere. Although I was Japanese, the kind sisters who ran the church extended the same warmth and cordiality to me as they would any other in their congregation. I spent many evenings in communion and found that the church afforded the only solace in a time of cruelty and hardship. It changed my perspective substantially and I tried to reciprocate the kindness the sisters showed me, not only to them personally but also to the local people. My brother and the other soldiers in the barracks poured scorn on my attempts belittling me for being too 'soft' on the vanquished. Nevertheless, I persevered knowing that what I was doing was right.

We had been only a few months in Singapore when Japan surrendered. We were stunned and could hardly believe that the Emperor did not want to fight to the bitter end. Many of my colleagues could not bear the utter humiliation and shame and committed hara-kiri. I chose to wait hoping that the Emperor might change his mind and that we would fight on.

Singapore erupted into chaos and turmoil during the weeks after the surrender. There was no army or police force to control the looting. I stood by the sisters and with the assistance of my brother, protected them from the unscrupulous mobs that roamed the streets. For some, the end of the war brought more pain than the war itself.

The British ships finally arrived after many long days

of gratuitous suffering and a semblance of order was restored.

The remaining Japanese soldiers were quickly rounded up and it would be our turn soon. My brother and I were just outside the convent when a group of British soldiers came to take us away. The group of five was headed by a Captain and a Sergeant. We were armed only with our traditional samurai swords and my brother was in favour of charging them and dying as honourable soldiers. I, in lamentable misjudgement, persuaded him to submit to the mercy of the British. We raised our arms in submission and prepared to lay down our swords. Without warning, the Captain, pulled out his revolver and shot my brother in the back. I can recall the tragic scene to this day; the look of hatred on the Captain's face, my brother twisting in mid air and holding on defiantly to his sword and finally crumbling to the ground. Such treachery, such cowardice and callousness to strike an unarmed young man in the back. The Sergeant who was carrying a Lee-Enfield pointed its muzzle at my brother's head. Coughing and spluttering my brother uttered the two words to me, which I shall never forget.

"Kill him!"

Then the Sergeant shot him dead. I stood frozen in disbelief at this iniquity feeling the mounting rage urging me to kill them all. If only I had not dithered and hesitated. The opportunity for immediate action was lost. I could not avenge my brother in the face of insurmountable odds.

As the Sergeant aimed his revolver at me, I ran away unashamedly, dodging and weaving. The shots from the Captain and the Sergeant ricocheted around me. I believe it was only with the grace of God that I reached the safety of the jungle.

I hid in the tunnels and a bunker that we had dug in the hill under the church. Their existence was known only to the Kempei Tai and I was safe for a while. The anguish of losing my brother without raising a hand to help him almost compelled me to take my own life but I meditated through the night and decided the best course would be to avenge his death. The next day I set about planning to deceive the British into believing me to be dead.

I exhumed a body of a Chinese man who had died recently and covered it with some old rotting Japanese uniforms I found in the bunker. I carried the body and left it in the jungle by the edge of Changi Road. I left my dog tag on the body. Less than a week later the British had found the body, noted my identity tag and the search for me was over.

Fortunately there were enough combat rations and fuel in the tunnel to last for several months so I stayed hidden and only came out after sunset for several weeks. The jungle had a plentiful supply of fruits and the occasional small game to sustain me through all these years but even then I had to rely on help from some friends. Some of the locals remembered the kindness I had shown them during the Occupation and gave me some food sometimes.

I hardly left the jungle in the first few years. When I did, it was to go to church for prayer and meditation with the gentle sisters. They were kind and supportive. In their eyes I had been forgiven and accepted by the Lord.

I was sent to protect them in their time of need and now it was their turn to reciprocate.

But I could not forget, Jenkins San. My beloved brother had been killed and his dying words haunted me to this day. How can his soul rest in peace after such a cruel death? It was the Lord's will and it was the Lord's guiding hand that led me to do what I had to.

The ugly incident could not be forgotten but it was not foremost in my thoughts at least. Several months had gone by and with the sisters' help I achieved some form of peace of mind but it is God's will that the memory of my brother's untimely death would resurface again. By chance, no not by chance but by the grace of God I stumbled on photos of my brother's two killers. I had friends who worked in the RAF and saw the killers in a British Armed forces magazine.

Both had been promoted soon after the Surrender. They were now Major Hughes and Warrant Officer Class 1 Ben Pyke. Major Hughes had left the country so I concentrated my efforts on Ben Pyke. It wasn't difficult to locate him as he was the Sergeant major in an army camp in Changi.

After a month or so of shadowing him I ultimately managed to corner him walking home alone one night. After so many years the fire of my vengeance had cooled and mercifully, I made sure his death was swift. A single stroke of my sword decapitated him.

Although many British soldiers who were stationed here occasionally returned to Singapore, I did not expect Major Hughes to return. My brother's dying wish was partially satisfied but if the Major did return, then it would be the Lord's will. I kept my eyes and ears open through friends in the area, for any visitors from Britain to the British armed forces bases in Changi. I was not expectant or hopeful but neither was I going to ignore any information that came my way. I just had to perform my duties as the Lord sees fit. As it so happened, the Lord delivered him to me.

A few years later Major Hughes arrived. I had to fulfil my Divine obligations. You already know the events leading up to his death since you were almost a witness but what no one realised was that I was responsible for only his death and not the others at Changi Air Base.

During the years when I lived as a recluse in the jungle, I had doubtless left myself exposed to curiosity. Bits of rumour accumulated to eventually unmask my existence in the jungle to the likes of Ah Seng, who lived close by. With the aid of his powerful friends from the Barisan Socialis, he was able to ascertain the objective of my enquiries about the British. It was not long before they conspired to use me to further their own ends. Ah Seng approached me in the jungle saying that Major Hughes would be returning to Singapore soon and providing me with the exact dates and times when he would be in Changi Air Base. On the fateful night in Changi, Seow Kow had followed me into the air base unbeknownst. It was he who killed first the two guards I had left tied up and then later shot the Sergeant in the land rover.

It was part of Ah Seng's plot to incriminate me in the other murders so that I would comply with his wishes. A few days after the murder of Major Hughes I was invited to his house for a meeting to discuss the terms to smuggle me out of Singapore and back to Japan. I regret my naiveté and failure to see through Ah Seng's deception. I committed a grievous error and agreed to meet him. If I had refused then so many of the tragedies which unfolded would have been prevented and so much misery averted.

His Barisan friend was with him at the meeting and he produced a false passport and documents that would ensure my safe passage back to Japan. I foolishly believed them. They could see I was completely taken in and overjoyed at the prospect of going home. Once more I would be able to touch snow, to see the lovely colours of cherry blossom in the spring, to behold the splendour of the mountains of Japan and to be with my own kind.   Then they unveiled their true intentions and spoke at length about Beethoven 96. It would be just another killing, they said, of a man who had caused great suffering. The removal of an anti-Christian who hated the Japanese they lied. I refused to agree to their terms but they threatened they would report me to the authorities. I would be charged with four murders and would definitely hang they argued. I explained that I was a soldier and not a killer. I had avenged my brother's treacherous death and had no desire to kill innocent civilians. Still they pressed me, reminding me of my obligations to them and still I refused. Eventually they comprehended that I was adamant and could not be moved but I had known too much about their fiendish schemes. I would have been killed there and then but the Barisan man was squeamish and ironically did not want to have any blood spilt in his presence. I was tied and left in a room at the back of the house. I managed to use my teeth to unlatch the window and jump out and by a twist of fate, our paths crossed once more, Jenkins San.

You saved me from certain death by helping me that night. My code as a warrior demands that I can only repay you with gratitude and *sumimasen*. Apology without end for my deeds. I know where and when the important state visit will be and I can guess where Ah Seng and his men will position themselves for the assassination. I will be there ready for them and I will repay their treachery with interest.

Shun-Ichi Sato

24. Voices - Kingmakers

Finally resolved

Yes.

But not in the way you expected.

It rains only one way. Down from the heavens. A divine cleansing.

Are the Hartsons safe for our purposes?

Yes. On their way to Aden via the steamer to Colombo. It won't be in their interests to talk to either the Singapore or British authorities now that they are suspected of being communists.

I'm surprised you managed to persuade Mrs Hartson.

Yes. A single-minded and calculating woman but such a person bends to the force of circumstance easily. She comprehended the overwhelming odds and had no scruples in doing what we wanted her to do.

So the Hartsons can be disregarded. Ah Seng and his triad have exhausted their usefulness and were paid in full. Sato is similarly silent.

No one realises that we watched Ah Seng and Seow Kow being disposed of by Sato and then moved in.

Sato was too fast and was only wounded before he

escaped. The official version that Sato and the two gangsters killed each other suits us but I can't help wondering what would have happened if either party guessed that the other was a gambit.

They were pawns who did not need to be persuaded to be sacrificed. They were manipulated into a position where there would be only one viable course of action.

Sato wrote a confession. It might be damaging if someone reads between the lines. They might find out about the Japanese legacy.

Sato's confession makes interesting reading but it is misguided and hardly damaging.

Misguided?

The origins of Beethoven 96 started with us. We suggested it to the communists, through our plants and in such a convoluted way that it cannot be traced back to us. They really believe Beethoven 96 was their own invention.

Yes, they wanted power so much that they were blind to our manipulations.

But it wasn't the communist threat that had to gain prominence.

No, we had to demonstrate British ineptitude convincingly. British incompetence would be blamed for failing to discover the plot. We, and not the British, stopped the assassination. The security provided by the British would now be regarded as inadequate and our power will have to be enhanced.

It won't be long before Britain agrees that our present internal self government status is inadequate and that Singapore is quite capable of managing entirely by itself.

Full independence within five years?

After this, it is more likely to be two years.

What about the Japanese promises of compensation for Sato's involvement?

We can expect a substantial sum.

A million?

Millions.

Good

Do you think Inspector Prem suspects?

He's told me personally that he suspects other involvement.

But you still intend to remain his partner?

Yes!